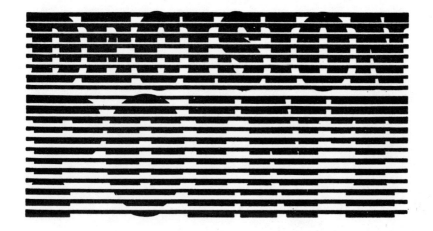

Books by Blaine M. Yorgason and/or Brenton G. Yorgason

Decision Point
The Greatest Quest
Seven Days For Ruby
Family Knights****
Becoming
The Eleven Dollar Surgery (Church History series #1)
Bfpstk and the Smile Song***
The Shadow Taker**
The Loftier Way: Tales from the Ancient American Frontier
Brother Brigham's Gold
Ride the Laughing Wind
The Miracle
The Thanksgiving Promise (paperback - movie version)
Chester I Love You (paperback - movie version)
Chester I Love You
Double Exposure
Seeker of the Gentle Heart
The Krystal Promise
A Town Called Charity, and Other Stories About Decisions
The Bishop's Horse Race
The Courage Covenant (Massacre at Salt Creek)
Windwalker (movie version - out of print)
The Windwalker
Others
Charlie's Monument
From First Date to Chosen Mate
Tall Timber (out of print)
Miracles and the Latter-day Saint Teenager (out of print)
From Two to One*
From This Day Forth*
Creating a Celestial Marriage (textbook)*
Marriage and Family Stewardships (textbook)*

Tapes by Blaine M. Yorgason and/or Brenton G. Yorgason

Caring and Sharing (Blaine M. Yorgason - two taped talks)
Things Most Plain and Precious
    (Brenton G. Yorgason - two taped talks)
The Joyous Way (Blaine & Brenton Yorgason - two taped talks)
Rhinestones and Rubies (Brenton G. Yorgason - two taped talks)
The Miracle (dramatized tape of book)
Charlie's Monument (taped reading of book)
The Bishop's Horse Race (taped reading of book)
Becoming (dramatized reading of book)
Chester I Love You (dramatized tape of book)
The Greatest Quest (dramatized tape of book)
Life Passages (Blaine M. Yorgason)
Little Known Evidences of the Book of Mormon
    (Brenton G. Yorgason)

*Coauthored with Wesley R. Burr and Terry R. Baker. **Coauthored with Carl J. Eaton. ***Coauthored with Tami B. Yorgason. ****Coauthored with Margaret Yorgason.

DECISION POINT

A Novel

BLAINE M. YORGASON

Covenant Publishers, Inc.
Salt Lake City, Utah

For those who are coming -
may I have left them only
goodness

With appreciation to

Jerry L. Glenn
Wiley F. Smith
Douglas Stoddard
Larry L. Smith

Introduction

It is early morning, and the sun is bright upon the land.
There are three men who are in the Cove on Big Lost River,
standing widely separated but in line. There always are,
whenever they come. Three and no more. Yid Francom, and
two others whose names and faces he does not know. Nor
does he know anything else about them; nothing but that
they are always behind him in line. And that is important,
though Yid hasn't the faintest idea why. Only he knows
somehow that he needs to be first. It is just as though,
whenever he absolutely must have something from the
white-haired old drummer, so-called because he must drum
up his own sales business, Yid finds himself in the midst of
a race that he doesn't even know is being run. Of course, so
far he has always won, which astounds him more than he can
say. But still ...

So he awaits, with eagerness, the opening of the
drummer's business. Finally the canvas lifts, and Yid Francom steps forward to the side of the iron-tired wagon. From
the smiling old sales clerk he orders harness hames and a
butter churn. Taking these on credit, and smiling his grati-

tude, he leaves.

The second man steps forward to the open window of ... a large automotive van. From the smiling salesman he orders shock absorbers for his pickup, and a new radio antenna. Taking them also on credit, and expressing his sincere gratitude, he happily departs.

The third man steps forward to ... the flexi-side opening in the freight module. From the joyful dispention he orders a time-lock, and green, yellow and buff food rolls for planting. Taking them on credit, and expressing his deep appreciation to the man who dispenses, he also happily departs.

This happens many times, and then one day for some particular reason there is a great mist, and the men get their order in line mixed up. Instead of obtaining from the drummer, salesman or dispention the things they need, they are each given products that were meant for the others, and great confusion develops.

Thus the story begins--

• PART ONE •

THE HUSBAND

1

With a sudden trembling of nervous excitement, Yid Francom pulled his two-horse team to a halt. A single light beamed out of the darkness ahead of him on the Ketchum-to-Challis freight wagon road, and he could see that it came from a lantern hanging suspended inside an unchinked log barn.

His heart hammering and his body trembling from something more than the chill of the September 1899 evening, Yid considered what he was seeing. Ahead was Sage Creek, that barn on Sage Creek belonged to Amber Wiggins, and the light meant that she was awake and out there. It also meant, at least more than likely, that she was having some problem that she might need help with. And he, Yid Francom, was the only man around who might help her.

For the past several weeks and months, Yid had thought longingly, blushingly even, of the widow woman who was now in the barn before him. At first he had tried not to think of her, at least in the way his mind seemed to take him. But the harder he had tried, the more persistent her image had become. So finally, in complete frustration, he had given in and allowed his thoughts to wander. And wander they had, directly to Sage Creek where he now was.

Nor was Amber Wiggins a grandmotherly sort of old widow woman with iron-grey hair, spider-web skin and a proper black shawl draped over her bony, hunched shoulders. No, sir, by Tophet. She was, in fact, the most beautiful woman, in a savagely feline sort of way, that Yid had ever seen. Her face was gorgeous, her hair fine and silky, and her form wickedly enticing. But more than that, she was dainty and petite, her voice was small and quiet, and perhaps most significant of all, she obviously liked *him*. Or at least she acted like she did, and had done so ever since her husband had been killed in that cave-in at the Custer Mine up at Challis. She smiled radiantly whenever Yid did the least little courtesy for her and her baby son, and she was constantly heaping praises and compliments upon him whenever they happened to be in the same vicinity.

So Yid had spent many pleasurable hours, in the midst of his own trials and difficulties, in considering her. And to his complete surprise he had very quickly concocted a regular situation, or drama, in which he and Amber Wiggins were the only participants. In that drama he always saw her in a particular place, on a particular day. They were engaged in sweet, private conversation, and Yid knew all the lines of that conversation by heart.

Of course he would have blushed to have that conversation spoken aloud; but truthfully, his fantasy dwelt on the fact that he was delighted to be...well, to be on intimate terms with her.

Yid felt terribly guilty about what his mind was doing, but to be perfectly truthful, he didn't really *want* to stop it. He was certain that he could have stopped his thoughts had he wanted, but Amber's beauty had put his mind into gear, and to his surprise, these dreams of her were enjoyable. They were in fact a sort of release from his daily troubles, and the more he thought of it, the more he felt that he deserved such a release.

And that Amber Wiggins ... My, oh my, oh my! What a person to have sweet dreams about!

So he had been thinking of her that night while his team had plodded along the darkened road toward the Cove on the Big Lost River. He had dreamed of her, he had listened in his mind to her sweet and gentle voice as she had spoken with him and told him, over and over, how proud she was to be with him, and he had longed for that dream to become real.

But now...

Trembling, Yid pulled the team to a halt outside Amber Wiggins' barn. Taking a deep breath to steady his nerves, he climbed stiffly down from the old springbed wagon, easing his creaking and tired joints. Carefully then he moved forward until he stood outside the barn window. From that vantage point he looked inside, and instantly his heart renewed its furious pounding.

Amber Wiggins, looking even more lovely than he had remembered her, stood alone in the flickering lantern light, her face streaked with perspiration. She was straining futilely to free an unborn calf that was coming breach, but the old cow wasn't helping, and Yid could see at a glance that it would be nip and tuck to save either the calf or its mother.

Moving quickly, he opened the door, took a deep breath, and walked in on the surprised young woman.

"E...evenin', ma'am," he said nervously as he averted his eyes to the floor. "Looks like you need help."

"Oh, Yid," Amber Wiggins cried, stepping back from the half-born calf. "I...I mean, Mister Francom," she stammered, blushing. "Where did you come from? And how did you know that I needed you?"

"I was p...passing by," Yid declared, his voice low with nervousness, "and I saw the light. I figured there must be some trouble, so I stopped. You...uh...you have a block and tackle here?"

"Block and tackle?"

"Right," he declared, his confidence already growing.

"You know, a rope with two pulleys that's used to pull things? Do you reckon you could fetch me such a thing?"

Amber Wiggins stood, uncertain. Suddenly she smiled and ran into the tack room at the far end of the barn. Seconds later she was back with a small block and tackle, which she handed to Yid.

Meanwhile he had rolled up the sleeves of his shirt, greased his arms with some handy axle grease, and had reached in around the calf, working another small rope so that it was around the tiny animal's shoulders.

He quickly hooked that rope to the block and tackle, secured the other end to a post in the barn wall, tied the old cow more snugly to the far wall, and commenced to pull.

His efforts brought a bellow of protest from the cow, a cry of fear from Amber Wiggins, and, finally, a newborn calf into the world.

Still working quickly, he cleaned the nostrils of the small animal, cut its cord and tied it off, and then lifted it to its feet.

The calf swayed, toppled, was picked up again and again by the gentle Yid Francom and the thankful Amber Wiggins, and after about ten minutes was leaning awkwardly with its muzzle against its mother's udder.

"Looks like that'll do it," Yid declared, smiling with relief. "Critter's pretty as a little red wagon."

"Oh, it is that," Amber Wiggins agreed. "Yid, I mean, Mister Francom, you have such a special way with animals."

"I...I reckon," he declared, embarrassed again. "And...and call me Yid, please?"

"All right...Yid. Oh, but look at you! All dirty and covered with blood and grease. I'm so sorry..."

"It's nothin', ma'am."

"Yid, call me Amber. Please?"

"I...I... Well, alright, A...Amber. Like I said, it's nothing."

"But it is. Come to the house, this minute, and let me clean you up. You won't be traveling anywhere, not looking like that. I won't have it."

Yid thought of arguing. He didn't feel comfortable about going to Amber's home. Not at all. It was disconcerting enough just being alone with her in her barn. Besides, how would he ever explain ...

"Just follow me," Amber insisted as she took the lantern off the overhead nail. "I'll light the way."

She started for the door, and still Yid hesitated. But he did want to get cleaned up, and he really didn't know of another place where he could do it. Besides, Amber was already out the door, her comely form well lit by the lantern she was carrying.

Dumbstruck, Yid was still staring at the closely clad loveliness of her figure when she turned back and smiled beckoningly. At that, the poor man's will shattered instantly against the radiance of her expression, and he followed.

Shortly Yid found himself in Amber Wiggins' small cabin, a sanctum he had never before seen the inner side of. Amber prepared a basin of warm water, and before long Yid was scrubbing himself thoroughly while his mind whirled with wonderment and concern.

Here it was the middle of the night, he was alone with Amber Wiggins, and...and...

He was so aware of the woman's presence, now beside him, now behind him, but always near, that he could hardly think. He tried to picture other things in his mind, but beyond brief glimpses of distant, hazy events, he couldn't conjure up much at all. Over and over such mental efforts would be gone and he would be in that imaginary, private place of his fantasy, with Amber Wiggins holding him tightly.

Controlling his thoughts, more than ever before, seemed totally impossible, and Yid Francom wondered, as he furiously scrubbed, if he cared. Would it matter, really, if he just let things take their course? Would it...

"Yid, I have one of my husband's shirts here. Why don't you take it, and leave that one for me to wash. It's the least I could do."

Dumbly Yid nodded. Then he hurriedly dried himself,

and snatched the shirt from Amber's outstretched hand.

"You'll never know how much I appreciate your help with that calf," the young woman said quietly. "Without you, I think that maybe I would have lost both it and the cow. That would have been a disaster, especially for my little boy. By the way, did you notice if it was a heifer or a bull?"

"I...I..." Yid stammered, entranced by the woman's large and questioning eyes. "I didn't."

"Well," Amber laughed easily, "it doesn't matter. I'll go check on the little creature in the morning. Right now, finding out doesn't seem awfully important."

Yid, fumbling with the buttons on the borrowed shirt, nodded silently. And he did his best to keep his eyes away from the woman.

Slowly Amber Wiggins walked to the bed and sank onto it, where she wiped back from her face a strand of long blond hair. "My goodness but I'm tired," she sighed, falling back upon the bed with her arm up across her eyes.

"I...I'll bet," Yid mumbled as he stared at her, his eyes arrested by her form, his heart pounding with desire. "That s...sort of thing takes it out of a person mighty quick."

He continued to stare while the seconds dragged by, and he was truly frozen to the spot. Nervously he licked his lips, wondering what he should say, what he should do. In his mind he could hear his imaginary conversation, but he had never imagined, not ever that he might actually be alone with Amber Wiggins like this.

What he had ought to do, he knew, was get out of there. Right that moment. But she looked so lovely lying there, so terribly inviting. And somehow it seemed to him that she was only waiting...

The baby, in a small bed next to the larger one, stirred restlessly. Yid's eyes shifted from Amber to the baby, and then quickly back again. In the iron stove some burning logs settled a little, and then the room became incredibly quiet.

Still frozen in place, Yid pictured in his mind what he

should do; how he should walk to the door, open it, and get on his way to the Cove. But on the other hand, something within him whispered, he might just as easily walk to the bed, take hold of Amber's hand, and say something soft and pleasant. It would be easy, even more so than he had ever imagined it would be. All he had to do was to put his one foot out ahead of the other ...

"Yid," Amber Wiggins said, her eyes suddenly flaring open, "please excuse me. I'm being terribly rude."

Quickly she pulled herself to her feet before the startled Yid Francom. Then she smiled and walked toward him. "I think it must be this country that makes me so tired," she sighed. "I love it, but it is so harsh, and it does take its toll on a lone woman."

"Y...Yes, ma'am."

"Why do people ever choose to live here, do you suppose?"

"Why?" Yid responded, his love for the land suddenly filling him with enthusiasm and the courage to speak. "Because there is no land like this high western country, not anywhere in the world. To attempt to describe it is hopeless. Worse, it's downright profane. Nobody who hasn't seen it will believe you. Anybody who has will resent you trying to tell him about it. I reckon it's best to see it as sort of a sacred thing, or anyway past easy describing, like motherhood, or young love, or being free as a kid, or growing old with dignity. It's just too big for the eye to get around, or the mind to capture. Mrs. Wiggins, ma'am, you can quote all the words ever put down on paper about it and not begin to tell the truth about this Big Lost country."

He paused, and they both were quiet.

"Why, Yid," Amber finally spoke, "you are a poet."

"No, ma'am," Yid responded, his voice soft and gentle-sad. "I'm just a mostly useless dreamer."

"Dear Yid," Amber replied gently, placing her soft hand on his quivering arm, "thank you so much for your help. If you want anything from me, anything at all, you have only to ask. You know that, don't you?"

Dumbly Yid stared at her.

"Don't you?" she repeated, her eyes wide with expression.

"I...I reckon I do."

"Good."

Amber Wiggins smiled up at him, reached up and touched his face with her fingertips, and then Yid realized with a start that she was leading him.

"Mrs. Wiggins? A...Amber, I mean?"

"Yes?"

"I...I sure am glad I g...got here. In time, I mean."

"So am I," the woman stated sincerely.

"I...I...uh..."

"Yid," she said then, a pleading in her voice, "sit down with me and say something sweet and gentle. With my husband dead and gone, I get so scared and lonesome I could cry."

Yid jumped at the abruptly offered, dreamed-of invitation, but Amber's hand on his arm steadied him, and at last he found his voice. "I...I know that feeling too, ma'am," he finally said. "I know it like you can only know something you've lived with all your life. Lonesomeness is like a woman, I reckon. You can't..."

"Lonesomeness *is* a woman, Yid. This woman. Now, please..."

She deliberately teased his hand then, as she took it in both of hers, and then slowly she leaned toward him.

With a sound that was meant to be an "excuse me but good-bye," but which Yid decided later had probably sounded more like the death squeal of a young rabbit, he jerked back from the startled woman. Then he spun around, tore open the door, and fled into the darkness.

He ran until he came rather abruptly into contact with the back of his wagon, and there he stopped, trembling and breathing heavily, while he listened to the sound of Amber Wiggins' soft "good night and come back real soon" from somewhere behind him.

"Merciful heavens," he mumbled as the cold night air brushed across his face. "You poor, sorry fool. Do you realize what you were thinking? What you were wanting to make happen? Why, Yid Francom, how stupid can you be?

"What do you think you would ever tell Mincy? You do remember your wife, don't you? Or the Lord, you numb-skull? How would you ever kneel down and tell him what you'd done? Why, Paul the Apostle wrote about you, yes he did, when he called you a traitor, heady, high-minded, a lover of pleasure more than a lover of God; creeping into houses and leading captive silly women laden with sins, led away with divers lusts..."

Yid shook his head in total disgust at his weakness, and with a muttered oath he stumbled to the front of his wagon, climbed onto the seat, and cracked the lines. Startled, the team, still having spirit enough to cut and shower back shoe sods with the driving dig of their start, lunged into their traces. Within fifty feet the span was going at full gallop, and the wagon was back on the dark road, heading once again in the direction of the Cove.

"By jings," Yid mumbled then as he rehearsed in his mind the events of the past few moments, "the touch of that woman's fingers shook me like the swamp fever. But she surely acted like she liked me. And what she said, about me having anything I wanted...

"Of course I'm powerful glad nothing happened. I don't want to go through the hell that would come with fracturing a commandment like that. Why, I'm no adulterer. I'm a better man than that, any time, any where.

"Besides, I'm married to a real good woman, and I couldn't hurt Mincy that way, either."

Yid paused, his gaze drifting off into the darkness of the Big Lost country night through which the wagon was bouncing. "But doggone it," he finally declared emphatically to the darkness around him, "that Amber Wiggins is surely a hot-blooded woman, and I do think that she likes me plenty."

2

Just as Yid reached the last low ridge before the drop to the river below, the three-quarter moon came up from behind the Pahsimeroi Mountains. Gently it bathed in soft white light the wagon road, and Yid, his mind yanked from dreams of Amber Wiggins with the amazing beauty of it all, pulled his team to a dust-raising halt.

Down below curved the darkened hollow of the Cove, nestled between two sweeping arms of Swensen Butte. South across the Big Lost River, above the night-black stand of cottonwoods that crowded the roily water, rose Bartlett Point. And beyond that stood Porphyry Peak and the other hills that rose to become the White Knob Mountains, suddenly brighter in the moon wash than the star-shrouded sky against which they had been planted.

Yid needed to get down into the Cove, he knew, for he had to be first in line, come dawn, to catch the drummer, who had his new plow. But there was time and a little to spare for dreaming; so he wrapped the lines of his two mares around the brake handle of the old spring bed, rose stiffly to his feet, and inhaled deeply of the chill mountain air.

How he loved this land, this high desert country he and Mincy had come to settle! It was in truth a place of unreal beauty. A wild place, and a brooding and lonely place, too. Full of solitude and splendor and frightening silence. It was an unbelievable jewel of lush meadowgrass, endless rolling sage, cottonwood, pine and fir, cedar and bending willow, all set in a fantastic mounting of platinum water, harsh gray-black rock and raw blue sky. The impact of it struck a man simultaneously dumb, humble, sad and afraid. It left him shaking his head and thinking inside himself, by Tophet, it *is* beautiful. And it left him, too, with a deep and poignant ache of wanting to tell, so bad that it hurt like a heart pain, just how truly wonderful and mind-staggering was this great work of the Lord's, this long lonely valley that men called the Big Lost River country.

That, to Yid Francom, was good.

And there was something else that was good, too. In fact, most always Yid felt puffed up as a frog in a cream can whenever he thought on it. And he thought a great deal, in his own quiet way, of this and that and the other, never giving his mind a chance to rust out or shrivel up and blow away. And in that way, many things were made clear to him. Many questions were answered, many mysteries made transparent. But the greatest mystery of all was likely going to remain forever unsolved in the mind of the smallish and troubled man.

He had seen other men, had watched and studied them, and he knew. Some were rapacious rascals who made social capital of their natural good looks and inherent lack of social compunction. They had no more morals than a stud mustang. But still, they were men; handsome, eager, entirely courageous, and most any beautiful woman's, just for the asking.

Then there were others, not so handsome, maybe, but male in every lean molecule of their bodies. There was nothing about such a man that a knowing woman would want to change; they were too fascinating. Nor was the fascination purely physical. Such a man's character was hard and compelling, and little doubt as deadly as the polished barrel of an Army Colt. Withal, such a man was dangerous, saturnine, exciting, and able to read women as though he had written the original book about them.

To his dying day, little Yid Francom would remain convinced beyond doubt that Mincy could have had any such man for the least beckoning of bold eye or cocked eyebrow.

Why, then, in the name of a supposedly just and reasonable heaven, a bewildered Irish-American tailor-turned-plow-follower would be asking himself till the end of his days, had she chosen to wind up in a rough-hewn fir cabin down off the hill from Willow Creek Summit in the same beautiful sage-choked Big Lost River country of north-central Idaho that he himself loved, with a bedraggled, drowthed-out specimen like Yid Francom?

And that was the bare-boned fact of it. Mincy had consented to come into *his* life, and with him into *this* valley, and Yid would never totally understand why.

With a long sigh he sank back onto the wagon bench. All that being true, and it being also true that he loved Mincy with all his heart, then why did he persist in harboring such insidious thoughts his lovely, fair-haired widow neighbor?

Into his mind came once again the haunting image of Amber Wiggins, and with a fair degree of objectivity, Yid placed his wife beside her and began to compare. Tall, short; dark, fair; loud, quiet; happy, serious; his wife, not his wife ...

In disgust Yid kicked against the footboard of the old springbed. What was the matter with him? Why was he not more able to control his heart and his mind? Was it that he didn't love Mincy? No, of course that wasn't it. No man ever had a more loving wife, and he honestly felt the same about her. So what was it, then? Was he ashamed of her? No, that wasn't it, either.

Of course there were a couple of things about her that he didn't care for, and a couple more things about her that were, well, *unusual* would be the best word to use. Mincy, as sweet and domestic a wife as she was, could also out-plow him, out-plant him, out-harvest him, out-milk him, and out-do him in most everything else on the farm, too. Further, she outweighed him by at least fifty pounds, and stood taller than him by almost a foot. As folks occasionally said, probably more tongue-in-cheek than otherwise, they made a rather remarkable pair.

On the other hand, the poor girl couldn't bake decent biscuits, and she couldn't sew for sour apples. Oh, once in a while she pushed a needle through some fabric, all right. But that wasn't sewing. Not by a long shot it wasn't. Why, with the least flick of his wrists Yid could have out-sewn her six ways from Sunday. Of course he never had, not since they had been married. Somehow it felt, to him, an unseemly thing for a man to out-sew his own wife.

And Mincy's biscuits were awful! Hard and heavy as any biscuits he had ever tried to chomp down on. Of course, if a man was ingenious, a use other than eating might be found for them. If he could get a rifle with a big enough bore, for instance, those biscuits would make tolerable good ammunition. As it was, they were real handy for wearing the beaks off most chickens, slinging after the calf when it got into the garden, and holding down the house when high winds blew down off Dickey Peak. But they weren't good for eating.

Yid grinned at his own humor, lifted his eyes and stared off into the night. His horses, Peaches and Cream, stood patiently, swishing their tails at a swarm of late-season mosquitos that had chosen the horses as their pre-dawn breakfast hosts. But ignoring both the horses and the insects, Yid continued to follow his thoughts.

Those things about Mincy did bother him, but truthfully they weren't that bad. What was, and what troubled him more than he could say, was her quick anger. Why, Mincy had a temper hot enough to smelt ore. And if she ever got going, her vocabulary would sizzle the grass for miles around. Bare-handed she could beat any dozen pumas or three dozen Indians in Idaho; she-grizzlies with cubs abandoned their babies and fled from her; and there wasn't a white man in all the northwest who could stand up to her in an out-and-out argument. Yes sir, when it came to temper, Mincy was a person who ought to be avoided.

Yid had never grown accustomed to that, and even though he had only seen her lose control once, and that in his own hapless defense during a hoorawing some teamsters were giving him down in Blackfoot, it did bother him. Yet withal, his wife was a fine woman, and Yid was certain that he loved her.

"So then," he muttered disgustedly as he unwrapped the lines from around the brake handle and took up the slack, "why in Tophet am I building castles in the sky with the widow Wiggins?"

Peaches, Yid's right wheeler, lifted her head in response to Yid's voice, and tossed her head and snorted. Cream, the left wheeler, didn't notice a thing, and probably wouldn't have, even if Yid had yelled in her ear. She was either the densest, or brightest and most concentratingest horse that Yid had ever owned, and he couldn't decide which.

"Peaches," Yid said, "I'm right happy that you're paying attention. Maybe you can help me. You see, a man who is loyal to his wife, and who considers his marriage vows to be honorable and binding, ought never to even think of another woman. And especially he ought never to think of her in the way that I find myself thinking of Amber Wiggins. Why, the whole idea of such disloyalty sounds empty as a church on a Saturday night.

"Worse, the Good Lord told us that thinking such things was just as bad as doing them. So I'd give most anything to get her out of my mind, and quit. Why, my goodness, I hardly know that woman, and here I am replacing thoughts of Mincy with inappropriate dreams of her. It isn't right, and I know it. So from now on I won't think of her any more. That's a promise."

A bat fluttered close above Yid's head, swooped upward, and darted off into the darkness. Off in the hills a coyote yipped, and the alert mare raised her head again, listening.

Yid listened too, and as he did so, he realized that his thoughts had once again returned to the lonely cabin on Sage Creek. He could see the Wiggins widow clearly as she stared out into the night, fearful of what might be out there, wishing with all her soul that Yid would return to be with her, wishing that he and she...

"Aw, nuts!" Yid growled with a wry grin as he cracked the lines against his horses' backs, sending them forward toward the Cove and the drummer. "Why fight it, Peaches? After all, it's mighty pleasurable, thinking on that widow woman. And besides, what possible harm can a little dreaming now and then ever do? None, and that's a sure fire cinch!

"Now giddap there, and let's go see that drummer."

3

The morning mist was thick enough to chew before swallowing, much worse than Yid had ever seen it, and he had a difficult time finding the drummer's wagon. As he clucked his team forward he wondered at the mist, trying to decide why it had become so thick. It was not terribly cold, so it wasn't like steam from the hot springs. And though mists frequently hung over the Thousand Springs area on early fall mornings, he hadn't often seen them here along the river. But nevertheless, here the mists were, thick as pea soup, and he was having a devil of a time finding the old salesman's wagon.

He managed it, though, finally, and after leaving his team some distance off, stood waiting in silence for the old man to lift the canvas side and open up for business.

Casually he looked around him, wondering where the horses were that the drummer used. He had never seen the animals, and had always assumed that the drummer knew of some secret pasturage near by. Of course today they could be ten feet away, and he wouldn't know of it. But he couldn't hear them, either, so he was certain they must be staked some distance off.

Now Yid looked behind him, and with surprise he realized that he was alone on that count, as well. The two men
who were always behind him, were not there, and that
troubled him. Not a lot, actually, but it did bother him a
little. Where were they, and why did he feel so totally
alone? Of course maybe they were there and he couldn't
see them through the mist. But he should have been able
to at least detect movement.

Turning back to the wagon, he stood alone with his
thoughts. Once again, as he had for perhaps the hundredth
time, he rehearsed in his mind the events of the night
before. But already those events were changing, becoming
an entirely new mental drama or scenario in which Amber
Wiggins' desires for him ran almost unchecked, and where
the only restraints upon her wantonness were his laugh-
ingly declared commitments to his wife, Mincy.

"Yid," he could hear Amber pleading in his mind,
"please..."

"I'm dearly sorry, ma'am, but I am married," Yid would
reply with a smile.

"It doesn't matter!" Amber would feverishly declare.
"Hold me...hold me..."

She would then force herself into Yid's resisting arms,
and he would graciously submit.

But in his heart of hearts Yid knew that should such a
thing ever really happen, he would fight valiantly to resist.
He would run just as he had run the night before. He
couldn't hurt his wife that way. Nor did he want to. But
that didn't mean he couldn't dream...

With a start, Yid realized that the canvas had been rolled
up, and that the drummer was standing above him, waiting
in silence.

"G...good morning," he stammered to the old salesman,
feeling somehow embarrassed at what he had been thinking. But he didn't understand that, either. Why should he
be embarrassed by his own private thoughts, especially in
front of the aged drummer.

The old man remained still, and Yid wondered at that,
for in the past the man had always been so warm and

friendly. Besides that, it was crazy how thick the mist was. It swirled up in waves around him, yet so far as he could tell, there was no wind, no breeze, to move it.

Eerie, he decided. Downright eerie. He was glad that it was finally coming on sunup. He could hardly wait for the sun to burn the mist away.

"I...uh...I broke my plow yesterday afternoon," Yid explained, still feeling unexplainably guilty. "Hit a rock, I reckon. I was hoping that I might get another one... on a note, and pay for it when the crops sell?"

The old drummer remained silent, and Yid wondered again what had happened to erase the man's customary smile. But what did it matter anyway, he decided? If the old man smiled, it was fine. If he didn't, it was also fine. What did he care if the man turned cold as a banker's heart? Just so long as he was able to obtain a plow and get back to the farm.

"I...I reckon that my bill is getting a little big, but...uh...well, do you have a plow here in your wagon that I might buy? Please?"

For a long moment the drummer looked down at him from his lofty perch. And Yid was certain, for an instant, that he could see tears in the old man's eyes. But the mist was thick, he couldn't be sure, and when he tried to see more closely, the drummer turned his back and moved away into the wagon.

Nervously Yid stood, waiting. A moment passed, then another, and he thought suddenly of Mincy. He'd better be getting back, or she would raise the roof.

Angry? She'd likely be mad enough to chomp a chunk out of an axe. She'd see Amber Wiggins' dead husband's shirt on his back, too, and that would make things worse than ever.

Maybe he should stop in at Amber's on his way back and trade shirts again. Maybe if he didn't spend any time...

But no, that was a fool's idea, and he knew it. Why, he had barely escaped disaster the night before. What on earth made him even consider entering into that lioness' den again? No, he would wear the shirt and face the music at home. That would surely be the most easy way to deal with it.

But Amber Wiggins would never get angry with him like Mincy would likely be. Of that he was as certain as he was that she had taken his hand in hers, or that the morning was misty, or that the old drummer was still rummaging around in the back of his wagon, taking his own sweet time about things.

Unaccountably irritated by the old man's slowness, Yid stepped forward to see if he could get the drummer's attention and spur him on a bit. But as he did so his feet and ankles slammed into something hard that the mist had kept hidden. Glancing down, he felt his heart suddenly begin to hammer.

There before him on the ground, still with the grease and brown paper wrapping upon it, was a new McCormick Farm Implements plow — *his* new plow. But the drummer's wagon was as it had been, still as death in the early morning mist. And Yid had neither seen, nor heard, anything of the old man since the fellow had turned away into his wagon.

Cautiously Yid looked behind him. Nothing. Not a soul could be seen. Bending over, he peered under the wagon. Still nothing. Stepping around the plow, Yid took hold of the wagon side, pulled himself up and leaned into the interior.

Nobody.

And worse than nobody, *nothing*!

The drummer was gone, and even more incredibly, the wagon was empty! Where, only moments before, there had been stacks of wares, now there was nothing but the bare boards that made up the sides and bed of the wagon.

Suddenly Yid felt as alone as if he had been Adam in the Garden of Eden before Eve was created, and he wanted nothing more than to get away from the Cove, and fast.

Puckering his lips, he whistled for his team. Or rather, he tried. But try as he might, he could not get out a whistle. Again he tried, and then again and again. And at last, with valiant effort, a squeaking whistle came out. Then he stood quaking in the misty silence of the morning, afraid to move, waiting for his horses to bring the wagon to him.

Finally, and with great relief, he heard the plodding of his team's hooves and the creaking of the old springbed, and he could hardly comprehend his further relief when the two horses loomed out of the mist, coming toward him.

"Peaches," he sighed. "Law, but I am glad to see you and Cream. Now whoa. Whoa up, there. That's it. Stand still, while I get this plow into the wagon."

The horses stood obediently, and Yid worked his arms under the heavy iron tool. Straining, he lifted it, staggered to the back of the wagon, and toppled it onto the wagon bed.

"Blasted drummer," he grumbled. "Least he could do was stick around to help me load it. Well, I won't do him any favors with the broken one, either. I'll just roll it off and leave it lay. He can load it any way he can. If he won't..."

And then, once again, Yid Francom was stricken speechless. Feverishly he looked around, anxiously, fearfully. But it did no good.

His old plow, the broken one he had hauled all the way from home, was gone from the wagon, gone as though it had never been there at all.

For another second Yid stood, perhaps two, and then he scrambled onto the seat, took up the reins that had been looped around the brake handle, and with a frantic snap he set his team into motion.

"Come on," he whined anxiously, "giddap! This place is making me nervous."

The team responded, and the wagon lurched out of the Cove. And Yid, if he had only looked back, would have seen the man who had always stood second in line behind him. That man was moving slowly forward out of the mist and up to the open window of the automotive van, and he was doing it almost as if he could not see clearly where he was going.

And in the van, the white-haired salesman was standing solemnly, waiting to help.

• *PART TWO* •

THE WIFE

4

Mincy Francom stood just inside the door of her home on Arentson Gulch, watching the early sunlight slide down the side of the West Hills, slowly turning the blues to gold and the misty night to morning. Outside under the eaves a myriad of birds greeted the new day with a cacophony of song, and beyond in the pasture the calf bawled to the world that it was time and past for his breakfast.

She smiled at that, for she knew that once again the calf was going to be disappointed. It had long since grown past the need for its mother's milk, and the old cow had also long since stopped paying the least attention to the cater-wauling of her maturing offspring.

A mountain bluejay caught her attention then, and with another smile she watched its antics. Known everywhere as robber jays, the bold birds often flew right into her home and took food from her table. This particular bird seemed to be sneaking up on her, hopping from fence pole to fence pole in an ever closing approach to her open door.

"Say there, you old thief," she called softly. "What do you want to do that for? Here, take this crust of bread and be off with you, and stop those wicked ways."

Tossing the bread into the yard, Mincy laughed delight-
edly as the jay frightened away an opportunistic chicken,
took up the crust, and fled to the roof of the barn.

Still laughing, Mincy turned to face the rows of empty
fruit jars that had to be filled. With a step made light
because she knew that her husband would be on his way
home, she walked to the sideboard, took up the paring
knife and a peach, and proceeded to peel it, slice and pit it,
throw the pit into the slop bucket, and slide the halves into
the first open jar. Ignoring the slippery feeling on her
hands, she took another of the ripe fruit from the pan and
repeated the process. She did not think about what she was
doing, however, for there was no need to. This was her
third year of canning for herself and her husband, and the
process had become automatic.

Instead, she thought of Yid, and of how hard he was
trying to make their lives better. For instance, he had
purchased these peaches from a freighter who had hauled
them all the way up across the lava desert from Blackfoot.
They must have been expensive, but knowing how much
Mincy enjoyed eating fruit, he had not minded. He had
simply done it, just as he tried so hard to do everything else
for her.

Nor was it easy for him. Mincy understood that, and
loved him the more for his efforts. She thought then of the
first day she had seen him, on that street corner in Battle
Mountain, Nevada.

She had had a pretty rough life up to then, having been
orphaned and generally mistreated since her parents'
deaths by most of humanity. Of course, she couldn't really
blame folks for that. She *was* bigger than normal, and her
folks *had* been somewhat notorious. Besides, most of her
schooling had been the sort she had given herself, and she
was terribly self-conscious about that, as well as her lack of
social graces. Thus she had done a lot of drifting from one
cooking or scullery job to another, and had never been able
to find much happiness.

Then she had met Mister Yid Francom, and her life had
changed. That day, September 1, 1896, she had been stand-

ing on a corner, without money, emotionally spent and defensive, and seeking any way she could find to get on to Winnemucca and hopefully another chance at life.

He had been standing a few yards away when she had first noticed him staring at her. When she had asked him what he had wanted, he had stammered some silly reply and had hurried away.

The next day, after spending the night asleep in the livery stable, she had been astounded to see the runty little man staring at her again.

"Here," she had called to him, "why are you watching me?"

Instead of answering, Yid had simply stood, slack-jawed and grinning, and inadvertently giving her a good look at him.

And in no way was she impressed. The little man was pale, sickly looking, and could not have reached near six feet, even with the help of his three-inch boot heels. His weight would not have exceeded 140 pounds even with his pockets full of desert sand. His eyes, large and heavily lashed, were an odd shade of green. His sensitive mouth was delicately drawn and red as lip rouge. His hair, long, soft and curly brown, was unkempt, too much. In fact, the only thing that Mincy liked about him was that he made her feel so immediately superior that she was sure, should she snap her fingers, that he would roll over on his back, all fours waving, in the attitude of craven surrender.

Mincy broke off her belligerent regard of him, satisfied that she was once and forever in charge of the situation, at least as far as the runty, staring man was concerned. And once again she concentrated upon finding a free ride out of town.

For hours then she had ignored the man, but finally his own scrutiny of her had become more than annoying. She simply couldn't tolerate knowing that he was standing off behind her, staring. It was going to end, by thunder, even if she had to pick him up and throw him into the street on his ear. That, at least, would give him the message.

Only, just when she had been about to take out after him

and thump him good, the runt had disappeared.

Breathing a sigh of relief, she had relaxed, and was just starting to attempt to hail down another freight wagon when around the corner the little man had come in a fringed surrey. And to her further surprise, he had pulled the team to a stop before her.

Letting no opportunity slip by, Mincy had stepped forward. "Are you by chance going on to Winnemucca?" she had asked politely.

"Ma'am?" he had questioned, softly, gently.

Instantly Mincy had realized that the man had that disconcerting habit of looking at a person without letting them catch him at it, and of appearing to listen politely, while actually paying no attention at all. "I said," she had replied, politely enough, "that I need a ride to Winnemucca. Is that too difficult to understand?"

"No, ma'am, not hardly at all. I mean, I reckon I understand, all right."

Mincy's ears had grated on his twang just as her eyes had grated upon his form, and she had determined to bring him up short.

"Good. Then I trust that you will be a gentleman and help me find a ride."

"Yes, ma'am. And given the chance, I will get you a little repair, as well."

Mincy had lifted her chin.

"I beg your pardon!"

"No offense, ma'am, but sleeping in stables and going hungry day after day isn't very kind to a woman."

"Indeed it is not!" she had snapped. "Now if you will just kindly find someone who can take me..." She had started to ask about a ride again, but he had cut her off with his shy smile.

"Shucks, ma'am, I'll do better than find you a ride. I'll take you to Winnemucca myself."

Moving quickly then he had stepped from the rig and reached to pick up her straw suitcase. But Mincy would not surrender it to him. Seizing it firmly, she had faced him down.

"Mister, please be good enough..."

"I'll carry it for you, ma'am."

His hand had found the handle of the suitcase then, and in consequence, her hand. The touch of his thin fingers was as unsettling as the twang in his voice. It sent a shiver through Mincy that she did not like. Yet she found herself, because she really had no choice, giving up the suitcase and climbing into the surrey with the strange little man.

For an hour he had driven in silence, while she had wondered who he was, where he was taking her, and what on earth he wanted.

Finally, and to her eternal, dumfounded amazement, he had spoken.

"Name's Francom," he had said. "Yid Francom. T...there's new land opening up for homesteading... in Idaho. High-up bottom land, good water, and enough of a growing season to do."

His voice had been very quiet, and even sitting in the buggy seat next to him Mincy had had a hard time hearing.

"T...trouble is," he continued, "settlement is only open to couples. Married couples, th...that is."

"So?"

Yid had looked up at her, and then quickly away. "So...I'm... I ain't never been henpecked, but I'm hankering to try it. I...I mean I'm... unattached."

"That doesn't surprise me. So what?"

"I heard that y...you were, too. Unattached, I mean."

Realizing the ridiculous direction the conversation was heading, Mincy had laughed. "Are you proposing marriage?"

Again Yid had looked at her, and for the briefest of an instant, he had grinned. "You're a f...fine looking woman, Miss Mincy. I'd be honored if you were to say yes."

Mincy had snorted. "Hogwash! Who told you my name?"

"It...it doesn't matter. Most folks in town know it. I'd sure admire owning a farm."

"So that's it? You want a farm? Why don't you just go buy one?"

Yid had shrugged, and then looked away. "It... wouldn't

come with... with you, I reckon."

Now Mincy had really looked at the small man. Suddenly angry, she had ordered him to return her to town.

"W...what's wrong, Miss Mincy?"

"I won't be made fun of, that's what! You'll sucker me into agreeing to this, and when we get back, I'll be made the laughing stock of the town. No siree, little man. I've been laughed at before, I've been laughed at enough, and it won't happen again. I promise you that!"

Yid had stopped the surrey and had turned to face her. "You... you don't think I mean it, do you."

It had been a statement, not a question, and Mincy had instantly agreed. "No, I do not. Now take me back."

"If I...if I agreed to drive us to Winnemucca, straight off, so we could get married up proper, would you believe me then?"

"Right now? Without going back to town?"

"Sure as chokecherries taste tart. You see, Miss Mincy, I do want a farm. But worse than that, I want a wife. I've been watching you since you first came to town, months and months ago, and I've been wishing... Well, if you'll have me, I'd admire to marry you."

"Why me?" Mincy had asked suspiciously.

"Uh...well...I..." Yid stammered. "Oh, gosh, ma'am, I don't think I've ever seen anybody more pretty than you. Why, you loom up like a tin roof on a sunny day, and I never saw such honey-soft eyes..."

Smiling at the memory, Mincy whipped out a peach stone, tossed it into the bucket, and slid the halves into a jar. Then she took up the hot sugar water and poured it over the fruit she had bottled. That finished, she pulled linen over the jar tops, tied them down, and dipped them in beeswax to seal them. Then she took up another peach and resumed peeling , her mind still three years back in the past.

"You can cut that blarney out right now!" she had declared emphatically. "I don't believe a word of it."

"But it's true, ma'am," Yid had declared. "Every loving word. And besides, I think you'd give birth to some fine sons. I'd admire to be a father to some fine sons, myself. Will...will you do it? Marry me, I mean?"

Mincy had stared at the small man, uncertain. She wasn't impressed with him, not at all. And she surely didn't want any of his sons. But on the other hand, he was offering her an out, a way to escape the hopeless misery in which she was bogged.

"You seem mighty anxious, Mister Yid Francom," she said at last. "Might it be that you can't find anybody else?"

Yid had looked at her, startled, and then slowly had dropped his eyes. "I...I..."

"Well, out with it. I asked you a question."

"I have tried to marry one or two others," he responded quietly, "and my offer has been declined. But I...I have thought of no one but you since first I laid eyes on you, most of a year ago, and I will never think of anyone else again. Not if you say yes, I won't."

Mincy had sighed with resignation, and had kept her eyes on the far horizon. "Saying yes wouldn't hardly be fair to you, Mister Francom."

"Why wouldn't it?" he had countered, quickly, sincerely.

"Because I don't know you...don't love you. If I said yes, it would only be to make my own life easier."

Now Yid had looked at her again, his green eyes wide with sympathy. "Miss Mincy, I thought that was the whole entire point of two folks getting hitched up together."

"Stop it," Mincy had declared emphatically. "You've got to listen to me. You see, my background isn't the best, I don't have much schooling, and to tell the truth, I've had *no* other offers of marriage. From age fifteen I waited eagerly, from age eighteen I waited hopefully, from age twenty I waited prayerfully, and since I turned twenty-three, I have simply stopped waiting. That's why, if I was to accept your offer, I'd be taking unfair advantage..."

Mincy had stopped, her eyes and protest arrested by the tears that had welled up in Yid Francom's large green eyes.

"Law, Miss Mincy," he had declared softly, sorrowfully, "I'm sure sorry that you've had such pain."

"But that isn't what I meant..."

"Miss Mincy," Yid interrupted, "other men must be blind as weanling bats not to see what they've been missing. Why, to tell the truth, if you was to say yes, the advantages would be all mine. And ma'am, I surely hope that you will."

Yid had given her an appraising, pleading sort of look, and once again she had shivered a little with wonder about the small man. But then he had sighed and smiled pathetically. She saw that, was suddenly filled with a curious warm buzzing that somehow enabled her to see herself happily married to this man, and her heart was won.

"I reckon I'll do it, Mister Yid Francom," she said after drawing in a deep breath to steady herself. "And I'll do my best to make you a happy man."

"You've already done it," Yid had beamed. "And I promise that I'll do the same for you."

Then he had whipped his team into action again, and that very day, in Winnemucca, Nevada, Mincy had become a married woman.

Slipping the final remnants of the peach halves into the last mason jar, filling it with sugar water and sealing it tightly, Mincy wiped her hands on her apron and stared out the window. It was already afternoon, and the breeze was banging the barn door, which was hanging loosely by one hinge. A few feet away a section of fence, not yet even three years old, had broken down and had never been repaired. Off down in the bottom where the stream came out of the irrigated fields, what remained of the salt blocks gleamed in the afternoon sun. They had not been gathered in out of the weather in all the months since their cattle had been put on summer graze, and now the salt was nearly gone, wasted.

With a sigh and a smile of love and sympathy Mincy took off her apron and stepped to the door. Out back the cow was bawling with a full udder, and of course Yid, when he had left, had not even thought of who would milk her. Nor had he thought of who would do the rest of the chores.

And that was her dear, sweet husband, through and through. Sweet and gentle and kind as any man she had ever known, a wonder with animals and children, and a pathetically awful farmer.

Mincy's smile of love grew wider. How could his inability to farm really matter, at least in the big scheme of things? He loved her, he tried his best to make the farm productive, and he did everything in his power to make her life happy. What more, she thought with a slight chill of pleasure, could a woman such as herself ever want?

And of course the answer, other than the sons and daughters that both he and she longed for but which had never come, was nothing.

No, she thought as she stepped out into the yard to get about the chores, truthfully she could ask for nothing else. She was a happy woman, and she knew that, because of Yid Francom, she would remain happy for the rest of her natural life.

PART THREE

THE DECISION

5

"Honey-darlin'," Yid said the minute he stepped through the door after returning with the new plow, "I...I reckon we had ought to make us a little medicine."

"A little *what*?" Mincy giggled after she kissed him hello. "I declare, Yid, that I never heard *anybody* talk like you do. Why, you sound like you just walked out of a cow camp!"

Yid, ever the opportunist for making folks smile, and desperately wanting Mincy to smile now, took her comment in mock tragedy. He scrunched down like a wet dog that has just tried to slip into the warm kitchen and had the door slammed on his nose. About then, most anybody else would have taken instant pity on account of his sorrowful expression. But Mincy was giggling too hard, and she took none at all.

"I swear," she gasped, "that... you talk funnier than any man I ever met, my poor, departed grandpappy included. How you think of those things, when you aren't even a cowboy, is beyond me."

"I've done a little riding, here and there."

"You must have," she declared, still smiling. "But you've never told me about it. If the story is as funny as the language you learned, then I surely want to hear it."

"Funny," Yid wailed fervently, his act picking up momentum, "you think I talk funny?" Then, his shoulders further hunched, he acted like he felt worse than ever.

"You want a story, woman? I'll tell you a tragic tale that'll have you weeping worse than Thousand Springs Valley in the springtime, and that's a promise. You see, I growed up kicking from ranch to ranch with my poor, departed, widowed father, an emigrant Irish tailor who hawked his talents with a needle just like a patent medicine doctor hawks his alcoholic wares. And I tell you, the lingo of them salty fellers on those ranches flowed like blackstrap molasses into my brain, quick to run in, worse than impossible to clean out."

"Law, honey-darlin', I've been working steady on my grammar for three solid years; in fact, three years to this very day. I've managed to cast aside a tolerably large portion of my *ain'ts* and other such nefarious customers, and I hardly ever say *reckon* anymore. But such speech habits as I've accumulated are more than middling hard to break.

The conversation became a game then, with Yid playing picked on, and Mincy doing the picking. They played it often in their lonely conversations at the solitary cabin, reversing the roles at will, and it was an unusual but highly enjoyable way for them to draw closer to each other. Nor did any of their harangues often drift far from the absolute truth.

"Well," Mincy glowered fiercly at him, showing forth her own knowledge of country grammar, "I don't feel like weeping, just rejoicing. All I can say, Yid Francom, is that it's a mighty good thing we don't have kids. I want them book-learned and brung up halfways fit, and not talking like uneducated scalawags and carpetbaggers. Mercy, but I wish you'd hair up and at least *try* to adopt a little education in your grammar."

"By jings," Yid allowed in total agreement, "I reckon I should ought to do that, all right. After all, education's like a mother's love, or a married lady's morals. A man doesn't dast question either one in public. You come out against education, you just ain't going to get elected in this Big Lost country. A man might better stand in favor of being kind to Claude Johnson and other nefarious horse thieves, refusing to dance when young 'Fiddling Bill' Lambson tunes up his fiddle, or maybe giving free whiskey to the Indians down at Fort Hall. Tell the truth, I'd rather run on a ticket of kicking stray dogs and pistol-whipping little old ladies than to utter a derogatory word about book learning."

Yid paused, scraping at his chin.

"Still, honey-darlin', concerning my grammar, it's no bet. I'm just a slat-ribbed, uneducated galoot what has no more chance of talking fine and Eastern-fancy than a leppy calf has of wintering through on ice crystals and creek-bed moss. And since there obviously ain't no better in this marriage, I reckon you'll just have to keep on taking me for worse."

Mincy and Yid eyed each other, and finally, almost simultaneously, they broke into laughter. Off down toward the little butte and Thousand Springs a crow called out, and then again. Back behind the barn the calf bawled plaintively, and then Mincy was bit by a horsefly. Slapping at it, she giggled some more, and finally grew serious.

"Did you have a good trip, sweetheart?"

Yid dropped his eyes. "Well, I got the plow."

"Oh, good. I was worried that the drummer might not have one. Looks like you also got a new shirt."

Yid closed his eyes and took a deep breath. "Yeah, I...I did, at that."

"I'm glad, dear. You've been needing a new shirt something awful. Listen, I'll bet you're hungry. Sit tight, and I'll rustle something up."

Raising his eyes, Yid looked at his wife. "Uh...I need to get at the chores..."

"No you don't," Mincy said, smiling, "I got the peaches bottled early, so there was plenty of extra time. Now just you relax, and I'll have some supper ready in a snap."

Yid sat back, but there was no relaxing in him. Not when

his wife was full of so much love and kindness, and he was so full of lust and deceit. And why was he like that? Why, when he was married to such an a wonderful person, did his eyes and his mind continue to dwell upon other women? Or rather, *another* woman. What was there about Amber Wiggins that he found so fetching? How was it that she could...

"Yid, what's wrong?"

Startled, Yid looked into the eyes of his wife. "What?"

Mincy came slowly to him. "Something is wrong, sweetheart. What is it?"

"I...I... uh, nothing, honey-darlin'. I reckon maybe I'm just tired."

Standing, Yid walked past his wife to the door and looked out. He wanted to tell Mincy. But how could he? He was so ashamed, so embarrassed. Besides, even if he did tell her, what would that change? Mincy would probably love him less, and he'd end up thinking more about Amber Wiggins than ever. And Yid knew that he was going to do more dreaming about the widow Wiggins. She was simply too beautiful, too alluring, for him to want to stop. Why, even now he could see her, lying on her bed with her arm up across her eyes ...

"Yid, that isn't a new shirt, is it," Mincy said suddenly, breaking in on Yid's daydreaming.

Yid did not turn to face his wife. "No...it isn't. I...borrowed it."

"You borrowed it?"

"Yeah... from... Amber Wiggins. Her cow was delivering a calf breach, and I stopped to help. It sort of messed up my shirt, so she gave me this one until the other gets washed."

For a long moment Mincy was silent. "Did you save the calf?" she finally asked.

Yid nodded. "Both the cow and calf are fine."

Mincy put her hands gently on Yid's shoulders and began to massage them. "I...I'm glad you were there to help. You are so good with animals."

"Some say that."

Yid continued to stare out the door, ignoring his wife's

gentle fingers. What was wrong with him? Why couldn't he just relax and enjoy the evening with Mincy? So what if he had his private daydreams? They didn't need to interfere with his marriage, or with his wife's happiness, either. The one couldn't be so bad as to so thoroughly foul up the other. Could it?

No, of course not. But if that was right, then why was he feeling like he was? By jings, he was acting touchier than a teased tarantula, and that wasn't like him, not at all it wasn't.

"Yid?"

"Yeah?"

"Sweetheart, what is it?"

Pulling away from Mincy's gentle fingers, Yid turned and walked back to the table. "I thought you said you were going to fix me something to eat."

For a moment Mincy looked startled. But then, without another word, she stirred up the fire, sliced some fatback and potatoes into a pan, and put them on the stove to fry.

Sadly Yid stared at the table while Mincy set out a plate and cup and again busied herself over the stove. The sun was low in the afternoon sky, and where it slanted through the window the dust particles danced and moved in and out of the light. When he had been a child in his father's tailoring wagon, he had loved to play with that dust, blowing gently, or drawing his hand through it to stir it into swirls of commotion. But now the dust bothered him, even irritated him a little. There was so much of it in his home. Good grief! Couldn't Mincy keep *anything* clean? Why, Amber Wiggins' home was spotless, and ...

"Is she...that much prettier than me?"

Yid's head jerked up. "What?"

Mincy took a deep breath. "I asked if you thought... Amber was so much prettier than me."

"Mincy, you know better than to even ask a fool question like that. Of course I don't!"

"Then why...can't you stop dreaming about her?"

Yid dropped his head to hide his surprise. How on earth had Mincy known *that*? How could she possibly know that he had been thinking so intimately of Amber Wiggins? And even at that very instant, too. It was almost as though she could read his mind.

"Mincy, honey-darlin', I don't know what you're talking about."

"Yid," Mincy said gently, "don't make it worse by lying. A woman knows these things. I...I can feel what you are thinking."

And for a fact, Mincy thought, she *had* known. She wasn't certain exactly how she had known, or exactly what, even, but she had known *something*.

Why, Amber Wiggins had set her feather for her husband, and for some time the widow's enticements had been as obvious to Mincy as the fact that the sun rose in the east in the morning. Yet Yid had been amazingly slow to notice it, and Mincy had truly admired him for that. As he himself might have said, he apparently wasn't of a mind to glance slanchwise for anything short of the Second Coming. For a fact, in the face of Amber's almost obscene obsequiousness, Mincy had finally concluded that the Savior would have had to show up on the handlebars of a bicycle being ridden by a tame bear, to draw so much as a blink out of her husband. He had seemed that true.

But now...

"Yid," she pleaded gently, carefully, "please tell me what happened."

His eyes almost hollow, Yid looked up at his wife. "I'm telling you, Mincy, *nothing* happened!"

Mincy shook her head stubbornly. "Yes it did, sweetheart. I can tell. Maybe it wasn't anything terribly serious, but Amber tried to make it that way, didn't she."

Yid looked at his wife in wonder. Her intuition, or whatever it was, was amazing, simply amazing.

"I...I finally ran," he said quietly, with deep mortification. "I had to."

"I knew you would," Mincy declared with relief.

"But honey-darlin', I almost didn't. I came so close..."

"But you ran, sweetheart," Mincy exclaimed, "and that means you won. Oh, I'm so proud of you, of your strength and courage. You are the most wonderful husband a woman could ever have."

Yid stared at her, his heart aching more than ever. It wasn't fair what he was doing to her. It truly wasn't fair. Only...

"Mincy, that ain't...isn't all."

"What? But..."

"The rest of it is that I can't stop thinking of her. She's in my mind, every hour, every minute, most nearly every second. I reckon it's like a sickness, or something. It just won't go away."

"But it will, Yid, if you just keep trying. I know it will."

"I don't know, honey-darlin'. I do try, but thoughts of that woman just won't leave me alone."

Yid took a deep breath, wondering if he should continue. But he had to. He owed Mincy at least that much.

"Mincy," he almost whispered, "it's maybe even worse. See, I...I don't know if I *want* to stop thinking of her."

Mincy stared at her husband, unable to even respond.

"I...I don't know why that's so," Yid said quietly. "It's just that when I get discouraged or something, first thing I know I'm thinking of her..."

"And feeling better?" Mincy questioned tragically.

"Yeah," Yid affirmed. "And feeling better."

"That's because she is so pretty," Mincy declared sorrowfully as she turned slowly away. "Much more than me. I'm so big and ugly..."

"That's not so!" Yid declared, rising to his feet. "Mincy, you're a beautiful woman, and I've thought it since that first day I laid eyes on you. Why, sure, Amber Wiggins is pretty. But there must be ten million pretty women out there in the world, and every one of them is more ornamental than useful. Shoot, Mincy, not one of them is beautiful like you are, inside *and* out. Besides, you're the woman I'm married to, and like I've told you a thousand and one times, I asked you on purpose. It wasn't an accident, and all this coyoting around the rim about it and Amber Wiggins and you being not as pretty as her ain't going to change things one little bit."

Mincy, her eyes wet with tears, looked fervently at her husband. "Do...do you mean that? I mean, truly mean it?"

"Sure as they dance in the Grand Prize Hall," Yid responded with equal fervor. "Mincy, I don't know what's been ailing me lately, but from this moment on, she's over. Thoughts, dreams, visions, the whole she-bang, are only about you. It's just you and me, and no widow women or anyone else will ever get between us again."

"Oh, Yid, I'm so glad that you are..."

"Unless," Yid averred with a sly twinkle as he interrupted his wife, "that someone else should happen to be a tiny, bitty, wee one with a mop of lovely dark hair just like his mother's."

"Oh, Yid."

6

The next morning, September 2, 1899, the morning of Yid's and Mincy's third anniversary, the plow broke again. Not ten minutes down the first furrow, it broke.

In complete frustration Yid stared downward. "By jings," he said in disgust as he kicked at a huge clod of soil, "why does it always happen to me?"

Dropping to his knees, he took hold of the broken share and moved it back and forth. "They sure don't make 'em like they used to," he muttered as he fingered the sheared metal. "Trouble is, now what am I going to do?"

Sitting in the plowed earth, Yid took off his hat and wiped his brow. It might be September second, but by day it was hot as August second, and maybe then some. Off down the valley a crow wheeled over the Little Butte, and Peaches stomped her hoof, impatient to be moving.

"Aw, take it easy," Yid growled at her. "Can't you see I'm trying to think?"

The mare stared at him, swished her tail in a nonchalant circle and turned away again, to mimic Cream, her motionless companion.

Yid watched his horses, broke off a stick of dry sage to pick at his teeth, and considered.

This was bad, mighty bad. At this high elevation, he didn't have a whole lot of season left for field work. Of course he had his hay in the barn and stacked out back, and the ditches were already dug that would bring the water to this new forty acres that he was trying to get grubbed out and ready for planting. But doggone it, if the plowing wasn't done before snowfall, they'd never on this green earth get the grain drilled next spring in time to harvest it. And if they didn't have grain to sell to the Ketchum freight line next fall, he and Mincy might just as well board up the cabin and sign the deed back over to the bank. It was that critical.

"By Tophet," Yid growled as he threw a small dry clod of earth off into the brush, "that'd be a fine how-de-do! Wonder how Amber Wiggins would feel if I had to pick up and leave..."

Startled, he actually blinked. There he was, thinking of Amber Wiggins again, not by design, but just because that was where his mind had gone.

But why? He'd promised Mincy, and he'd meant every word of his promise. He wasn't going to sit around and let the devil play with his mind anymore. No sir. He and Mincy were happy, and it was going to stay that way. So why had his mind gone where he had promised both himself and his wife that it would never go again? He didn't know, but it wasn't going to stay there.

"Giddap," he barked to his team as he rose to his feet and took up the lines again. "Let's get this broken plow back to the cabin. Then maybe I can figure what to do about it. Now come on, Peaches, let's go!"

Ten minutes later the team had gone only a few yards, Yid was scrunching along on his knees trying to hold up the broken plowshare so it wouldn't dig in wrong and throw the whole shebang out of kilter and into the horses, thus causing them to bolt, and he was more frustrated than ever.

"Law," he mumbled as he pushed back his hat and

wiped his brow for the umpteenth time, "this doesn't hardly seem worth it. Man sure ought to be able to make a living easier than this."

Peaches looked at him again, Yid looked back at her, and in his mind he saw Amber Wiggins, smiling sweetly, inviting him...

"Well, for the love of pete," he growled as he stood up. "What is the matter with me? Why is that widow woman all I can ever think about? What on earth happened the other night that caused this?"

Of course nothing *really* had happened, but Yid had found it next to impossible to convince his mind of that fact. Ever since then, even despite his promise to Mincy, his thoughts had made the event into something more and more explicit and titillating.

And truthfully, because he couldn't get the experience, or the imaginations of it, out of his system, his burden of guilt continued to grow. Guilt, he had quickly discovered, had not helped things between himself and Mincy. As a point of Big Lost country fact, guilt, and the thoughts that caused it, had made things stink worse than a week-old wolf-killed carcass.

"Come on," he encouraged himself as he strained against the plow handle to tilt it sideways, "I'll hold it like this, and maybe..."

And that was when Yid first saw the writing. It was burned into the underside of the plow handle, almost like it had been stamped with a very small brand. But of course it had not been. Only why did it smell like newly burned wood ...

Twisting his head so he could read it, Yid slowly mouthed out the words.

> *Verily I say unto you as I have said before, he that looketh on a woman to lust after her, or if any shall commit adultery in their hearts, they shall not have the Spirit, but shall deny the faith and shall fear.*

Slowly Yid lifted his eyes, looking around him. There was a strange pounding in his head, and a knot of fear gripped his belly. Who had written this? How had it come to be on the handle of his new plow...

The drummer. It musy be the drummer. He'd done this. Somehow the meddling old fool had become suspicious and was doing a little preaching. He'd probably even fixed the plow so it would break again, the crazy, senile old man. Well, he wasn't going to get away with it. No sir, Yid was going back to that Cove and give him what for. And he was going there immediately, too.

Angrily he yanked up the plow, and with a vicious slap of the lines sent the team up out of the field toward the cabin. And with each step he took, he became more resolute. No one was going to tell him what he could and couldn't think. Nobody was going to preach scripture at him. Especially not someone like that old fool drummer.

He would think what he wanted, by jings, and if it happened to be that he wanted to consider the incredibly female charms of Amber Wiggins, then that was exactly what he would do.

And Yid could see her ever more clearly as he marched, that lovely, haunting visage of the woman who seemed to be waiting down on Sage Creek for him to return.

"I'm telling you, Mincy," Yid growled as he reached the cabin, "the drummer gave me a defective plow. I was paying attention, and I didn't hit any cussed rock, either."

Mincy dropped to her knees next to the broken plow. "Can we fix it?"

"I don't reckon we can. If I hadn't accidentally burned up the bellows last month, then maybe I could smith it, but I burned up those consarned bellows..."

Yid stopped talking and watched as Mincy moved the share back and forth.

"Something sheared it off," she muttered thoughtfully. "Question is, what do we do now? We've *got* to get the ground ready for early drilling, and that can't be done without a plow. Is there someone in the valley that we could borrow one from?"

Slowly Yid shook his head. "Not hardly, Mincy. Them that has plows are using them. Besides, other than Al West, who *is* using his, the next nearest neighbor is Jack Bascom, and you know he has already loaned his plow to Dan Richardson. We both heard them talking about it."

"So what do we do?"

"I'm going back to that old drummer, Mincy. That's what I'm going to do. It's his fault, and he owes us a new plow. I aim to see that we get it."

Mincy looked quickly up. "Do you think he would have another one? How many plows can a drummer possibly have in one wagon?"

Yid, for the first time in two days, remembered the totally empty wagon he had left behind him in the Cove. There would be no plow there. There would be nothing at all. Not unless the drummer had returned with new stock.

Suddenly Yid smiled. Of course! That was surely where the old fool had gone when he had left the wagon so suddenly the day before. To get more stock. Most likely he had come back by now, and it was even more likely that he would have obtained another plow.

Besides, and Yid almost chuckled when he thought this, when he passed Sage Creek on his way to the Cove to get the plow, he might also see Miss Amber again.

Yid grinned even more widely. "Well, honey-darlin, he'll have a plow. Now I reckon I'd better get cracking if I want to get back by tomorrow."

Mincy looked deeply into her husband's eyes. "Yid, sweetheart," she pressed gently, "are you sure that's the *only* reason you want to go to the Cove?"

"What are you asking?" Yid questioned as once again he saw before him the provocative, enticing form of Amber Wiggins.

"I'm asking," Mincy said gently, honestly, "if you're having trouble with thoughts of Amber again?"

"Now why would you think that?" he growled, suddenly feeling nervous as a bit-up bull in fly time. It was scary how Mincy could see through him. Were all women like that? Was Amber? Did she also know what he had been thinking?

"I know," Mincy continued quietly, "that the road goes

right past her place, and you seem awful anxious to be off in that wagon again. A person can't help but wonder..."

"Doggone it, Mincy," Yid argued, "you know it's the only road."

"It is unless you go down past Al West's, and over the Bar," Mincy responded.

"That's a long way around to the Cove, ain't...isn't it?"

"Yes, but maybe safer for you, if you know what I mean."

Yid stared at the ground, thoroughly upset. It was bad enough that the plow had broken and that the old fool drummer had tried preaching to him and that he couldn't get his thinking about Amber Wiggins under control. But it was worse that Mincy could see it all so easily and then treat him like some little kid who'd been caught with his hand in the candy sack. By Tophet, being treated like that didn't set well with him at all.

"Woman," he said, glowering, "you and a few other folks are sure enough riling me."

"I'm sorry, sweetheart. I don't mean to. I...I'm just worried."

"Why?" Yid snapped, using his anger as a whip to subdue her, to beat her away from his conscience and guilt. "You afraid I might leave you? By Tophet, Mincy, I told you last night; Amber Wiggins is out of the picture, and I'm sure as bear grease is slick not planning on stopping there today. Like I said, I intend to *stay* married to you.

"Now I'm going after that conniving drummer,and you're going to wait here until I get back. Hear me, Mincy?"

"I... hear you," Mincy said slowly, distantly.

For a moment there was silence — a terrible, uncomfortable silence that Yid could hardly bear, for he knew that he had deeply wounded the woman he loved. And so at last he spoke.

"Mincy," he said, shuffling at the dirt with his boot tip, "I'm sorry I've given you all this pain. I reckon I've had me a few problems, but I want you to know that I love you, and you're the only one for me   Always.

"Now, we have a broken plow here, and some plowing that needs mightily to be done. Do you want me to go after that old drummer again, or not?"

"You're leaving it up to me?" Mincy asked, surprised.

"I am."

Mincy laughed. "That's some decision you're leaving me, Yid Francom."

Yid grinned sadly.

"Of course you must go," Mincy instantly declared, "and you must take the Ketchum freight road, because it is the shortest. I'm so sorry, sweetheart, that I doubted you."

Yid squeezed her hand and kissed her softly. "No need to be sorry, honey-darlin'. It was my fault, not yours. *Adios.* Reckon I'll be back as soon as I can."

Quickly Yid walked away from his smiling wife, and as he moved the team into place over the tongue of the old springbed, he smiled.

"By jings," he muttered as he hooked the tugs to the singletrees, 'I can beat this thing with my thoughts. I know I can. With a woman like that to stand behind me, there's no need to ever look slanchwise at Amber Wiggins again. Or any other woman either, for that matter. No sir, and that's a bob tailed flush against no bet at all, no matter how the deck is cut."

Grinning, Yid finished harnessing the span to the springbed, climbed aboard, took up the lines, and with an airy whistle he touched the horses with his whip.

"I love you," Mincy suddenly called to him from the doorway. "You hear me, Yid Francom? I love you."

"I love you, too," he called back sincerely, joyfully, and then he leisurely lined the team out for the hazy distance of the lower Big Lost River valley.

"Law but it's a beautiful day," he muttered as the wagon passed out through the open pole gate. "Things sure would shine a little brighter, though, if I could take Miss Amber on a picnic this afternoon..."

Surprised at the totally unexpected thought, Yid snapped closed his mouth. Wh...what had he said? Had he...discussed, even with himself, that widow woman

again? Of course the answer was yes, but Yid didn't understand that at all. Especially he didn't understand when, not
two minutes previous, he had vowed that thoughts of
Amber Wiggins were out of his life for good. Obviously he
had been wrong, but why?

And then Yid knew. Or at least thought he knew. On
down the valley some ten miles or so, a faint wisp of smoke
hung clearly visible in the afternoon air. That smoke came
from the cabin on Sage Creek, the cabin which housed a
terribly fetching young widow woman who seemed to
have an amazingly high regard for one Yid Francom.

Which regard, Yid grinned to himself, was appreciated if
not clearly understood.

And that, he suddenly realized and just as suddenly
admitted, had exactly nothing at all to do with his beloved
wife, Mincy. He and she were happily married, and would
remain so forever, for he would most definitely stay true to
her.

But such marital circumstances surely didn't need
to keep a man from looking, from enjoying, from
savoring, from dreaming, and maybe even from spending
a little innocent time together with the lovely Amber
Wiggins ...

"Yid," Mincy suddenly called from back near the porch,
"stop! I'm coming with you."

Surprised once again, Yid turned back. Mincy stood
where she had stood before, but her arm was in the air
signaling to him, and she was already lifting her right foot
to start forward.

"Sweetheart," she cried again, "I've changed my mind!
I'm coming with you!"

Instantly, perversely determined that he would go alone
so that whatever might develop between himself and
Amber could, Yid turned his back once again upon his
wife. And with a Blackfoot warrior screech for his team to
proceed forth *huyee-hoto*, he laid about the ears of the two
horses with his fifteen-foot bullwhip, handling it like a
schoolgirl's quirt.

The chargers hit their collars cowboy style — from a

droop-headed shuffle to a back-humping run in three jumps. Those horses had been eating oats out of a nosebag most of the summer, and both of them were as full of scat as a catnipped kitten. How they ran! And Mincy was left strangling amid an acrid cloud of horse dust and disillusionment, smack in the middle of her chicken-scratched yard.

The manner in which she then emerged from her eclipse made Yid wonder from then until snow melt the next spring. With no outcry of foul play, in fact with no audible complaint whatever, Mincy simply proceeded to run down on foot a span of gingered-up horses in full gallop. Once abreast of the springbed wagon's front wheels, she seized the seatbox hand irons, vaulted up beside Yid, and grabbed the lines from him. Then she lifted both horses practically clear off their tugs and threw them back on their haunches for a twenty-six-foot sliding stop that flung Yid down between the horses, stood herself straight up on her feet, and set a local Big Lost country record for dead-run haul-ups that Yid spent the rest of his life trying to equal and never did come closer to than thirty-eight feet and seven inches. And even doing that, he turned over the wagon and killed eleven chickens and a sleeping dog. While the chickens didn't matter, the dog was a good friend of his, and the little tailor-turned-farmer never did completely forgive Mincy her patent responsibility for the murder of the canine. However, that was six months later and another story altogether .

For the present, Yid lay where he had fallen between the quivering rumps of the team. There, eyes tightly closed, he kept muttering over and over again, "I'm dead, by jings, I'm dead!"

"Now Yid," Mincy called down to him in a pleasantly diffident voice, "if you will please cease conducting your own sad funeral and climb back up here, we shall embark at once for the Cove.

"Ah, no, Yid," she protested as Yid crawled back up and reached for the lines, "I shall pilot this fool wagon the remainder of the way."

Whereupon, and before her companion could object, Mincy tossed Yid's bullwhip into the dirt, clucked gently to the span of horses, and sent the surprised hitch into a honey-smooth road lope that would have done credit to any four Wells Fargo horses ever foaled.

"By Tophet," Yid muttered as he stared in amazement at his wife, "I don't believe it. I had no idea you could galvinate like that. You got across that yard faster'n a lizard off a hot rock. The last time I saw anything move so swift and shameless was the night Wond'rous Wayne Boss went to treat his saddle gall in the dark after a particularly arduous game of five-card-draw with Bernell 'Preacher' Christensen. He got the sheep-dip out of the tackroom medicine chest instead of the bear oil, was painfully perturbed as I recollect, and didn't slow down his scampering and howling for over an hour."

"Poor fellow," Mincy responded quietly. "Who won the hand?"

"I don't rightly know. Why'd you change your mind about coming with me?"

Mincy looked off down the valley. "I just had a feeling, I suppose. Whatever it was, I got to thinking about you and Amber Wiggins, and suddenly I could see, plain as day, that you were thinking about her, too. That made my decision. I...I just couldn't let you face that sort of temptation alone."

Yid scowled thoughtfully. Something was squirrelly about Mincy's ability to read his mind as a peach orchard boar, but he couldn't put his finger on it. Not yet, he couldn't. But it would come, and when it did...

Meanwhile, no old drummer, nor yet any one woman on God's green earth, wife or otherwise, was going to prevent him from conducting his own sweet daydreams. No sir, he'd entertain and fantasize whatever he wanted, about *whoever* he wanted, and that decision was final as the end of the railroad line in San Francisco.

"Well," he said almost sweetly as he settled down beside his wife, "come right on along, then. All's we need to do is get to that drummer by dawn's first light. Otherwise I'll never be first in line to get a new plow, and you know, honey-darlin', that I *have* to be first in that line."

"Happy anniversary," she responded softly, gently ignoring her husband's grousing.

And Yid, his conscience at last pierced through, grumbled a "happy anniversary" in return.

And with a slight smile of total understanding, Mincy nodded and gazed ahead.

7

"Yid, this place is frightening."

Feeling as apprehensive as his wife felt, Yid visually searched out the fog-shrouded Cove. But though it was broad afternoon daylight, the area was so thick with mist that he felt suffocated, overpowered by it, and he could see very little at all.

"This stuff ain't natural," he said uneasily. "It was bad the last time I was here, but not like this. Why, it's darker than the insides of a black bear's paunch."

"Does it ever lift?"

"Law, Mincy, I don't know. Normally the sun burns it off shortly after daylight. But this? All I can say is that I reckon it can't possibly stay here forever."

Mincy shivered beside him. It's like a...a haunt."

For a moment neither Yid nor Mincy moved, and the silence of the Cove was ominous. Finally Peaches stamped a hoof impatiently, and that seemed to be a signal.

"Well," Mincy declared, doing her best to shake off her nervousness, "we've come this far; we might as well finish it. Besides, as they say, daylight's burning...somewhere. Where does the drummer park his wagon?"

"Uh...it's mighty hard to tell."

"What do you mean?   You've been here often enough. Don't you know where he camps?"

"I...I do, sort of. It's usually off over that-a-way."

Yid swung his hand in a small arc that covered maybe a fourth of the compass, and Mincy shook her head in amazement.   "That's pinpointing things to a fare-theewell, all right. I take it you don't really know?"

"Well, I've always found him, Mincy, but he does move around some. And in this fog? Law, I can't hardly tell."

Mincy smiled. "Then I suppose we start exploring."

"I reckon we do," Yid agreed, and with a gulp of apprehension he shook the lines. Peaches and Cream responded, and soon were dragging the wagon forward into the thickening gloom.

"By Tophet," Yid growled to himself as the wagon creaked forward, "it's harder to see right now than it was when I flailed the mares out of Amber's place the other night. Doggone but I wish I hadn't been in such a hurry to get away. She and I could have really..."

"Yid," Mincy suddenly said, breaking the ominous silence, "how can I help you?"

"Help me what?"

"Stop thinking of Amber.   I know you had some thoughts when we passed her place, and you look like you're thinking of her now. What can I do to help you stop?"

"Humph," the surprised Yid grunted, having nothing better to say.

Mincy reached out and took her husband's hand. "I know you want to stop, sweetheart, and there surely must be some way that I can help. Tell me what it is, and I'll do it."

Listening to Mincy's voice, Yid knew that she was being absolutely sincere. She wasn't angry, she wasn't even disgusted. She was simply doing her best to assist the man she loved to crawl out of a very difficult, and what she considered to be a terribly filthy, situation.

"Honey-darlin'," Yid responded, "I...I don't rightly

know how you can help. Seems like, if I do change, it's mostly got to be me."

"Are you saying that you might *not* change?" Mincy asked quietly.

Yid squirmed uncomfortably. "Well, I didn't mean that exactly."

"Then what did you mean?"

"I mean...well, doggone it, Mincy, it's kind of confusing. You know I'm going to be true to you, and I know it, too. Nothing on this earth, or no person either, including Amber Wiggins, could ever palaver me into being unfaithful to you. Those being the nailed-down facts, I can't see how a stray thought, here or there, can hurt either one of us."

"But Yid," Mincy argued, "such thoughts are lustful, and Jesus says they are just as wrong as adultery."

"If they're so wrong," Yid countered, "then why do they come so natural to a man's mind? The Lord made my think-box to work like it does, not me. I just naturally think about women, and I enjoy it. Neither do I *try* to bring those thoughts inside. They just sort of get rounded up and herded in by themselves. I truly can't stop them.

"Besides, before we got married it was natural and reasonable for me to look at all the women I saw, and believe me, I did look. Just like I looked at you. I never did nothing with those women, though, beyond looking at 'em and maybe dreaming a little. That being the case, why should I feel guilty for doing the same sort of thing now? I may be married, but I'm just as harmless as I always was, and maybe more so. Tell the truth, I don't think I should feel guilty for doing what comes so natural."

Mincy looked at him without speaking, but Yid could see the deep pain in her eyes.

"By jings, honey-darlin', don't look at me that way. I love you with all my heart, and I'm doing the best I can to be a good husband. "

"I...know you are," Mincy said as she turned away. "All I want to do is help, but I...I just can't help feeling somehow betrayed."

"I'm not betraying you, and the best way you could help me would be to stop pestering," Yid declared. "Or to stop throwing Amber Wiggins' name at me every time you see me dreaming. I *might* be thinking about fishing, you know, or riding the far-off hills. I do have other dreams than Widow Wiggins."

"So you...you want me to stop trying to help?" Mincy asked.

"That's the purr-dee truth." Yid affirmed. "One of these days I'll just naturally stop, all by my lonesome. You'll see. Until then, well, there's no point in even worrying about it. My occasional dreams *can't* make any difference in the big picture of our lives."

"But what if they do?" Mincy pleaded, her voice growing more desperate.

"They *can't*. There's nothing real in a man's thoughts and dreams to make a difference with. That's why I say that the whole issue is foolishness.

"Now," Yid concluded with finality, "what say you and I get looking for that sorry old drummer?"

Moments later they heard the team splash into the small stream that ran through the Cove, and then with a lunge the wagon bounced out the other side and up over the bank. There Yid pulled the animals to another stop.

"N...now what?" Mincy asked, her voice subdued.

"Now I need to be sure where I am," Yid answered. "By Tophet, it's thick enough in this mist to slow down a bat. Let's see. There should be a clump of cottonwood just to our left, but I can't see anything."

"Good heavens, Yid, there are trees all around us."

"I know, Mincy, but I'm looking for a particular grove."

"Where is it?"

"By jings, woman," Yid declared, feeling unaccountably upset, "if I knew, I'd go there directly."

" It looks a little thinner off that way." Mince replied hopefully, pointing. "Maybe we should look there."

"Or there or there or there," Yid said, pointing in various directions. "If I could just see that consarned grove..."

For long and agonizing moments Yid directed the horses back and forth through the mist and the trees, looking for that one particular grove of cottonwoods. "By jings," he finally said, "I'm beginning to feel like someone stole my rudder. Or like the mist has addled my think-box. Or maybe like I'm stumble-drunk as a fiddler's clerk. Doggone it, Mincy, finding that drummer is getting skimpier'n tracking bees in a blizzard.

"What I don't understand," he moaned then, looking hopelessly around him, "is that always before I've been able to point right to his wagon. Last time it took me a spell because of the mist, but it sure wasn't like this."

"Have you thought that he might not be here?"

"Sure I've thought of it," Yid snapped. "But he's always been here before, every single time I needed him. If I could just find those trees."

There! Ahead of him, through the mist, was the very clump of trees he had been looking for all along. He whipped the team forward, and soon they brought the wagon to a stop under the spreading boughs of the exact cottonwood where he had parked so many times before.

But now he looked around him, shaking his head in dumfounded amazement. "I don't understand it," he muttered. "I for certain sure don't. I *know* we've been past here two or three times in the last hour. Law, Mincy, how could I have missed it?"

"Maybe because your mind is so taken up with other things," Mincy answered softly. "Things that you ought not to be dwelling on..."

Instantly madder, as he would have said, than a bear-swatted beehive, Yid leaped from the wagon into the mist. "Find your own way," he snarled at his wife. "That, or stay here by your lonesome. It makes no difference to me. By Tophet, I'm gone!"

Then Yid turned away and disappeared, after only a step or two, into the thick and swirling mist.

"Yid?" Mincy called.

Yid did not answer.

"You've no call to be upset, Yid. You asked questions, and I was only trying to help you find the answers."

Grinning maliciously, Yid remained silent, knowing that he was well hidden by the mist.

Anxious, Mincy climbed down from the wagon and took a few steps into the fog. But then she stopped, moved a few steps in another direction, halted, went a third direction, and finally knew that she was hopelessly and totally lost. In fact, she could not even see the wagon she had just left somewhere behind.

"Yid," she called, "please? I love you with all my soul, sweetheart, and all I want is to know that you love me the same. I...I don't think I can bear it, knowing that you are...are thinking of another woman. Can't you understand that? Now that I know what you're doing, I feel like I'm being stabbed, beaten down, destroyed. Surely that can't be the result of righteous or acceptable thoughts."

Yid, not more than a dozen feet from his wife, stared into the gloom.

"Don't the scriptures say that we need to put off the natural man?" Mincy continued. "Don't they say that the natural man is an enemy to God? That's what they say, Yid, and the Lord must surely have been talking to those of us who think that being natural is being right.   Thinking what comes naturally wasn't right back then, not according to Paul. And it can't be right for you, either."

Mincy was probably right, Yid knew. But what was he to do? He'd tried to get rid of his thoughts — really, truly tried. Only they wouldn't go away, and any more, it just didn't seem worth the effort. One day they would go away by themselves, he knew that. But until then, what was the big deal? Like he had explained, it was only imagination and dreams, and they were nothing at all. And nothing, he reasoned smugly, could hurt nobody, Mincy included. She should surely be able to see that.

"Yid, please, I'm lost. Sing out, so I can find you."

The mist was thicker than clabbered milk, soupier by far than he had ever seen it, and Yid was not surprised that Mincy had become lost. In fact, it felt like it was burning his nostrils, or clogging them, it was so heavy.

"Yid?"

Mincy's voice sounded more fearful, and Yid's conscience pinged him. He was hurting her, something he had never wanted to do, and he didn't like the feeling it was giving him. That, above all else, wasn't right .

Cautiously he moved through the mist toward her, careful to see where he was placing his feet. But he was a hunter, and a good one, so it was easy for him to move quietly.

"Yid, please?"

Now Yid smiled again. She was near, not more than four or five feet from him. He'd give her a good scare and tell her again that he loved her. He wouldn't even say anything about his thoughts. That way maybe they could get on about the business of getting a new plow and getting back to work, and he could go on with the pleasant daydreams that he was so learning to enjoy...

Whump!

With a scream of fear, Mincy spun and drove with her two fists straight into Yid's face. And Yid, with not a second to react to the fact that he had walked right into his frightened wife, found himself flat on his back with his head spinning like a loco catawampus and his whole body so weak that he couldn't lick his upper lip.

To say he was surprised would have been a century-staggering understatement. Mincy had never hit him before, had never even come close. Yet now it had happened.

"Mincy," he whined from where he lay, "why'd you hit me?"

"I'm sorry," Mincy whimpered as she bent down. "Oh, Yid, I'm sorry. I didn't mean to hit you."

"Well," he growled, feeling angry in spite of the fact that he knew it had been his own fault, "you did, and now I'm here on the ground. Look at all this blood. Law, woman, you trying to put me to bed with a pick and shovel?"

"Sweetheart," Mincy declared from directly above him, "I...I'm truly sorry. Here, let me help you."

Rolling away from his wife's outstretched arms, Yid

pushed himself up off the ground, drew his feet under him, and was in the act of standing up when a dead limb, hidden by the mist, snagged into the front of his shirt.

There was the sound of fabric tearing, Yid saw a button go flying off into the mist, and instinctively he pushed the limb away.

Instantly Mincy gasped with surprised pain, and Yid heard the sound of more fabric tearing.

"What happened?" he snapped.

"I...I don't know," Mincy responded. "This limb came out of nowhere and tore my blouse something awful. It snagged my skin a little, too, but I'm fine. Are you all right?"

"Yeah, except for a bloody nose and a lost button. Do you have a handkerchief?"

Yid listened as Mincy groped around in her bag. "Here," she finally said. "Did...did you find the drummer?"

"Not hardly. Reckon we'd best get moving, hadn't we."

Taking Mincy's hand, and feeling comforted that she was still willing to give it to him, Yid moved slowly forward into the gray void of the mist.

"See anything?"

"Yep. Mist, mist and more mist."

Mincy giggled quietly, and for some reason that he didn't understand, Yid felt a little shiver of pleasure. He enjoyed seeing his wife happy, and there was nothing he had ever heard that was so infectious as her laugh. Yet only moments before, he had actually relished causing her discomfort. Why was that? What was getting into him, that he wanted to hurt her, to lash out ...

"What's that?"

"Where?"

"Right in front of you."

Yid looked, and suddenly realized that he was seeing, at some distance before him, a man, or rather, the back of a man. Whoever it was, he was facing a huge, white wagon of some sort, and he seemed to be upset and protesting something to another man, who stood in a large open window.

"Oh, no!" Yid muttered as he tried to hurry. "He's ahead of me in line!"

And then, as Yid and Mincy drew nearer, they saw writing on the side of the wagon, strange writing, and both stopped short in amazement.

Automotive Parts, the writing said, whatever that meant, and beside the writing was a window .

Suddenly Yid's breath was stilled. The second man, standing in the window of the strange wagon. It was the drummer, *his* drummer. Only the fellow was dressed funny, and he was not smiling, not speaking .

"Yid, what is it?" Mincy whispered.

"I...I don't rightly know," Yid whispered back. "I...I think that I lost my place in line, all right, but then that isn't the drummer's wagon, either, so I can't tell."

Slowly he stepped forward once more, wanting to get even closer, to see who the man in front of the window was and to hear what he was protesting. But the mist swirled up around him again, momentarily blinding him, and he could see nothing.

When the fog thinned at last, Yid realized with a sinking feeling that the man who had been standing in front of him had gone. So too had the drummer and the wagon-like object with the writing on it. Instead he could see, and his heart hammered with a hollow ache of fear at the sight of it, a shiny sort of metallic object looming out of the mist where the funny-looking wagon had been.

Carefully he stepped forward, held out his hand, touched it, and felt the smoothest, softest metal he had ever felt in his entire life.

"Yid..."

"Shh!"

In the instant silence that followed, Yid stepped directly to the strange object, and then walked along the side of it, his hand brushing it lightly as he passed. It was metal, all right, or at least he supposed it was. But it was like no metal he had ever seen before, or felt.

Kneeling, he tried to feel under it. But the object went right to the ground, and even seemed to be buried a little in the earth.

Standing, he reached upward, but could find no indication of a top. Nor could he see any sign of wheels.

"Mincy," he whispered, "can you reach above this thing?"

"You...you want me to *touch* it?"

"I'm touching it, honey-darlin', and it hasn't bit me yet. Just see if you can reach the top."

Yid felt Mincy straining upward behind him, and just as she reached her full stretch, her blouse tore a little more. Then the metal in front of Yid began to fold in upon itself.

Mincy fell back with a cry of alarm, and Yid stared in open mouthed silence as the metal before him seemed to dissolve into nothing. Then a large window stood revealed. But even more amazing, the old drummer, *his* old drummer, stood framed in that window, still silent, still unsmiling.

But the old salesman was different, too, or at least his clothing was different. In fact, it was even different from what he had been wearing only a moment or so before when Yid had seen him through the mist.

Now his clothing was shiny, or more aptly put, shimmering, almost as if the fabric itself were alive. Nor did it have a distinct form, but hung almost as if it were a multi layered robe, or many robes worn one above the other. And the man's face glowed like it had a lantern behind it, a very bright lantern.

"H...howdy," Yid stuttered as he stared upward.

He was greeted with silence, total and absolute.

"Yid," Mincy whispered from behind him, "is that *your* drummer?"

"As ever was," Yid answered in a low voice, and the look in his eyes when he said it put a chill up the ladder of Mincy's backbone that she could feel clear up between her shoulder blades.

"Th...that's a mighty fancy wagon you have there, mister," Yid persisted.

The drummer continued to gaze downward without speaking, and Yid felt Mincy's presence at his elbow.

"Uh...we broke our plow...again." Yid declared, feeling more out of place than a pig in a pawnshop. "I...I think the one you gave me was...was defective. We were...uh...wondering if we might have another...until our grain comes in next summer, I mean. Then we'll pay right up. I've got most of a hundred acres in hay, and with a new plow I can do another forty or so in grain. We have some mighty pretty land up there, gorgeous as a fresh spring morning, and I reckon that the farm is going to be a fine one. Why, you should see the mountains that have us boxed in..."

Still the drummer did not move, and now Mincy nudged Yid's arm.

"He's not listening," she whispered urgently. "Just ask him flat out, and tell him that he needs to take the broken one back."

Yid nodded his understanding. "My wife, Mincy — this is her right here. I don't think you ever met her. Anyway, she says that there ought to be some sort of guarantee on the plow. I mean, we only had it two days."

Yid stared in consternation as the drummer, without any change of expression, turned back into the...the...whatever-it-was that he was in, and began to go through his merchandise. Suddenly he turned back, placed two small black containers upon the counter before Yid, and straightened.

"Uh." Yid coughed, looking at the small cubes, "I...uh...I needed a plow. Those ain't precisely what I had in mind."

But the drummer did not move. He did not respond, or smile, or make any indication whatever that he even knew that Yid was speaking to him. Yet he did cry, and Yid, gazing up at him, had the distinct and uncomfortable feeling the drummer was weeping *for him*.

Dropping his eyes in embarrassment, Yid's vision automatically focused on the small boxes. Then, unaccountably, he found himself reaching out to take them up and look at them. He hadn't meant to do that; he hadn't even thought of it. He was just, suddenly, picking the two boxes up and holding them in his hand.

For an instant, no longer, he looked at them. Then he

looked up at the Drummer to protest, to declare that he hadn't meant to pick them up, to complain that they in no way would take the place of the plow he needed.

But to his shock, fear and total consternation the side of the ... the...machine or wagon or whatever it was closed. It was all metal again, soft and glowing metal, and there was no one there.

No one .

8

"Yid, what are you doing?"

"I d...don't know," Yid whispered while his heart hammered with fear. "That old geezer was here, I saw him! Didn't you?"

"The drummer? Of course I saw him. But why on earth did you let him give you those little boxes?"

"Mincy, I didn't have no more choice'n a rabbit in a hound's mouth. I didn't want them, not any more than you did. For a fact, I didn't even mean to put my hand out to take them. Now let's get out of here, afore that old drummer decides he wants to give us something else we don't want."

"But...but I don't think we should go," Mincy stated. "We need to know if he has a plow or not, and I don't think we should leave here until we find out. Here, let me knock."

And then Mincy's voice grew still. Where the metal object had been, where only a second or so before something had stood glowing in the muted light, there was only mist — swirling silent, but mist nevertheless. Not only the weeping old man in the funny clothes who stood within the object, but the crazy metal wagon itself, were gone.

"Y...Yid?"

But Yid, instead of answering, was puckered up again, doing his best to whistle for the horses.

Mincy, seeing her husband's futile efforts and realizing instantly what he was trying to do, placed her two fingers in her mouth and blew out a whistle of her own that would have brought judgment day itself down upon them, happen the Lord would have been there to sanction it. But He wasn't, at least that they knew of, and neither Yid nor Mincy were ready to die yet anyway.

Yid, staring at her, shook his head. "Law, woman," he muttered, "where'd you learn to do that? You likely pierced my eardrums, drove insane a whole family of field mice who might have had the misfortune of choosing that unlucky moment to pass by, sent a hundred yards of willows to shivering like they were in a high wind, and knocked the smallest branches from the limbs of the nearest dozen cottonwood trees. Woman, you did some damage with that whistle."

"Maybe," Mincy smiled shyly, "but it brought the horses."

And for a truth it had, on a snorting, head-shaking, ear-pricked gallop.

"Get aboard," Yid ordered as he tossed the little boxes into the back of the springbed and took hold of the lines. "Hurry up, doggone it. And no more whistling. I'm deaf as a drowned rattler, and there's no telling what else we're going to run into in this fog that I might have to listen in on."

Mincy, completely amenable to Yid's suggestions, clambered up onto the wagon seat. Handing her the lines, Yid followed.

"What about the broken plow?"

"How's that?" Yid yelled, cupping his hand to his ear.

"I said," Mincy yelled, "what about the..." And then she sensed what Yid was doing, and started to giggle. "You heard me," she gasped finally. "Now answer me."

"By Tophet," Yid replied with a grin made smug by his success, "we'll bring it back some other time. And what are you laughing for, anyway? This is spooky business, woman." Then he whipped the lines against the horses' backs.

"It certainly is," Mincy agreed. "I'll tell you what. Let's find a blacksmith down to Houston who can repair it. Or Arco, if need be. Now that I think on it, I don't imagine a two- or three- day trip away from this cursed valley would be a bad idea."

"No, for a fact it wouldn't," Yid agreed, feeling more shaken by his recent experiences than he cared to admit. "Fact is, maybe we had ought to go all the way to Blackfoot and make a week's trip of it. Sure ought to be a blacksmith there who could pump his bellows for a few minutes over that consarned plow. I..."

As Yid spoke of the plow, he turned back to look at it, and once again the hairs on the back of his neck stood straight out.

"M...Mincy..."

"What's wrong?"

"The p...plow's gone."

"What? But..."

And then Mincy too became speechless. The plow was indeed gone, and the only things in the wagon were the two small boxes that Yid had tossed into the back; the boxes that had been given them by the sad and silent drummer.

With a muttered oath Yid shook out the team again, urging them to even greater speed. And if he had looked behind him, he would have seen...

Nothing.

Yid had become last in the line. Out of place, in fact, as hashbrowns and fatback on a citified supper menu. And on top of that, he had also become once and thoroughly confused.

And as with him, so too with his wife. Mincy had no idea at all of what was happening. But this much she did know. Shortly before five o'clock in the afternoon of September 2 in the year 1899, the third wedding anniversary of she and her husband Yid Francom, there stood under the cottonwoods of the Cove on the Big Lost River the following mixed array; one worn-out springbed wagon; one mismatched span of mares, the first gingery and the other docile as a marmot in winter; and two adult Americans, the male so slight he couldn't pack an elk's tooth on a vest-pocket watch chain, and the female who was big enough, as Yid might have said, to shade an elephant.

Then, shortly *after* five o'clock on that same date, there was nothing and nobody standing or sitting under the cottonwoods of the Cove.

There was only the narrow set of iron-rimmed wagon tracks snaking off up toward the freight road to vanish among the vast and aromatic reaches of sage in the upper Thousand Springs valley. And by the time the sun was ten minutes further down the sky, the tough, pungent grasses were already springing back into place to rub out even the wagon tracks. Shortly, no mortal record remained that a man and a woman, desperately in need of *something* from the individual they erroneously called the old drummer, had been to visit him in the Cove.

PART FOUR

THE CRAZIES

9

Slowly the wagon rattled along through the slanting afternoon sunlight. The two mares, not in any hurry, nevertheless kept up a steady gait, and Yid had nothing to do but think.

What in the name of Hannah had he seen, he wondered? Or what *hadn't* he seen? What had happened to his plow, both this time and the last time that he had come to the Cove? How had that crazy message been burned into the handle? And why the ring-tailed devil had the crazy old drummer given him those two black boxes instead of another plow?

Hesitantly Yid turned to look back at them. Each was about two inches square, and both appeared solid. They also seemed to be identical, but without picking them up he couldn't be certain. And he didn't want to pick them up, not at all. Why, a man never knew what might erupt from boxes like that, and he didn't feel like taking any more chances. Not if he didn't have to...

"Why don't we see what's in them?"

Mincy's question startled him, and Yid looked quickly at her.

"I mean it," she pressed. "You keep staring at them. We might as well open them and see what the drummer gave us."

"You want to do it?" Yid asked defensively.

"I will if you want me to."

Yid did want her to, with all his heart he wanted her to do it. After all, this was a touchy situation, and a man never knew what might happen. Trouble was, opening them ought to be his responsibility, not only because he was the man, but because he had taken the boxes from the drummer.

"Well," he muttered under his breath as he crawled back across the wagon bench, "it's not being a coward that counts. It's getting caught at it. Reckon getting caught won't happen this time, anyway."

"Here," Mincy said at exactly the same moment, "I'll do it." And with that she leaned back to pick up the two boxes.

There was another sound of parting fabric as Mincy extended her stretching reach, and quickly she sat back up, holding her blouse together beneath her arm, trying to close the even larger tear.

"My goodness," she gasped as she worked to pull the gaping hole back together. "Everything I own is falling apart."

Watching her, Yid grinned and climbed into the back of the wagon, where he squatted to carefully study the boxes.

"This sure is a mighty big hole," Mincy murmured as she fumbled with the fabric under her arm.

"What?" Yid growled without looking up. "Quit mumbling into your chin stubble, Mincy. You sound like a dry-spell cow gumming a mouthful of prickly-pear cactus."

Spinning, Mincy gave him a white-sided, eyeballed look of absolute astonishment. "Wh...what did you say?" she asked incredulously.

Embarrassed, Yid quickly looked up and apologized. "I'm not meaning to be rude, honey-darlin', but I just didn't hear you."

Mincy's back-look instantly lightened. "Oh! I'm sorry. I was just fussing a little about this hole in my blouse. Have you opened the boxes yet?"

"Not hardly. But I will."

"Well don't hurry on my account, sweetheart. I'll drive the wagon until you want to take over again."

Once again Mincy turned her attention to the gaping hole in her blouse, and Yid sat back, considering her. She might have no more education than a country schoolmarm, nor no more public manners than the Governor of Texas being interviewed about the Alamo. On the other hand, she had more unadulterated brass than a Spanish-cast cannon barrel, more grit than a gravel-pit, and more ambition than a setting-hen in early spring.

All things considered then, Yid had to admit to himself that Mincy was a remarkable and lovely woman, tough when riled, but quick to forgive, and overall full of love for him and sweet as houndstooth candy.

Still, if it came down to pure good looks and passion-rousing excitement, which for some reason Yid was desperately craving, then she wouldn't hold a candle to the widow Amber Wiggins.

No, sir, by jings, Mincy wouldn't.

While Yid had been so critically appraising and comparing his wife with his amorous neighbor, he had also been unconsciously watching the two small boxes that the drummer had given him. Now, suddenly, his eyes focused on one of them. The other rattled around the wagon bed freely, rolling here and there as the wagon bounced along. But the one he was eyeballing, Yid suddenly realized, went nowhere. In fact, it didn't even bounce. It remained absolutely motionless, no matter what the wagon beneath it did.

His thoughts of the two women momentarily forgotten, Yid slid forward in the wagon bed. And then carefully he reached out and took up the motionless box. Cautiously he examined it, turning it this way and that. But though it seemed too light to be solid, he could find no way of opening it.

Setting it down, he took up the other box. It seemed a bit

heavier, but other than that it appeared exactly the same as the first one he had held. It had no seams, no apparent means of allowing him to get inside. Yet for some reason Yid was certain that the two boxes were hollow, and that somehow they could be opened.

Putting the second box back down, Yid again picked up the first, and suddenly he had the strangest sensation of lightness, of floating in the air. Quickly he lifted his hands and took hold of his head, certain that Mincy's blow had made him dizzy. But the feeling did not pass, his head did not really feel like it was spinning, and so slowly he lowered his hands.

Still the lightness persisted.

"Law," he said quietly. "I sure as Cuba sunk the battleship *Maine* last year don't recall ever feeling like this before."

"What'd you say?" Mincy murmured.

"Nothing, honey-darlin'."

Yid sat still, continuing to wonder at how he felt. The sense of lightness persisted, but it wasn't bad. In fact, it felt rather pleasant, like he didn't have so much weighing him down.

"Sure would like to see what's in this thing," he muttered then, looking more closely at the box. Instantly the black object, still in his hand, popped open, and Yid found himself staring at the interior.

For a brief moment he gazed, thoroughly surprised, and then he laughed. Long and loud he laughed. And Mincy, her hand still clutching her dress together, turned and stared.

"This...this is surely a caution," he gasped finally as he looked up at his wife. "Might even be the greatest hoorah of all time."

"What is it?"

"Just this," Yid answered, holding up the box with another chuckle. "It appears that fool drummer knew you had a problem with your blouse there. Take a look at what he gave us."

Yid held out the open box, and Mincy stared in surprise at a needle and a small spool of thread.

"Oh, for goodness sake!" she exclaimed. "Yid, this isn't right. We need to go back and confront that drummer. We need a plow, and we shouldn't let that foolish old man give us a needle and thread instead."

"Uh...Mincy..."

"Yes?"

"Seems like I recollect something about his being gone before we were."

Mincy's eyes widened. "My goodness, I'd forgotten all about that. Well, what are we going to do?"

"Do?" Yid smiled sadly. "Why, I reckon we're going to let the horses keep going while we open the other little box.

"Law," he said softly as he lifted it and turned it from side to side while Mincy watched closely, "here goes nothing. Box, I'd like to see inside of you."

Again, instantly, the box popped open. And Yid, as thoroughly startled as was Mincy, dropped it onto the wagon bed.

It hit once, bounced slightly, and came to rest upon its side. And then, from the box, a small round object rolled away and toppled to a stop near the side-board.

His face suddenly white, Yid reached out and took up the object. And then again he looked up at Mincy.

"By Tophet," he whispered, "this is crazy."

"Why?" Mincy asked, more alarmed at Yid's fear than at the box's opening by itself. "What is it?"

"A *button*, Mincy. Can you hardly imagine that? A strange button that could take the place of the button that got popped off my shirt back at the Cove. How could that old buzzard of a drummer have known I had lost a button?"

"Well," Mincy said thoughtfully, "you did stand directly in front of him. He likely *saw* the missing button."

"That doesn't wash, Mincy. I'd pulled my coat over it, just like you had your coat pulled over your torn blouse. Yet somehow that old man knew of both our problems. I'm more confused about all this than an armadillo in Alaska, but I'm also terrible afraid it runs deeper than it appears."

"What do you mean?"

"I mean," Yid said quietly, "that there's something serious stirring up our henhouse, and to tell the truth, I'm more than somewhat frightened by it."

"I...I don't understand."

"Then listen carefully. First I get a plow that has a crazy message burned under the handle."

"What? But I didn't see a message."

"I didn't show it to you. But that crazy old salesman burned some scripture into the handle of that plow he gave me."

"What was it about?"

"Oh," Yid replied, squirming uncomfortably, "it was just some verse of scripture."

"About...your thoughts?" Mincy asked quietly.

Yid stared at his wife. "Now how in thunderation did you know? Never mind. That ain't...isn't important. First the plow breaks, then a branch from out of nowhere pops off my button and tears your blouse. After that we finally track down the drummer, but he is different, somehow, and in a different sort of machine without wagon wheels."

"Don't forget that you got behind that other man."

"That's right," Yid affirmed. "I sure enough lost my place in line. After that, I stand before the old man, palaver a mite, ask for what I need, and he gives me...what I need...but which ain't what I asked for at all. Does that make any mortal sense to you?"

Scowling, Mincy shook her head.

"Nor me. But I allow there is a skunk in the woodpile around here somewhere. You know what else I think?"

Mincy shook her head.

"I think we'd better use this stuff the old man gave us, and pronto."

"What? The needle and thread? And the button? You mean not take them back?"

"That's exactly what I mean," Yid declared, not even understanding, himself, why he felt that they should use the items.

"But Yid, I think we need to go back and at least try to find that old man. We must have our plow."

"With half your body bulging like a puffball through that tear in your blouse?" Yid asked quickly.

Instantly Mincy reached back under her arm and drew the two seams of her blouse together. "I can wear my coat."

"Actually, you won't have to. I can fix the tear, happen you want me to."

"*What*? You sew? But you haven't... Wait a minute. You did say that your father had been a tailor. Was that funning, or did you really mean it?"

Yid shrugged. "I meant it, every word. I spent eight years as apprentice tailor to my father, and four more being a tailor. If you want me to give it a try, I reckon I could sew that blouse up easy. You wouldn't even need to take it off."

For a moment Mincy wavered. But then the thoughts of the drummer and her missing plow turned and set her mind. "I don't think we ought to use it, Yid. I can fix my blouse soon enough when we get home. Right now I truly think we ought to go back and find that drummer, give this stuff back to him, and get our plow."

"And what about your blouse *until* we get home?" Yid asked, feeling more anxious than ever that they use the things the drummer had given them, but still not knowing why. "A whole lot of you is showing through that tear, honey-darlin'. More than the coat can hide. We'll soon be passing Amber Wiggins' place, and then Dickey's, and who knows who we might meet on the road. Law, Mincy, you'll be drawing more stares than an albino badger with two heads and a sweet temper. Not in the memory of the most saddle-bent of the valley elders will there have been such a sight trailing up the Ketchum-to-Challis freight wagon road. Why, the news will likely be proclaimed over the pulpit at church, passed among the young scholars at school, whispered of and snickered over at next Friday night's fandango down at the Grand Prize Hall."

Self-consciously Mincy looked again at the gaping tear.

"See?" Yid declared triumphantly. "It's mighty bad, Mincy. But I can fix it, certain sure, and we'll still have plenty of this thread left over. I can even sew that button onto my shirt. We can always tell the drummer that we used it, and that we'll pay for it or get him another spool and button to take its place our next trip to the Cove."

"You don't think he'd mind?"

"Law, no. A button's a button, and a spool of thread is a spool of thread. We can even pay him for a larger size if you'd like, just to make certain he feels good about the deal."

"Well," Mincy reluctantly agreed, "all right. But hurry. I'd feel like dying if someone saw me all exposed like this."

Smiling with a strange feeling of peace, as though he had just accomplished some terribly important goal, Yid took the needle and thread from the small box. And that was when he saw that beneath the thread was tucked a slip of paper, folded over. Ignoring it, he went to work, and with deft fingers he pulled the two portions of Mincy's blouse back together and stitched them into place. The task did not take him long, but nevertheless the stitches were small and fine, and soon the blouse looked good as new.

Mincy admired his work, ran her fingers along the seams, and admitted with not a little pride that Yid *was* a good tailor.

Nodding with satisfaction at his wife's compliment, Yid took up the strange button from the floor of the wagon, and with a few more stitches he secured it onto his shirt, just where the old button had rested earlier that morning.

"There," he said as he tied the thread securely with the needle, "that ought to do."

And Yid, looking back at his wife, realized for the first time that she was no longer seated on the wagon bench. She was, in fact, seated comfortably about six inches *above* it. And she was enjoying the smoothest ride of her rough-shod young life.

10

"M...Mincy?" Yid squeaked as his startled voice tried to reassert itself upon the world. "Mincy, what are you *doing*?"

"I'm not doing anything," his wife replied sleepily. "We hit this smooth stretch of road where I wasn't getting jolted to death, and I decided to take a nap."

His heart hammering, Yid looked at Mincy's slumped form, and then he reached over and ran his hand across the wagon bench beneath her, just to be sure.

Yid was frightened, and maybe more than frightened. Again he ran his hand across the wagon bench. And then again. But it made no difference how many times he tried it. His hand touched nothing but the rough wood of the bench. Mincy was seated comfortably, her chin resting in the palms of her hands, some six inches above the wagon bench, in mid *air*!

"M...Mincy?"

"Yes, sweetheart?"

"Woman, for pity sake, open your eyes."

Mincy finally did, and then she turned and looked back at him, her face reflecting her confusion.

"What is it, Yid? What's wrong?"

"Law, Mincy, you...you're *floating*."

"I'm what?"

"Mincy," Yid cried out in an anguish of sincerity, "I mean it.You're up in the air, not on the wagon bench at all."

Now Mincy looked at him again. Suddenly her own eyes widened, then literally bulged with fear, and she began to scream.

"Dad-blast it!" Yid shouted desperately. "Don't get so doggone riled up. Nothing can be that terrible awful about floating. Now calm down, so I can figure this thing out."

But Mincy, still staring, still screaming, paid no attention to her husband's pleadings. Instead she brought her finger forward in a pointing motion, her entire hand trembling with fear.

And Yid, looking downward where she was pointing, suddenly realized that there was... there was light beneath *his* feet.

Further and even more confusing, his shadow did *not* start where he ended. Instead there was a small space, of say five or six inches, between the end of him and the beginning of the darkness of his shadow.

Suddenly filled with a feeling of endless falling, Yid closed his eyes, lifted his foot, and stamped it down desperately, trying to get it back into contact with the wagon bed.

But no, it wouldn't reach.

Again he tried, again and again, and as he tried, a feeling of horror choked him. He could not touch the ground. He could not even touch wagon bed bottom. He was suspended forever in the air.

At last, in desperation, he reached out and took hold of the brake handle. Then, holding it tighter than a baby's grip on a fresh-given candy stick, he pulled himself frantically against it.

Suddenly the air was filled once more with the sound of Mincy's shrieking and crying. Spinning, Yid looked, and to his amazement, he discovered the air was also filled with her. The poor woman was rolling and tumbling awkwardly while her hands and feet struggled vainly to find something solid to take hold of.

"Yid," she cried desperately, "h...help me!"

But Yid, clinging for dear life to the brake handle, didn't dare free a hand to reach out to her.

"Mincy," he instructed, "j...just put your hand out and grab hold of something."

"I'm t...trying, but I can't stop sp...spinning. Oh, Yid, what is happening?"

"I don't hardly know."

"Well, do something. Pleaseeeee..."

Yid, secure with his grip on the brake handle, suddenly realized how ridiculous Mincy looked, spinning and tumbling beside him, and he started chuckling.

"What are y...you laughing at?" Mincy whimpered from her low-level orbit.

"You," Yid howled. "Mincy, you look like that big old hot-air balloon I rode in down to Blackfoot!"

"Yid, please..."

"Law, Mincy," Yid cackled as he held to the brake handle, "I mean it. I've never seen anything so funny. I just wish I could hire you out to a circus. Of course we'd need to cover your bloomers a little, since you're showing more underside than a bull calf at branding time. But by jings, you could be a side show all by yourself. Maybe even the main attraction."

And with that he howled all the more.

Mincy, meanwhile, felt her hand brush across the wagon bench, and with all her strength she gripped the wood and hauled herself in. Then, twisting around upon the intently clutched seat, she turned to face her husband.

Yid, seeing her success, and seeing also the expression in her eyes, forgot instantly to laugh. He also forgot his own tendency to float, and pushed himself away from the brake handle, thinking to jump to the ground and escape from his molar-gnashing wife.

But he didn't jump, not even a little. Nor did he go to the ground.

"Oh, no!" he muttered as he spiraled wide-eyed up and away from the wagon. "Oh, no!"

And Mincy, holding tightly to the seat, forgot her anger and stared helplessly after her rapidly departing husband.

Higher Yid went, higher and farther away, until he could see quite an amazing distance around him. It was enjoyable, too, in a rather bizarre sort of way. In fact, in a strange way he actually liked the feeling of freedom it gave him. However, there was the wagon way down below him, growing rapidly smaller and more small. And there was Mincy clinging to the seat, crying out for him to come back to her.

Somehow it didn't seem right that he not be with it — with her. Only, how could he get back down ?

Suddenly a slight gust of wind hit him, and Yid began to tumble, exactly as Mincy had tumbled only moments before. It was not fast, but nevertheless the feeling was terrible, and he could feel what little remained in his stomach rising rapidly into his throat. Then more wind caught him, the tumbling grew worse, and suddenly he was swirled up and around and away in a rising thermal of warm September air.

Filled with unreasoning fear, and nauseated beyond belief, Yid finally retched. Only he was in the wrong position, and suddenly found himself choking, unable to breathe. Desperately he banged on his chest, trying to free the obstruction that had blocked his air. But it wouldn't break free. No matter how he struggled, it would not. And that was when Yid knew, with a terrible certainty, that he would shortly die.

His hand still against his chest, he tried again and again to breathe, could not, and as tears of pain and frustration and fear flowed helter-skelter from his eyes, he sobbed into the empty air that surrounded him.

"Dear God," he pleaded with forced and raspy whisper, "I'm sorry for all the bad. I...I'm even sorry I've had all those thoughts about Amber Wiggins. I won't ever... Oh, just let me be back on the wagon bench next to Mincy."

And in that instant, Yid was back.

"Wh...what happened?" he gasped after his throat had finally cleared itself and he had regained his breath.

"Yid?" Mincy squeaked in just as startled surprise.

"I...I... Was I up there? I mean, *really* up there?"

"You were." Mincy stated, her voice pleading for a modicum of understanding. "I saw you. I know I did. But...but how'd you g...get back?"

"I don't know. I... Mincy, how did all th...this happen?"

Dumbly Mincy shook her head. "While you were fixing my dress I felt awfully light and sleepy. The next thing I knew, I was... Oh, mercy, Yid! I'm frightened."

"So am I," the small man declared emphatically.

"Is this actually *possible*?"

Yid shrugged his shoulders. Then he reached down off the seat and took up the small black box. It had opened because he had said he wanted it to open, and he had come back to the wagon because he had said he wanted to come back. What in the...

Removing the small, folded paper, he opened it and read.

ANTI-GRAVITY THREAD

mfg. 2003

Use with caution

"What does it say?"

Speechless, Yid held it out for Mincy to read.

"I...I don't understand, Yid."

"Me either, but I think we are...floating...because we've used that thread."

"Oh," Mincy whimpered fearfully, "this can't be real. It can't possibly be happening." And accidentally letting go of the bench, she suddenly floated once again into the air.

"*Yid!*"

Quickly Yid reached out and caught hold of her foot, and then gently he dragged her back.

"You're all right," he said soothingly as he held his terrified wife and tried to calm her. "I've got you, honeydarlin', and you'll be fine. Now listen. I reckon I have this whole shebang about figured out. It works by thinking things at it, or maybe saying things."

Yid stared down at the button on his shirt. "I figure we sort of go where we think we are going, or say we are. Try it, Mincy. Think yourself someplace, and see what happens."

"Are...you sure?"

Yid grinned. "Not very. But law, Mincy, anything's worth a try if it'll help us understand what's happening. Now, I got back to the wagon either by praying, or by saying what I wanted to have happen. I was doing both when I was brought back here."

"Might it have been your prayer?" Mincy asked, her eyes wide.

Sadly Yid shook his head. "I don't reckon it was. I feel like too much of a sinner to get answered that wondroussudden. But maybe it was a little of both, my prayer *and* my instructions. Here, let me try it again.

"See that tree over there. I would admire to be sitting on the top of it"

Watching closely, Mincy finally shook her head. "Nothing happened."

"So I see. Well, let me think at it, then."

Yid did, with his deepest concentration. Yet still nothing happened.

"I take it that thinking isn't the way, either. Did you pray?"

Yid shook his head. "I didn't," he muttered. "I feel sort of foolish, even considering it. But if that's what I have to do...

"Lord," he muttered, "I know I'm a mighty unworthy specimen, but Mincy and I have this problem, and I'd admire Thy help. That old drummer gave us this thread that makes us float, and I think it also makes us go places. Trouble is, it ain't...isn't working proper. So if Thou doesn't mind, I'd admire to be sitting in the top of that tree over yonder, on top of the very smallest branches, right this instant."

Yid closed his eyes in apprehension, and opened them only when Mincy sighed deeply.

"Thank goodness," she whispered. "How would you have ever gotten back?"

Again Yid shook his head. "I don't know. But I can tell you this, honey-darlin'. That's how it worked before."

"Then why doesn't it work now? Does that paper say anything else?"

"I don't think so," Yid answered, lifting the small paper back up to look at it. "It just... Oh, no! This isn't right. It can't be..."

"What is it?" Mincy whispered fearfully.

"The writing," Yid responded as he stared at the paper. "Or that meddling drummer. You know how a moment ago this paper said something about anti-gravity thread? Well, now look at it."

Mincy did, and read: "He that looketh upon a woman to lust after her...shall not have the Spirit."

"I...I don't understand," she declared.

"Well, I do," Yid growled. "This is the same message that old man down at the Cove burned into the wooden handle of the plow we just took back. He's somehow got it into his head that he's going to save me from my thoughts. By jings, his brains must be thicker than calf splatter if he thinks these little messages are going to make me change. I tell you, I won't have him meddling like this. I..."

And that was when Yid finally saw the shocked expression on his wife's face. "What's the matter with you?" he muttered.

"I... I..." Mincy stuttered. "Did you just listen to yourself?"

"I reckon I did. Why?"

"Yid," Mincy said, "you are fighting against the very things you know are right. Doesn't a person do that when they have lost the Spirit? And isn't the old man right about your thoughts concerning Amber?"

Yid sputtered, but he had no ready response to Mincy's questions. Nor was he willing to examine them to see if she was right. Not yet he wasn't. Not until he had dealt with that meddling old drummer and his crazy anti-gravity thread .

"By Tophet, Mincy," he declared, filled with sudden realization, "you and I are being hazed into the wrong trail. Here we are floating in the air like so much thistledown, and we're worrying about Amber Wiggins. I tell you, it's a fool's game that old drummer has us playing. We've got lots more serious problems than my thoughts to worry about. Tons more. I suggest we get about figuring this mess out, and do it pronto."

Reminded, and looking downward at the space that yet remained between herself and anything else that was substantial, Mincy instantly buried her face in her hands. "Oh, Yid," she whispered brokenly, "hold me. Please hold me."

And Yid, just as frightened as his wife, but nowhere near so willing to admit it, put his arm around her and drew her close to his chest.

"Don't you worry yourself so much," he soothed as he stroked her dark and silky hair, "we'll figure this thing out. I know we will. We'll just stick together until we get 'er done."

Sniffing, Mincy reached up against Yid's chest with her hand. "Oh, Yid, sweetheart, I bless the day that you were born! I love you so much..."

But then, slowly, Mincy's voice grew still, and pulling away from her dumfounded husband, she stared around her in open-eyed wonder. She sat next to him in a small, low-ceilinged room off a cobble stone courtyard, which she could see through a dirty window. And before her, in a low bed, a woman lay writhing in the agony of childbirth.

"Yid," she whispered frantically, "what...where..."

But Yid, his hand on her arm, was rising slowly to his feet.

"Yid..."

"M...Mincy," he whispered, almost strangling on his words as he stared, "th...that's my mother. I...I think... Only, she is so *young*... so different from how I remember her. Law, woman, what have we gone and done?"

"Yid..."

"Mother," Yid called softly as he stepped toward the woman who lay on the bed. "Mother, it's me, your son Yid. Are...are you all right?"

But the woman, seeing Yid appear at her bedside, suddenly began screaming. Then a door burst open and a man ran frantically into the room. He was small of stature, but quick and wiry, and he took in the situation at a glance.

"Who are ye?" he asked, his accent heavily Irish. "Sure an' ye better be answering me. Do we know ye? Tis after escaping me memory, if we do."

Yid, frozen in place, simply stared.

"Ah. Tongue's stopped, is it? Then be gone, the both of ye. Tis our room ye be in, and as ye can see, the pains is bad on herself, and I think maybe it's surely her time. Now be gone..."

"F...Father?" Yid finally managed to stutter.

"What? What asked ye?"

"Aren't you...my father? Aren't you Henry Francom?"

"Aye, sure and I'm Henry Francom. But as fer bein' yer father, that can't be so. Herself has no' given birth before, and she won't, either, not unless ye take the woman and be gone. It's a grand pass we've come to in this country, where folks just walk in without so much as a by-yer-leave. Now be gone with ye, and let us be about the birthin' in peace."

In desperation Yid turned to Mincy. "You see," he whispered urgently. "You said the day of my birth, and by jings, here we are. This is Liverpool, England, and the year must be 1872."

"Is it peaceful that ye'll be leaving?" the little man asked, "or is it on yer ear that I must toss ye?"

"Fa...Henry," Yid pleaded, turning back to the man, "t...talk to me, please. Let me prove to you who I am. Is this not Liverpool?"

"Sure, and every fool knows that."

"And is it not 1872? September 20, to be exact?"

"Faith aye. Ye be right brimful of information, common information that is. Now be gone..."

The woman cried again, in pain, and the man turned to look down at her.

"The wee one is coming," he breathed. "'Tis demented the pair of ye must be, coming here at a time like this. Now be off with ye, before herself is hurt."

"One moment, sir," Yid cried pleadingly. "Please hear me out. You will set sail on the good ship John J. Boyd, and she will clear the coast of Ireland on the eleventh of No-vember. The passage will be stormy and slow but not dangerous, and you will reach the banks off Newfound-land the day before Christmas."

"Where ye got the ship's register I know not," the man snapped in anger and frustration, "but as for the rest of it, sure and ye be talking nonsense. November first the ship is to sail, and landed we'll be at Castle Garden, long before Christmas. Now off with ye, before I call a constable."

Desperately Yid looked around, trying to think of some-thing, anything...

"S...Say howdy to my uncle...your brother Yid," he whis-pered frantically. "And when the child is born, please name him..."

"Yid," Mincy whispered, moving in front of him and placing her hands against his chest to stop him and push him back, "don't say that. It isn't right that you be here, and it isn't right that you say such a thing."

"But why? This is my Fath..."

"I...I don't know why," Mincy stammered, interrupting him. "I just feel that we can't interfere with what has already happened. If these people are really your parents, then this whole episode is past and done. Your birth is already taken care of, and needs no help from either of us. Now please, let's go back."

"But...but how are we to do that?"

Mincy's eyes dropped. "I...I don't know that either. I just wish to heaven that we were back in our wagon..."

And before Mincy could even finish her sentence, they were.

11

For a long moment the two stared around them in silence.

"Law," Yid breathed. "My head's spinning like a hard-thrown broncobuster with his spur still in the stirrup. If that wasn't the confoundedest thing I ever saw in my life. I'd swear it had to be a dream, only I think I'm about as awake as ever I was. Mincy, honey-darlin', was what I think we just saw for real?"

"L...Liverpool?" Mincy whispered, "your mother and f...father?"

"Then you saw them, too?"

"Oh, Yid, what is happening to us?"

Sorrowfully Yid shook his head. "Honey-darlin', I...I wish that I knew. Somehow we manage to go places where even angels couldn't go, and I can't hardly imagine that any of it is real. I ain't even got the sense to figure out whether I'm awake or asleep, let alone whether or not we're floating in the air or what by jings else is going on."

"Well," Mincy admitted, "you must have been right about *one* thing, at least. I took us to Liverpool and back here again just by saying it."

Yid nodded solemnly. "I know...at least I reckon I know. Shall we try it again and see what happens?"

Mincy agreed, and so they tried. They surely did. Only, no matter how many places they thought of, no matter how many times they named locations off, she and Yid remained floating just a few inches above the wagon bench, right where they were.

Then Yid thought of the other box, the one that the button had been in. Spinning effortlessly, he reached down and lifted it from where he had let it drop.

In that box there was also a paper, folded, and Yid quickly pulled it free and read it.

"What does it say?" Mincy whispered, consternation filling her voice.

"It says, 'Go-Button, manufactured 2004, Use with caution,' just about like the other paper said about the thread."

"Go-Button?"

"That's right. But, I can't throw a loop over the sense of this thing at all."

"Go-Button," Mincy mused as she watched her husband's frustrated expression. "Go-Button. I wonder... Yid, I'll bet anything it's that button the drummer gave us, the one on your shirt. It makes us go places."

Yid looked down at the button. "Maybe," he said softly, pensively. "Maybe so. But if it is, then why hasn't it worked the other times we've tried it?"

"I...I don't...know..."

"Wait a minute," Yid exclaimed excitedly. "You had your hand on my chest; on the button, actually, and at the same time... Mincy, I reckon I know how to do this. I take hold of the button like this, and then say that I want to be home, for instance, in the chair by the stove, and..."

And Yid was sitting in the high-backed chair by the stove in his cabin on Arentson Gulch just under Willow Creek Summit.

"Law," he cried with astonishment, "it works! See, Mincy? I told you that..."

"Mincy? Mincy, are you here?"

Quickly Yid rose to his feet and looked outside. But he was alone, and the place had all the stillness of an abandoned farm about it.

Taking the button in his hand, Yid frantically stated that he wanted to be back in the wagon, seated beside Mincy. Instantly he was, and Mincy was looking at him with wonderment in her eyes.

"You...you went home?" she asked incredulously.

"Sure as cigars smell bad," Yid beamed. "Why didn't you come with me?"

"I... don't know. You just went without me, I suppose."

"I didn't mean to. We went together to Liverpool, so I thought... Wait a minute. I'll bet a dollar against a broken wooden nickle I know why. We need to be touching if we're to go together. That's the secret. Here, take my hand, and let's see. I want to be in the last meadow where I fished. There's a stump, and I sat on the gnarled old roots of that stump and caught a two-pound trout."

And instantly Yid and Mincy were seated on that root, or rather, they were seated six inches above it, high in the mountains to the west of their home.

"My goodness!" Mincy exclaimed. "That button actually works. I can hardly believe it."

"It works, all right," Yid agreed. "Law but it does work!"

Mincy squeezed Yid's hand. "Now let's go back, sweetheart, and get the button and this terrible thread back to the drummer."

"What?" Yid asked, dumfounded. "But Mincy, consider what we can do with these things. A man'd have to be more loco than a slept-on bedbug to give them back. That fool drummer gave them to us. I say let's hang onto them, at least for a week or so."

Mincy looked earnestly at her husband. "I don't think we should keep them, Yid. Somehow I know that they weren't meant for us. If we keep them it will lead to trouble. I know it will."

"But honey-darlin', think what we can do..."

"No, sweetheart, it's more important that I think about

what we *should* do. That includes giving these things back, getting our plow, and then getting the plowing done and the ground ready for spring drilling."

"But the Go-Button, and the anti-gravity thread?"

"Yid, they aren't ours, and you know that as well as I do. Now please take hold of the button and take us back to the wagon?"

"I ain't going to do it, Mincy. This is too good a chance."

But Mincy, equally as determined as her husband, suddenly reached for the button herself. Yid tried to spin away, but she gripped his arm, squeezed down, took hold of his shirt and button, and demanded that they be back at the wagon. And they were.

"There," Mincy sighed in grateful relief. "Now, let's turn around and go find that old drummer."

But Yid, more angry than he could imagine because of Mincy's insolent disregard of his authority, determined not to let the matter rest. He was tired of being so henpecked he molted twice a year. Instead, it would be awful nice to be with a woman who appreciated his talents, a woman who waited up ahead at Sage Creek.

"Turn around?" he questioned smilingly while his mind built in quick succession a hundred or more pictures of an incredibly beautiful, totally amenable, obedient-to-her-husband Amber Wiggins. "Woman," he concluded, "you obviously are confuseder'n a love-bit blowsnake sparking a hoe handle. I'm not turning around for anything, least of all that old drummer."

"What?" Mincy asked, and then almost instantly her mind was filled with understanding. "Oh, Yid, she's back again, isn't she."

Yid started at Mincy's insight, but said nothing.

"I can tell, sweetheart. That message the drummer wrote you was true, and that's why you keep fighting..."

Mincy continued, but Yid didn't hear her. Instead he had inadvertently glanced at the other paper, the one that had had something about 'Go-button' written on it. But now it no longer said that. Now there was another message, a bolder one, and Yid shuddered as he read: "He that looketh on a woman to lust after her...shall deny the faith."

"By jings," he muttered, "how does he *do* that? And how can he know..."

"What are you saying?" Mincy asked, realizing finally that Yid wasn't listening to her.

"I'm saying that I've had it with that old man. Look at this paper. That old fool has done it to me again."

Mincy slowly read the note, and then, ashen faced, she looked into the face of her husband. "Yid, I don't completely understand this, but I can recognize a warning when I see one. If you ask me, the Lord is warning you about yourself and Amber, and I think you should pay attention."

"The Lord? Law, Mincy, what does the Lord have to do with that old fool drummer? Why, when I get my hands on him..."

"Yid, don't say it. We already have enough problems. Let's just take these things back to him, and get on with our lives."

For an instant Yid hesitated, stopped by the tone of Mincy's voice. But then, filled with anger and determination, he plunged ahead. "*We* don't have a problem, Mincy. You do, maybe, but not me. For myself, I think that my problems might just have ended."

Carefully Mincy regarded her husband. "What... do you mean?"

"I mean, by Tophet, that this button is power, Mincy. Real power. With it I can go where I want to go, do what I want to do, see what I want to see."

Yid smiled and took hold of his button. "This is my ticket to dreamland, Mincy, and no nagging, pushy woman is going to make me give it back."

"But Yid," Mincy breathed, her face reflecting her pain, "Just like that poor old drummer, I only want to help. I want to stop you from denying the faith that bonds our marriage together. I love you, Yid, and all I want is for you to be happy."

"That's just the doggone point. I *am* happy. Especially now that I have this button I am happy. And that brings up another thing. I told you before, and I'll tell you one last time; I am sick to death of feeling guilty for finding a little pleasure in thinking now and again on Amber Wiggins. Between you and that old drummer, I have just about had it. Thinking those thoughts does no harm to anybody, and it's high time you realized that. Why by jings, woman, if I wanted to, I could say the word and I'd be in Amber's cabin right this minute."

And to Yid's horror, he was.

12

Startled, Yid looked around him. What had he done? What, with the short fuse that had so recently become part of his temper, had he gone and done?

Directly in front of his floating self, her back to him, Amber Wiggins sat on the edge of her bed, undressing her baby. And behind her, steaming with hot water and ready for somebody's bath, was her tin, floor-model, Sears and Rohbuck bath tub.

"Just a minute, honey-pie," Amber was sing-songing. "Mommy's going to brush her hair, and then you and Mommy will take a nice, warm bath together."

Instantly Yid felt the red of embarrassment creeping up his neck, covering his ears, and turning his cheeks into sheets of bright red fire. "Oh, no!" he mouthed silently as he hovered frantically perhaps six inches above the floor of Amber Wiggins' cabin. "Law, no! What'll she think if she sees me here when she's...she's... Oh, by jings, this isn't how the thing's supposed to happen."

And while Yid stared in terrified silence, knowing what was coming but uncertain of what to do or where to go, Amber Wiggins finished undressing her baby and began

brushing out her hair, all in blissful ignorance of his presence.

In a terrible fever of desperation Yid clutched the button
and thought of other places to be. But no matter how hard
he concentrated, he could not make the button work. The
command had to be spoken aloud, and Yid did not dare
open his mouth to do so. If he did, Amber would know of
his presence, and likely she would never speak to him
again.

"Law," he thought, "I'm trapped as a weasel in a woo-
dbox, with no more notion of how to get out of this cabin
than a baby chipmunk has of learning the three R's."

"But maybe," his mind cried out hopefully, "maybe I can
float up into the rafters. She would never look up there,
and I can hide until she finally leaves the cabin. Then I can
order myself away, and she will never be the wiser. And
besides all that, up there I can relax a little, and maybe
even..."

Yes, he declared to himself with a smirk of delight, he
had to get up into the rafters.

Suiting action to thought, Yid began enthusiastically
waving the air with his hands, doing his best to fly up and
out of sight.

It worked, too. A little. He lifted perhaps a foot higher,
so that he hovered eighteen or twenty inches above
Amber's floor. But it also happened that in his pushing of
air, he pushed some behind him as well as down below
him. In consequence of that, he found himself closer than
ever to the unsuspecting woman, and stretched out at a
forty-five–degree angle in the air.

Well, if he had been worried before, from that moment on he was more concerned than a wing-clipped duck
who had become lost in the Sahara desert. Another
foot or so and he would be directly over Amber's head,
and the thought of that situation purely addled his think-
box.

Squinting his eyes closed so that he would not stare
down at Amber and her mesmerizing brush-stroking of
silken-smooth hair, Yid once again began frantically beat-

ing the air with his hands, trying to get back, to get away ...

"Da-da? Da-da?"

"What is it, child?" Amber asked, sounding concerned. "Do you see something that Mommy can't see?"

Yid, now *truly* frantic, beat even harder at the air with his hands, trying to get back down, out of sight of the baby and maybe even behind the bath tub, the only object of hideable size within finger-winged range of his efforts. There, he reasoned pitifully, he might have a small, albeit very thin, chance of not being seen.

But his flying motions must have frightened the child, for it began to whimper.

And that gave Yid an idea.

No, it gave him a *great* idea. If he could get the baby to cry, really scream, then Amber would be forced to halt her current activities so she could comfort the child again. That being the case, while she was distracted and while the noise of the baby was loud, he would whisper fervent and hurried instructions to his button and be gone before she could discover that he had been there.

Immediately Yid put his wonderful plan to work, stopping his flying to pull faces at the staring child. He swirled his arms, swished his legs back and forth, and made hideous, grotesque faces. He used his thumbs, fingers, and tongue; he bulged his eyes and puffed his cheeks; he pulled his ears out away from his head; he pushed his nose up and into his face .

"Aaaaauuuugh!"

Arrested by the startled feminine gasp, Yid looked away from the staring baby and directly into the wide, gaping blue eyes of the comely Amber Wiggins.

He blinked once or twice. Amber didn't blink at all. He blinked again rapidly. Amber's eyes grew larger and wider and still didn't blink. Yid wanted to scream, he was so embarrassed and humiliated. And finally Amber did scream, long and loud and with incredible intensity.

And while she screamed, Yid stared at her in horror.

She was standing with her face not eighteen inches away from his own, her hair well brushed and her dress still

buttoned up to the collar-stays. Her eyes were wider than
he had ever imagined human eyes could be, and her mouth
and throat were working overtime with that formidable,
unbelievable scream of terror.

Instantly, but with a feeling that it was taking him forever to do so, Yid grabbed for the button on his shirt.

"M...Mincy," he stammered frantically while he stared at
the screaming, terrified woman. "I w..want to be with
Mincy."

And in that same second, he was.

13

"Stay back!" Mincy was shouting threateningly, her back to him. "I'm warning you..."

"But Mincy," Yid protested, thinking that his wife was talking to him, "I didn't hardly..."

And then, for the first time, Yid saw the half dozen men who sat their horses around the team near the front of the wagon. He also saw Mincy's warning glance, but he didn't understand it at all.

Floating forward, Yid stopped himself a little behind his wife, and then he stared at the men. One of them, he noticed only then, held a gun.

"Say," he questioned of no one in particular, "what in tunket is going on here?"

"I told you she had a man around here somewheres," one of the men snarled.

"Yeah, but who'd have thought he'd be in the back, asleep."

"Well," the man with the gun grinned, "now that I look more closely, I see that the woman — snort, snort — might have been telling the truth after all, when she said she was alone. This feller sure ain't much of a — ha — specimen."

The others laughed, and Yid felt the red starting again up his neck.

"By Tophet," he stormed, "that's enough of that palaver. Now be off with you."

And Yid was rudely interrupted by a shot from the man's pistol, which took his hat off and nearly blew him out of the wagon, just from the wind the bullet created as it sped past.

"Yid?"

"I...I'm all right," he stammered as he pulled himself upright next to the familiar brake handle.

"Aw, Snort, I thought you'd kilt him," one of the men whined.

"I did too," another averted. "Doggone, I thought he was going to miss all the fun. Sure glad he won't."

"Yeah, Snort, ain't we gonna put on a show for 'im?"

"Ought to," the last of the group agreed. "He's already woke up for it, and in a minute or so his ticket'll be punched permanent. Before he dies, it seems like a man ought to see him one last good side show."

"Yeah, Snort. We got us a good start on them fellows from Challis. Let's take us a little break here."

"All right," the one called Snort shouted as he sniffed and snuffed at whatever seemed to be clogging up his breathing. Then he waved his pistol at the men around him. "Cut the chatter."

There was instant silence, and Yid stared in amazement at the obedient men.

"By jings," he mumbled to Mincy, "it's easy to see who's speaker of the house in this congress."

"Shut — snort, snort — up!" the leader declared.

"That feller surely comes by his name honestly," Yid wispered to his wife, ignoring the order. "Further, from the beetled look his brow, a feller might assume, with some authority, that his head is stuffed with something like livery stable dust and cement. And that given thirty days to do it, he likely couldn't figure out how to pour creek water out of a wet boot with directions printed on the sole.

And for a fact, Mincy, that Snort feller looks like the smart one of the bunch."

Mincy giggled and the man with the gun looked sort of confused, but that didn't stop Yid from being worried. The man was big and burly, and with his bedrock brain he would be about as safe to fight as standing barefoot in front of the runaway Oregon Short Line down at American Falls.

"Mincy," he whispered, "crossing that feller could be as dangerous as crimping dynamite caps with your side teeth up at the Yankee Fork Mine. Why, making a wrong move could lead to the rigors of mortis as short and swift as shooting yourself in the roof of the mouth with a caliber .54 Hawkins buffalo gun. So do be careful with your temper."

"Well," she whispered back, "what should we do?"

"I don't hardly know. I..."

"I told you two to shut — snort, snort — up." Snort thundered. "A couple of you boys grab that there woman, one of you — snort, snort — plug the man, and let's get outa here."

"You lay a hand on me or my husband," Mincy thundered, unable to restrain herself any longer, "and so help me, I'll tear your arms off."

"Ain't the old bag a mean one?" a man laughed. Two or three others joined in the merriment.

"I don't know, Snort," another man declared tauntingly. "This big sister looks tougher'n old boot leather. And she's uglier'n the south end of Karl Barton's northbound mule. You actual sure you want to drag her along with us?"

"Beggars can't be choosers," another snickered. "She'll do 'till something better comes along.

Yid, listening, could hardly comprehend what the men were planning. Yet they had the gun, and he and Mincy had nothing with which to defend themselves. Still, he couldn't just stand by and watch while they shot him and took Mincy.

"You fellers are sure right about my wife," he suddenly declared, floating up beside her. "She's a bad one, and that's saying it nicely. Why, her pa was so mean that he had to sneak up on the dipper just to get himself a drink of water. He had a disposition that would make an upset bobcat look like a monk in a charity mission. Tell the truth, hers is worse, and she is meaner. So you fellers have at her if you want, but remember that I gave you fair warning."

For a moment the men stared, and then the one nearest Mincy guffawed and reached out for her leg.

"Don't you touch me, you miserable..."

And then Yid stared in amazement as Mincy dodged the man's hand and struck out with her huge fist, swinging a blow that would have, under normal conditions, felled Paul Bunyan's big blue ox.

Trouble was, both Mincy and Yid had forgotten, for the moment, that she was weightless, and that conditions were not altogether normal. That blow struck home, but instead of the man going down, Mincy was catapulted off the seat of the wagon by the force of her own blow, and away she went, sailing out over the heads of Peaches and Cream and the staring outlaws.

"Yiii...Yiii...Yiii,' she cried as she flailed at the air. "Yiii... Yiiiid..."

The men, dumfounded, stared as she passed noisily overhead, while Yid thought about the fact that if he didn't go after her and bring her back she might sail on her way forever.

Grabbing his Go-Button, he ordered himself to be at Mincy's side. Instantly he was, and as the expressions on the faces of the men below grew even more amazed, he ordered himself and Mincy back onto the wagon.

"Th...they're *ghosts*." one of the men shouted.

"Ain't no such thing," another replied. "Leastwise, I don't think there are."

"Then how'd they do that?"

"Where'd they go?"

And while the men were still looking around the sky in confusion, wondering where he and Mincy had suddenly gone, Yid deposited his terrified wife next to the brake handle. Mincy couldn't help him out of this scrape, he now understood, and so it would be up to him to help them both. Quickly he ordered himself onto the back of Snort's horse, and then he set himself for what he knew would be coming.

"Hey! What the..."

"Snort," a man yelled frantically, "he's behind you."

"D'ya think I don't know *nothing*?" Snort growled angrily. "The consarned little idjut's quicker'n a — snort, snort — greased cat. Git your arms off of me, you little..."

And with that, Snort broke free and swung around, backhanding Yid with a glancing blow that mostly missed and wouldn't hardly have hurt a baby. Only Yid, being weightless, was sent flying off toward the clouds at an alarming rate of ascent, even for him.

However, he was not hurt, only launched, and he had sailed only a few hundred feet before he finally realized that.

"By jings," he shouted, suddenly angry. "Now you tinhorns've gone and riled me proper. Just for that I'll tie your ears in knots. I'll tear enough hide off the bunch of you to half-sole a herd of elephants. Just you keep on settin' there gaping, you mangy coyotes, and I'll..."

"Hey, boss," a man below him shouted with excitement, "look at him go. I never knew you could hit like that."

"I...I do it right regular," Snort declared, his voice filled with wonder that was quickly becoming pride. "Why, you'd ought to see what happens when I *really* —snort, snort — smack 'em."

"H...honest?"

"Honest Abe. Why, you just saw it, didn't you? All of you did. I hardly hit that little runt. Just think what would have happened if I'd really clobbered him."

"Yeah, boss," a man agreed. "I'm thinkin', and I'm glad you're the boss. Gee, fellers, would you look at the little runt go? I tell you, it makes a man proud, working for a man like the boss here."

Snort, in the midst of enjoying the accolades from his wondering men, suddenly found himself once again entwined between the weightless but gripping arms and legs of an instantly returned and highly incensed Yid Francom.

"Think you can smack me?" Yid snarled angrily into Snort's left ear. "Well, you overgrown, lump-eared babboon, I'll learn you a thing or two..."

"Smack him, Yid," Mincy squealed from where she still clung for dear life to the brake handle. "That's it. Hang on, and sock him a good one!"

"Shut up, woman." one of the outlaws ordered.

Instantly Mincy turned on the man who had spoken. "Why, you miserable excuse for a bunkhouse packrat, do you want me to wrap myself around you like my husband did to him? Do you?"

With her threat, Mincy stepped — or floated — up onto the wagon seat, and for the first time the man saw that she was hovering in the air about six inches or so above solid terra firma, or at least its wooden, wagon bench representation. Prior to that, the folds of her skirt had covered the space of air, but now it was visible, and the outlaw, shaken clear to his uncut toenails, dropped his lower jaw and panicked.

"S...S...S...Snort," he stuttered as he dragged his horse back away from Mincy and the wagon, "I...loo...look..."

But Snort was having troubles of his own, and neither he nor any of the other men paid the least little shred of attention to the stammering soul who had belatedly discovered Mincy's elevated status.

" Confound it!" Snort swore. "Git off of me, you little vermin."

Then suddenly he worked his hand free of Yid's ganglylimbed entwinement; the hand that held the pistol. Instantly he had it raised and pointed behind his head at Yid's middle.

His hand on his button, Yid quickly ordered himself onto the neck of the horse, facing the outlaw. Then he watched with satisfaction as Snort fired harmlessly over his own head.

"Missed," Yid declared then as he reached up and tweaked Snort's nose. "Didn't anybody ever tell you that you couldn't hardly shoot ghosts? Now boo!"

Snort started fearfully, and then his face bulged with

anger. "Why, you miserable little — snort, snort — lice-infested mouse," he declared as he brought the pistol around and drew down on Yid. "Now you die for sure."

But Yid had already ordered himself onto the man's horse who sat next to Snort, and from there he watched as Snort fired his pistol into the back of his own mount's head, killing it instantly.

"Well," Yid declared smugly as he watched both leader and horse hit the earth resoundingly, leaving the horse dead and Snort unconscious, "you sure enough didn't miss that time, Mister Snort."

"Yiiiee!" the man then screamed who sat directly in front of Yid. He had only that moment discovered he was riding double, and it unnerved him. With another screech he pitched from his horse, landed on all fours, and scrambled off between the rearing and bucking legs of a couple of other animals.

And then things among the remaining outlaws got quiet as a winter-froze stock pond. Men and animals sat still as a funeral procession waiting for the casket to arrive, and into that silence wafted the stentorian breathing of the laid-cold Snort.

"By jings, that's the windiest outlaw I ever listened to," Yid announced. "You reckon the altitude's what got those gusts up in him, Mincy?"

"No," Mincy replied.

"The pure air, maybe?"

"No."

"Likely it's the atmosphere, then. What with that roll-your-own cigarette he just dropped, too much Taos lightening, and none of these fellers having taken baths in the last year whether they needed same or not. Phew! It's something whiffy around here."

"Yes," agreed Mincy. "But it's not that either."

"Could be the lung fever?" asked the wizened Yid hopefully. "Or maybe some sort of Montana or Idaho epizootic?"

Mincy shook her head. "No," she said again.

Yid walled his eye and gave his wife a long, hard look,

showing that he wasn't getting mad yet. Just furious.

"By Tophet," he gritted, nearly forgetting altogether that he had set out to have a little laugh at the outlaw's expense with his and Mincy's funning. "If it ain't the altitude, nor the stench, nor yet the air, and if it ain't some new and un-discovered disease, what do you think *is* the matter with him?"

"The poor man has a cold," Mincy said sympathetically.

"*What?*"

"You heard me. He's caught a cold, and his nose is stuffed."

Yid, still in the outlaw's saddle, or rather, about six inches above it, nodded slowly, understandingly. "You're right," he declared unselfishly. "His nose-blocked snorting has hold of him, all right, and he sure enough sounds like the lead engine on the Durango-to-Silverton narrow-gauge express."

Then Yid grinned and continued. "Puts me in mind of a girl I courted once. Beautiful creature, too. Yellowest hair I ever saw. Anne Welker her name was — Anne 'Buck-snort' Welker.

"But it wasn't no cold in her, Mincy. No sir, it was the laughter that brought her snorting on. Why, about the time that woman was laughing hard enough to raise a good sweat, no matter what about, then her snorting would com-mence. And it would commence in serious, eye-popping earnest. Furthermore, it was a persistent sort of snorting. Once it had the bit in its mouth, so to speak, it was a sure-fire runaway, and there wasn't hardly any roping it and snubbing it down. She was a snorter, all right, and like I said, this feller does put me in mind of her."

With that solemn pronouncement Yid glared at the ring of silent, fear-frozen badmen. Then he took up the reins and swatted the horse, intending to ride to Mincy and the wagon. But once again he had forgotten that he was weightless, and as the horse moved out, Yid was literally blown out of the saddle by the breeze.

The remaining outlaws, staring as Yid slowly turned a somersault in the air before them, could no longer contain their fear. And Snort, who had by this time regained consciousness and extricated himself from beneath the saddle of his dead horse, looked up just when they looked up.

And well he did. Yid was spinning slowly above them in the air, like a slow-swimming, other-worldly cherub. And Mincy was quite literally a sight to behold, herself. She stood, towering above them all, and above the wagon as well, a feminine destroying angel apparently come down from the heavens above to wreck vengeance upon the wicked. She had the most horrible scowl that any of the outlaws had ever seen, and even Yid blanched with fear when he saw her.

"Th...they...they're *haunts*," one of the outlaws cried "I tell you, th...they've got to be."

Or...demons." another declared.

"But...I d...don't believe in haunts or demons," a third responded.

"Me n...neither," a fourth declared. "But...but..."

"Well I believe." Snort snorted with authority. "I ain't never fit no ghost before, and I ain't fighting none again. One of you boys give me your horse."

"Git yer own horse." one of his men called. "Come on, boys, let's ride."

"No, boys, don't — snort, snort — leave me... please..." the leader pleaded to the departing horde. But it did no good, for the band of horsemen spurred and whipped their mounts into flight down the road.

"Boys." Snort cried as he hoofed it down the trail after them, "please stop, boys..."

Yid, finally enjoying himself and quick to see the rare opportunity, gave the order to his button to be on the road directly behind the rapidly fleeing Snort.

"Boo," he wailed gleefully. "Boo!"

With a terrified scream Snort redoubled his efforts, and the last Mincy and Yid saw of him and his crowd of murderers and thieves, they were beating up a sizeable bank of dust along the Ketchum-to-Challis freight road. Of course Snort's cloud of dust wasn't near as sizeable as the others, for he was trailing considerably and using only his own two feet to tromp it up with. But his efforts were still admirable. They surely were.

Triumphantly Yid looked up at Mincy, and to his horror he saw that the wind stirred up by the passing and departed horses had caught Mincy in its whorls. She was spinning and tumbling along in the backwash of the departed outlaws, crying out to her husband for help.

With a sigh and a slight smile, Yid took hold of the button on his shirt and ordered himself to be with her.

And to Mincy's tremendous relief, he was.

14

"Well," Yid said, grinning, "happen you don't want to go back to the wagon, we could play this here tumblebug game for a spell longer."

Frantically Mincy grabbed his arm. "T...take me back," she pleaded, and almost instantly it was done.

Then, from her seat above the wagon bench, Mincy looked at her husband. "Yid," she said forcefully, bravely, "I don't even pretend to understand what is happening to us, but I do have a pretty clear idea of *why*."

"And that is?"

"Your lusting. Merciful heavens, Yid, admit that the things you are thinking about that woman are wrong, and change. Then we can stop all this...this whatever it is, and get on about our lives."

Yid said nothing, only stared at the ground beneath the patient horses, and so Mincy looked away. She wished desperately that she understood her emotions, understood how she was feeling about the man she was married to. She loved him more than she could say, but she didn't know if she could bear for much longer the pain he continued to inflict upon her.

But in addition to that, she didn't understand why he was behaving like he was. In all the three years of their marriage, he had never been erratic. Always, until the past two or three months, he had been incredibly consistent; good, kind, gentle, soft-spoken, thoughtful, affectionate. In fact, for almost the entire first year after their wedding, Mincy had been afraid to allow herself to believe that Yid was totally sincere. Only time had finally convinced her that his goodness was real.

Suddenly, however, since Amber Wiggins had become so obviously available, Yid's moods had gone up and down like a hand-top, the toy that some folks were now calling a yo-yo. And, she could clearly see, the more time passed without Yid taking control of his thinking, the more time he was spending on the far and discouraging end of that same yo-yo string. The old drummer, with his strangely given messages, was right. Because of lustful thoughts, Yid had lost the Spirit and was denying the faith that had made his and Mincy's marriage so wonderful. For a fact, the two of them were truly drifting apart.

Only what could she do? Yid became irate when she reminded him of things, and if she didn't remind him, then he became more and more enmeshed in the mind-trap he seemed to have set for himself.

Of course she could always go and see Amber, but Mincy didn't feel right about that, either. In fact, so far as she could tell, Amber was only a secondary problem. Mincy's marriage and life with her husband would survive only if Yid, and Yid alone, made the decision that it should.

And to help him do that, Mincy soberly concluded, she was going to have to spend a little time turning the other cheek. Until everything had gone way beyond helplessness, if it finally did, she would simply need to love him and do her best to support him.

Mincy thought all of this and almost smiled, considering how ludicrous it was that she should be so rational about Yid and the entire mess of their marriage when she was actually floating six inches above the bench of the wagon. And that didn't even take into account the absolutely impossible way of traveling that Yid's button had provided, and the equally impossible places it had taken them.

If someone had asked her, she would have had to say that she was having a dream of some sort, or maybe that she had been hypnotized. The trouble was, she could not seem to wake herself up from it.

"Yid," she finally said, drawing a deep breath before-hand, "I...I, well, thank you. I'm glad that you came back to help me with those men."

"You're welcome," Yid replied sincerely, relieved at his wife's tone of voice. "But I was glad to get back, too. Where I went was awful. Amber Wiggins was fixing to take a bath, and..."

"She was *what?*"

"I mean," Yid hastened to explain, "that without even meaning to do it, there I was in her cabin. And she was getting ready to give herself and her baby a bath. I couldn't no more think of a way to get out without her knowing I was there than nothing. So I tried to scare her baby so it would cry, but that didn't work at all. She saw me then and started screaming and I grabbed the button and said I wanted to be back with you, and I was. I'll tell you, Mincy, I sure didn't mean to take up her invitation to return again that way."

For a moment Mincy stared at Yid. Then she closed her eyes and shook her head, trying to clear her mind. "Sweet-heart," she finally said, "don't you see what that woman is doing?"

"What do you mean?"

"Yid, you're so good-hearted blind that you can't even see the real Amber Wiggins. You don't see the well-prac-ticed art of the averted glance, the purposely accidental exposure of the shapely calf, the furious blush, the startled half-parting of the lips upon being caught staring, the inno-cently lingering touch, the leaning close for just the sugges-tion of a mad moment's whiff of foreign eau de cologne, the deliberate let-slip of the softly-called first name, the stammering apology for the same boldness, and all the other artful mixed bag of tricks whereof few wantons and no nice women exceed the talents of George Wiggins' shapley widow.

"No, you don't see those things at all. But I do, Yid, and I can tell you with all sincerity that Amber is doing her best to destroy you and me. And you're leting it happen, sweetheart. With all these thoughts of yours that you refuse to control, you're actualy encouraging that destruction. And that's what that old drummer, bless his heart, has been trying to warn you of."

"Mincy, you can't be right! Why would she do that?"

"Because she needs a husband, Yid, a free hired hand to run her farm and do all the work on that huge place that George set out to do and never finished."

Mincy continued her explanation, but Yid had stopped listening. Instead he was seeing a team of dog-tired work plugs pulling a broken-down plow through an endless field of hard earth and sage, while a poor, scarecrow-like image of himself staggered along after them, trying desperately to cling to the plow...

"And I love you, Yid," Mincy was concluding. "Please know that. I do love you, and I know you can do it."

Yid gazed at the woman who sat next to him. Then he slowly dropped his eyes. "Mincy, I've been a poor, miserable, sorry fool, one who ain't got the least possible notion of what he's doing."

"Yid, please don't talk like that."

"But it's true, honey-darlin'. You love me, and I know you do. The drummer tries to help me see that, and I get all riled up. Then you try and help me change, and I won't listen. Fact is, Schiller described me years ago. 'Against stupidity the very gods themselves contend in vain.'"

"Sweetheart," Mincy pleaded, "don't be so hard on yourself..."

"But it's true," Yid said quietly. "Of course, Schiller was a surgeon during the War between the States, and likely used the knife too much. Matthew said the same thing better in the New Testament."

"What are you talking about?"

"Guidances from the Bible on the general subject of bullheadedness and yours truly," said Yid. "Same as the old drummer has been trying to get me to understand."

"Such as?" asked Mincy softly.

"'They be blind leaders of the blind,'" quoted Yid just as softly. "'And if the blind lead the blind, both shall fall into the ditch.'"

"Can you say it in English?"

"I reckon," Yid agreed gently. "It goes like this. Neither me nor Amber Wiggins knows what the devil we're doing or where that same evil fellow is leading us, but if I keep going, it's likely going to take at least me to grief. On the other hand, you do know where I'm headed. You see it clearly. Only somehow I can't make myself listen to you. Mincy, what do you reckon is the matter with me?"

"What the old drummer wrote you, Yid, on the plow and on those papers. You have lost the Spirit. That's why I've been so afraid to say anything to you about it. I can't hardly talk to you any more."

"Yeah, I have been somewhat cantankerous."

"As a fly-bit Missouri mule," Mincy agreed. "But let's let it end where it is, and try to find our way out of this mess. Yid, look at the two of us. Do you really believe we are floating in the air?"

"Or that we saw my folks the day I was born, or Amber in her cabin, or those outlaw fellers from up Challis way?" Yid asked, continuing Mincy's question. "By Tophet, I don't know. My mind says it can't be so, but my eyes and ears tell me it is."

"They do," agreed Mincy. "Besides, I don't recollect *ever* sharing a dream with someone else."

"Nor me. But doggone it, the whole idea of us floating and zinging here and there faster than we can hardly even think it is daft as...as, well, as the sun rising every afternoon in the west, and then giving off a pretty blue glow."

Mincy giggled. "That'd be something, all right."

"But not hardly any more strange than what's happening to us. But if it's real, I'm sick nigh unto death of not weighing anything. Since I started floating I've had me more trouble than the entire Army of the Confederacy had during Sherman's march to the south. Honey-darlin', I'm going to take us all home with my Go-Button, *muy pronto,* so we can change our duds and get away from this miserable thread.

"Then, we will return to life as it was and celebrate our anniversary like we ought to. And there will be no more Amber Wiggins between us, I promise you that."

And so, while Mincy smiled with relief and wiped her thankful eyes, Yid spoke himself to the back of Peaches.

"You'd better take hold of the brake handle," he advised from where he floated above the horse's back. "I'd hate like blazes to leave you floating along the road here."

Quickly Mincy placed her hand on the upright brake handle. "Are you sure this will work?"

"Nope. But nothing ventured, nothing gained." Then, taking hold of Peaches' mane, and grasping his button in his other hand, Yid ordered himself, the team and wagon, and his incredibly patient, amazingly quick to forgive, wife, to be at their home under Willow Creek Summit.

"Thank goodness," Mincy sighed as she pushed herself away from the wagon and toward the cabin. "I can't wait to get out of this blouse and get back to normal weight."

"I'll water the horses," Yid declared. "Then I'll be right in, and we can decide what we're going to do next."

Mincy smiled and closed the door, and Yid, still astride Peaches' back, ordered the team to be at the small stream he had run through the far corner of the corral.

Peaches snorted and tossed her head a little at the second unexpected change of location in almost as many minutes, but Cream, without even a toss of her mane, simply lowered her head and commenced to drink. She was certainly one concentrating old mare.

Yid waited quietly, his mind contemplating anew the vast differences between the two mares. In a strange way they were like Mincy and Amber; in some things alike, but in most things vastly different. Not better or worse, just different.

Nor was he certain which of the two women could make him most happy. Probably Mincy, of course, with her steady love and forgiving compassion. But if excitement was what he craved, the nail-biting, knee-knocking, heart-pounding brand of excitement that was promised by the come-hither flutter of long eyelashes and the soft curve of ruby-red lips filled with seductive whispers, then Amber Wiggins was the ticket. And by Tophet but that woman was a ticket!

Yid stared off down the valley at the smoke that was floating in the air above Sage Creek. His firm resolutions were forgotten, his mind was once again racing with the problem of how he would tell Amber what had happened when he had ordered himself into her cabin.

Of course he had already forgotten Mincy's accurate appraisal of Amber's need for a farmer-husband to grub out and plow up her thousand and more acres. He had also forgotten that though he had put in his legal apprentice time for being a tailor, and had become a pretty good one, the last three years had seen him hard-pressed to even come near being a poor-to-average farmer.

Yes sir, he had forgotten all of that, being persistently and pleasantly enamored by Amber's fiery good looks. In the hour of need, Yid's think-box had surely fled south for the winter. Or been fried to a chitling crisp by Amber's feather-soft touch on his arm and cheek. Or cracked wide open and spilled out to dry by his own bone-hard, bed-rock deep stubbornness.

Whichever, his memory was long and surely gone, as was his promised repentance, and in a moment's time Yid was back to his old and singularly narrow-viewed dream; the deceptively fine looks and amorous disposition of Amber Wiggins.

She would likely still be upset by his appearance in her cabin, all right. But then, she might not be upset at all. In point of fact, she probably wasn't. She was more than probably just disappointed that he had departed her premises so quickly.

Of course she might have been troubled a little by the fact that he had been floating in the air, but he could easily explain that and the Go-Button. In fact, suddenly he could think of dozens of possibilities that he and Amber could do together with the thread and the button, things that no one had ever done with *anyone* before.

By jings, with what he had ...

And suddenly Yid was flying off across the barn, swirling around at an alarming rate, caught in a dust-devil that had drifted down off Mahogany Ridge and crept up on him unseen.

"Oh, for the love of...," he muttered as he reached for his button, "I've got to get this thing sewn on with regular thread. A man just isn't any good without a little weight to hold him down. Maybe I'd ought to have Mincy bake some biscuits, and carry a couple of them in my pockets. They would surely keep me planted."

Yid was already back with the horses, enjoying a good chuckle over his memories of Mincy's biscuits. Peaches stamped her hoof with impatience, but Cream was still drinking, and so Yid waited, dreaming.

From on top of the barn a crow called noisily, and several flies buzzed around him and the horses. The scene was one of total tranquility, and Yid was enjoying it immensely, his thoughts plowing further the fertile dream of Amber Wiggins, when Mincy suddenly began screaming.

"Mincy?" he called out, "what..."

"Yid, help me. Please!"

Taking his button in hand, Yid ordered himself inside.

"All right, what's the big fuss about?"

"Oh, sweetheart, just *look* at me."

"What?"

Mincy pointed helplessly downward. "I'm still floating, Yid! Look, I've changed blouses, and I'm still in the air."

Dumfounded, Yid stared from a hovering Mincy to her hovering blouse, which was across the room from her, and then back to his wife. Then, slowly, he unbuttoned his shirt and removed it.

The shirt continued to float after Yid had pushed it away. But astonishingly, so did he.

"That doesn't make any more sense than square eggs," Yid declared. "If the thread makes things float, and if we take the thread away, then why the ring-tailed devil..."

"Because it's catching." Mincy wailed. "Oh, Yid, what if we are doomed to float from place to place as best we can, and to be tossed about by every little breeze that decides to blow, for the rest of our lives? We've caught whatever disease it has that makes that awful thread float, and now...and now... Oh, sweetheart, what are we going to do?"

"Well," Yid responded, thinking quickly. "*I* have a button, so I can always get back if I get blown away. But you? I don't reckon I know...

"Wait a minute! I do know how to solve this, at least temporarily. I'll fetch you a rope from the barn. Then you can tie one end around your middle and the other around a tree or the wagon or the porch or whatever, and if the wind blows you off, you can always haul yourself right on back again."

Mincy looked shocked. "What? But Yid..."

"Law, Mincy, that's just exactly what I'd do. Either that or fill my pockets with your biscuits."

Now Mincy's look of surprise gave way to one of pain, or sorrow, or a deeply disturbing combination of them both.

"Oh, Yid, you promised. Can't you hear what thoughts of that woman make you do? Or say? They make you mean, and nasty, and I don't know if I want to take very much more of it. Talk about the blind falling into a ditch. Yid, you're heading for the Grand Canyon."

"Tut, tut," Yid grinned, wagging his finger in mocking reprimand. "Don't lecture me, or I won't go fetch that rope."

Fuming, Mincy closed her mouth and folded her arms. Suddenly, though, her eyes widened.

"Yid?"

"Yes, ma'am?"

Mincy was thinking furiously. "Why don't we go see the drummer again? We could go there in no time with that Go-Button. And we both need this curse of weightlessness removed."

For a moment Yid thought of it. A trip to the Cove

would certainly be simple enough, and he couldn't wait to get shut of that thread

"Do you think the old man would take back only the thread?" he asked. "I do want to keep the button."

"He might, Yid. We could surely go see."

Yid considered the matter. If they found the old man, and if he very carefully didn't mention the button when he discussed giving back the thread, then he just might pull it off. And getting rid of that thread was something Yid truly wanted to do.

Besides, if the uncomfortable truth of the matter were known, he was feeling fidgety about the way he had been talking to Mincy, very fidgety. He had never treated anyone so poorly, and it appalled him, as he thought about it, to think that he had cast so far aside his mother's honored teachings. What mattered whether or not he dreamed of another woman? He loved Mincy anyway, he knew that she loved him, and by all that was right and holy he had ought to be treating her better than he had.

"All right," he declared amiably. "We'll go. Just get your blouse."

"But I already have on this other one."

"I know, Mincy. But I'm thinking that the drummer might want all the thread back, and I want the blouse there with us if he does."

Mincy nodded her understanding and struggled to where her clothing floated in the air.

"I'm ready," she said, smiling sadly. And Yid was awed by the radiance of even that sort of smile. Always he had been, always he would be. There was no one alive who had a smile quite as lovely as Mincy's. Not even Amber Wiggins .

"Good," Yid growled, forcing such thoughts from his mind. "So am I. Button, take me to Mincy's side."

Yid was instantly there, and grasping his wife's arm, he gave the Go-Button fresh orders to take them both to the Cove.

15

"I can't understand it," Yid stated, looking around. "No matter what time of day we arrive anymore, the Cove is filled with this foggy mist."

"Can you find the drummer this time?"

Yid grinned. "Sure enough. No matter how thick this soup is, the button can take us right through it. Go-Button, leave us be at the drummer's wagon."

Instantly they were beside the metal structure that they had seen earlier. Whether or not they were also in the Cove, was anybody's guess. The place was incredibly bright, so much so that it hurt their eyes even when they closed them. And the mist, which was bright rather than dark, was so impossible to see through that they could not see more than a foot or two in any direction.

But even the atmosphere seemed different, and both Yid and Mincy were immediately uncomfortable.

"Hurry," Mincy whispered, "this place feels worse than before."

"I'd say. A man sure wouldn't want to spend much time here."

"Well, then. Knock."

In total agreement with Mincy's sentiments, Yid banged on the side of the metal wagon, or whatever it was. But he couldn't hear the knocking and nothing else happened either.

"Yid, aren't you going to knock?"

"I did! Only no sound came of it. Watch, and you'll see what I mean."

Yid rapped again, soundly. And once more, no sound came forth.

"Y...Yid, I'm frightened."

"In those sentiments, honey-darlin', you ain't alone. I just wish I knew where in blazes we were. But I *don't* think we're in the Cove. I've been there a lot, and it was never like this."

"But that wagon object is here."

"I know, and that's what's roped my forelegs and thrown me. If I hadn't seen it before, then I might think..."

"Yid..."

But Yid Francom needed no yelped whisper from Mincy to get his attention. He had already given that, in its solemn, slack-jawed entirety, to the sudden opening in the metal object upon which he had been pounding.

"H...howdy," he stammered to the brilliant but unsmiling drummer, who stood silently waiting. "M...Mincy and I were j...just..."

"He knows, Yid." Mincy whispered urgently. "The drummer already knows."

"Knows what?" Yid whispered back to his wife.

"I...I don't know. Maybe everything you were going to say. Maybe even more than that. Look at his eyes, and you can tell."

Yid looked, and found himself seeing such incredible sadness as he had never before seen, never before even imagined. Desperately he tried to look away from the sorrow and grief, but he found that he could not. He was forced to look at the tears, and as they slowly fell Yid could hardly contain his own intense sorrow.

Yet, working desperately, he finally forced his eyes to

move away from the drummer's countenance. Only then did he begin to feel better.

A little.

"I...uh...I...last time, Mister Drummer," Yid stammered, holding up one of the small boxes, "you gave us this box of thread by m...mistake. We were uh...wondering if we m...might trade it back for our p...plow."

And to Yid's amazement, the box in his hand was gone. Just like that. Then he realized that the button he had been clutching was loose in his hand. And directly after that, beside him, he heard a startled cry and turned to see Mincy staring at her hand-held blouse, the gaping hole in it very evident.

Looking back up at the drummer he found, to his further and final consternation, that the opening had closed. The drummer, once again, had vanished.

"He...he's gone," he whispered.

"I can see that. Did... he leave us our plow?"

"I don't reckon I know. This mist is so thick... Mincy, this is mist. Real mist."

"So?"

"Well, a moment or so ago it was more like light, I think. Is that consarned plow here on the ground? Maybe we just need to look..."

"Yid," Mincy suddenly squealed, "I'm touching the ground. My feet are on the ground."

Mincy's voice was so excited that Yid grinned in spite of his nervousness. Then, intentionally, he stomped his own foot.

"So am I," he breathed in vast relief. "Feels good as warm milk on a cold night, doesn't it."

"I'll say. But I can't see the plow."

"Neither can I."

Suddenly Yid stopped, and his pounding heart jumped two speeds higher. This couldn't be happening, none of it could. Yet he was wide awake, he had to be, he was talking with Mincy, and so he knew that it was.

"Oh, oh," he breathed. "Oh, *oh!*"

"Wh...what's wrong?"

"Mincy, I...I think we're in neck-deep trouble, and sinking deeper by the minute. I just hope by jings that we ain't in quicksand."

"Oh, no! Now what?"

Yid gulped. "I just found another one of those black boxes."

"Is it...the same as the others?"

Slowly Yid shook his head. "No, this one is bigger."

"Are...are you going to open it?"

"I don't rightly know if I should, at least right here in the Cove. Here, give me your hand, and let's get out of this foggy mist and into the sunlight. Then maybe we can see what sort of fooforah we've been given this time."

Mincy shook her head. "I don't think we should take the box, Yid. I think we ought to leave it right here, and go."

Deep down, Yid agreed. But there was something about that box, something that seemed to pull at him so that he couldn't even consider leaving it behind.

"But what if it's valuable?" he asked for want of a better excuse for keeping it.

"It isn't a plow, and that is the only thing of value that we need. Now come on, sweetheart. Let's go. You know the trouble those other boxes got us into."

For a moment Yid vacillated. But at last, realizing the sense in Mincy's argument, he agreed. "All right," he said, tearing his eyes away from the box, "I'll leave it here on the ground. Now give me your hand, honey-darlin', and leave us be gone from this heinous bottom land."

Mincy gave her hand, Yid gave the Go-Button his terse and heartfelt orders, and they were back on the porch of their cabin.

Everything looked exactly the same as before they had gone. Peaches and Cream were still in their harnesses and Peaches was still stamping her hoof impatiently; the crow was still perched on top of the barn; flies still buzzed back and forth in the sunlight; and both Yid and Mincy had their feet planted firmly on the porch.

However, there was one small but entirely significant change. Or rather, there was one small but entirely significant addition. The black box that they had left behind them in the Cove? The one Yid had left so carefully there upon the ground? Well, it was positioned exactly between them, resting peacefully upon the porch floor.

And for a Big Lost country fact, it was also positioned open.

16

For a long and breath-held moment they both stared at the box in silence, and neither of them would look up at the other. Yid, thinking about it, decided at once that a man could very easily have sliced the silence and served it out in sandwiches, it was that thick. For some reason, things seemed very tense.

"Yid," Mincy finally whispered, "what is that thing?"

Yid took a deep breath. "I don't rightly know. Looks remarkably like a golden ball, though. At least it's round, and the workmanship is curious, mighty curious."

"What are you doing?"

"I'm picking it up. What does it look like?"

"But...but what if it...it *does* something?"

Yid laughed, but straightened back up without touching the object. "It didn't do anything before, back at the Cove. What do you suppose it might do now?"

"It wasn't open then," Mincy whispered. "Now it is, and it might do anything."

"Yes...I reckon it might. But how will I know if I don't pick it up and take a closer look?"

"Oh, Yid, must you?"

Yid looked at his wife, again amazed that she cared so very much. What was wrong with him, that he could not keep her love in his mind?

"Well, Mincy," he finally breathed, "*somebody* has to do it."

"Then let me," she declared. "You get behind the cabin, and..."

Grinning, Yid took her hand. "Not on your life," he declared. "I'll do it, and *you* wait behind the cabin until I tell you to come out. Now, rattle your hocks. I want to see what the paper underneath this thing says. Both times."

Hesitantly Mincy turned and stepped off the porch and around the corner of the cabin, and then Yid leaned down and gently touched the round ball.

Nothing happened.

Carefully he wrapped his fingers around it and lifted it a fraction of an inch, squinting his eyes tight shut as he did so.

Still nothing happened.

Slowly then he straightened, with the ball held gentle as a baby's breath in his hands.

"It's all right," he called then to the hidden Mincy. "I'm certain sure its safe."

Slowly Mincy came from around the corner, and then carefully she approached the porch.

"What...what is it?"

"Like I said previous," Yid replied, his voice low and quiet, "it's a round ball, a curious round ball."

"Are those things on it diamonds or rubies?"

Yid stared. "Law, do you think? To me they look more like colored glass, or something." Lifting the ball closer, he examined the colored crystal knobs that protruded from the surface. They were not large, there was one of every single color that he could think of, they were all of uniform size, and each was shaped with sparkling exactness like a cut gemstone.

"By jings, Mincy," he breathed, "could be they *are* real. Happen that's so, why, this ball is the startlingest treasure I ever laid eyes upon."

Gently Yid touched one of the stones, and to his surprise it depressed quite easily into the ball. Pulling his finger away, he saw that the stone returned gradually to its original position. And beyond that nothing else happened.

"So, what is it?" Mincy asked.

"By jings, I wish I knew," Yid responded. "Here. Hold it, and let me read what the paper says."

"Be careful, sweetheart," Mincy said as she gingerly took the ball.

Smiling reassuringly, Yid picked up the paper and read it carefully.

"Well?"

"Beats the goose down out of me. It says 'Future-Compass.' "

"That's all?"

"No, not exactly. It also says, 'manufactured 2089,' and 'use with caution.' Mighty like those other things."

"2089. Do you think those numbers mean years?"

"I don't hardly know. At least not for certain. If it is, we're a long way from it, and it's surely a different year from when the thread and Go-button came from. Law, maybe that's what Future-Compass means. It comes from the future."

"Or it shows it, maybe?" Mincy ventured.

"I don't hardly think so. This thing doesn't show anything at all, except these little stones. Doesn't seem like much of a compass to me. There isn't even a needle."

"Maybe it works by punching those stones."

"Maybe, providing someone is around who by nature is some reckless. You want to do the honors, Mincy?"

The big woman smiled mischievously. "If I did want to, would you let me?"

Yid grinned. "Not hardly, honey-darlin'. Reckon the job is mine."

"But...what if something happens?"

Yid's grin grew wider. "You've sung it many times, Mincy, though I suppose you thought it was only poor old Steven Foster's song. But like he wrote, life's a lot like the Camptown Races. Somebody bets on the bobtailed nag, somebody bets on the bay. And doggoned if the black with three stockings doesn't get up in the last furlong to win it going away. If we both had a dollar for all the long shots we've taken..."

"Like not putting a halter on your thoughts, maybe?"

"Maybe," Yid agreed, his voice growing even more quiet. "Though I still can't see what's so all-fired evil and dangerous about dreaming. Do you suppose the note has changed yet?"

"I...I don't know."

"Well then, leave us take a look. I... Aha! The old drummer is still at it. Listen to this, honey-darlin'. 'He that looketh on a woman to lust after her...shall fear.' "

Yid grinned. "Now I know that the old man is daft. I've never in my life felt less fear than I do right now. You saw me lift up that ball. Did that look to you like a man who feared?"

Slowly Mincy shook her head.

"Nor was it."

"How do you know that's what it means?" Mincy asked.

"Fear is fear, ain't...isn't it?"

"But what if you are wrong, Yid? Suppose that fear is just another step in the process of destruction that I believe is happening to you — to us? Suppose that it is not fear of immediate problems, but ultimate, eternal fear that the drummer means?"

Again Yid smiled. "Well, that is a gamble, all right. Howsomever, like the song says, I reckon a man gambles every time he gets out of bed."

"Seems like that goes for women, too," Mincy agreed. "A person might think she had everything going just right, and then get up in the morning, put her left foot in the thundermug of a shattering marriage, break her leg and have to be shot."

"Or anyways," finished Yid, grinning at Mincy's dark humor, "bow a tendon and get put out to pasture for six months."

"You think that's all our marriage ending means to me, Yid? That I'll feel a little pain for a bit, and then be fine?"

"I didn't say that, honey-darlin'. Fact is, I don't think we'd have any problems at all if you'd just stop talking about it all the time."

"Well, then?" sighed Mincy. "What do you suggest that we do?"

"I think," Yid declared easily, "that we ought to see if we can make this contraption operational."

Without another word Yid took the ball back, and slowly, carefully, he began pressing stones. He pushed until all of them had been depressed, and nothing happened. Again he punched, randomly, sometimes pushing two or three at once. But still nothing happened, except that the colored gems went in without difficulty and came just as easily back out.

"Maybe I need to give it an order," Yid muttered to himself as he turned the ball back and forth. "That worked dandy with the other boxes, and with my button."

Taking a deep breath, and feeling more than passing foolish for what he was about to do, Yid spoke directly to the ball. "All right, compass," he ordered, "show me the future."

Yid waited, but as far as he could tell, nothing changed. Except maybe that the day got later. Or that a fast-moving cloud bank scuttled closer. Or that he suddenly realized he was nervous. By Tophet, he was scratching at his feet like a centipede with the chills, and that was some nervous twitch, for a fact.

"Tell you what, Mincy," he said finally. "Whatever this doggone thing is, I don't think it works. Or if it does, I can't seem to throw a loop around it."

"Then why did the old drummer give it to us, Yid? I'm positive that he *wanted* us to have it."

"Well, it surely trailed us home. That seems like mighty good evidence, all right."

Mincy put her hand on Yid's arm. "Sweetheart, I am so frightened and confused. I would give anything in the world if we could just wake up from this nightmare, and find everything back to normal in our lives. I'm so sick and tired of chasing all these daft and crazy rainbows..."

"*Rainbows!*" Yid shouted excitedly. "By tunket, Mincy, that's it. A rainbow."

Mincy looked at him with consternation. "What? Yid, sometimes you make no more sense than...than... Well, you sure don't make sense."

"Could be I'm wrong," Yid agreed. "After all, I was wrong once or twice before in my life. But hear me out. A rainbow is color, ain't it? And each color is always in the same part of a rainbow. Now tell me, what is the first color?"

Mincy looked at him askance. "What do you mean, first?"

"I don't know. Top, I reckon."

"It's red, I think. But Yid, this is just silly."

"Could be, but maybe I'm right, too. Remember the Camptown Races. I have a funny feeling like this might be the bob tailed winner. After all, these stones have got to be for something. Okay, the red stone is pushed down. What's next in order?"

"Orange, yellow, green, blue and purple. I think."

"That's it? Just six?"

"Why?" Mincy asked, looking again at the ball. "How many stones are there?"

"I don't hardly know, but it seems like a mort more than six. Let's see, here is a red one, then orange, yellow, green, blue and,well, what do you know about those horses? Purple comes in dead last, in a field of just exactly six. As in horse races, just so in rainbows."

"Are you pushing them all down at once?"

Yid grinned. "Yes, ma'am, all at once. Why? Do you think I should do them one at a time?"

Mincy shrugged her shoulders. "From my vast experience with these things, Yid, I'd have to say that your guess is probably three times better than mine."

"Well said. Happen this doesn't work, however, we'll try it your way."

So, with the stones depressed, the two of them waited. Out in the yard the rooster crowed, Peaches stomped her hoof again and whinnied her distress at still being in harness, more flies buzzed, and nothing else happened. Except that the storm clouds got closer still.

"Law," Yid said with resignation as he released the stones, "sure as Al West trail-bossed twelve hundred ponies to St. Louis when he was sixteen, that wasn't it.

"Now," he grinned, his voice dry as the buzz of a diamondback rattlesnake, "let's do it your way. Red, orange, yellow, green, blue and purple. One at a time, down and up. There. Anything around here look any different to you?"

"No, but maybe it takes a minute or so."

"Could be, but I doubt it. Let's try it the opposite direction. Purple, blue, green, yellow, orange, and red, one at a time, down and up again.

"There," he grunted a moment later. "Still no ripples on the old beaver pond. Tell you what. I am going to put this useless creation back in its box..."

"Yid?"

Mincy's voice was little better than a gasp, and Yid hastily took his eyes from the ball to see what ailed her.

"Mincy? Are you all right?"

"Yid, look..."

Yid looked, and suddenly realized that the yard in front of him had changed. Either that, or it was no longer there. With eyes as steady as a crouched cat's, he watched, stretching off into the distance before him, a road. Or more accurately, he watched *two* roads. The one was well rutted and quite wide, and it was obvious that it was fairly heavily traveled. The other, which didn't run parallel to the first at all, was narrow, somewhat rocky, and overgrown with grass and weeds.

"Do you see that?" he asked quietly, almost reverently.

"Two roads? I see two roads. What do you see?"

"The same. Is that...a *rainbow* around that first road? The big, wide one?"

For a moment Mincy studied the scene before her. "It's colored like a rainbow," she finally responded, "but it surely isn't shaped like one. I'd say it's more like a ring of colored light. It's so bright, though, that I can hardly see the other, narrower road."

"Nor me either."

"Well?"

"Well what?"

"What do you think we are looking at?"

"Besides two roads? Beats the Christmas time turkey dressing out of me," Yid replied laconically. "I'm no forty-karat genius, though, and some things are more than a mite hard for me to grasp. Tell you what. Why don't you unlock your wheels, stop burning brake-shoe leather, and tell me what *you* think it means."

Mincy giggled, and Yid looked at her in wonder, amazed that she had the courage to laugh in the midst of such circumstances.

"How you ever think of such funny things to say," she grinned, "is beyond me. But I'm glad you do, Yid. Laughing makes me feel better about things."

"Good. Now what do you think?"

"I don't know either. However, if that's the future, it looks mighty like the present. In fact, it looks about like that road down near Barton Flats where it cuts up across the bar."

"You know," Yid responded with a satisfied grin, "it *does* look like that, for a fact. I disremember the trees being so far above the river, but everything else looks the same."

For several moments Yid and Mincy stood together, gazing out on the two roads, discussing what they were seeing. Above them the fast-moving, angry clouds spat out a bit of rain and then held back again, threatening more. But Yid and Mincy paid no attention to the short storm. Instead they watched the two roads, about which neither of them could see any change at all. Yet for some reason they found the stillness of the scene fascinating, and neither could take their eyes away from it.

Finally, however, the ethereal view began to dim and grow less distinct, fading slowly away. At last it vanished altogether, and the dusty yard appeared again.

Immediately overhead the tumbled clouds, black with afternoon lateness, still hovered, their undersides filigreed with glimmering lightening. Off to the east, the horizon sky was pale and pure green as the heart of the emerald-appearing stone on the ball. To the west it was deep-fired as the inner prism of the ruby stone. And everywhere, all about everything, lay the exciting raindust smell and misty yellow light of the thirsty earth.

Yid breathed the sweet aroma deeply, feeling the same gratitude and relief. Nothing crazy had happened. He and Mincy had activated the Future-Compass, had seen the view, and nothing else had occurred. Both of them had remained just fine. The bob tailed nag, at last, had come in first.

"So, what do you reckon happened?" he asked as he turned the golden ball in his hands.

Mincy shrugged. "Yid, I've no more idea of that than I do of all the rest of this craziness. But, if we aren't in the midst of a terrible dream, then I'd say we saw a vision of some sort. Only I've never even come close to having a vision, so I don't know if I believe in them either, except for prophets and such. What do *you* think happened?"

"Law, Mincy, nothing of much account, that's sure. Except that it rained on the still-harnessed team. I need to take care of them, and soon, or the harnesses will stiffen up."

"That's true. When we get a plow, the leather..." Suddenly Mincy stopped and turned back around. "Say, Yid, do you think maybe that other fellow got our plow? The one who was ahead of us in line?"

Yid looked at his wife, arrested by her tone of voice. She surely didn't act much like Amber Wiggins, nor look like her, either. But by Tophet, Mincy had something in her voice that sort of, well, it sort of made him feel all fluttery inside. Like maybe ...

"Did you hear me? Do you think he did?"

"I don't rightly know, Mincy. But whether he did or not, doesn't seem to matter an awful lot. He's gone to goodness-knows-where, I'm not about to go back to see that drummer, and I'd say that we are out one plow."

"Why can't you use the Go-Button?"

"To do what?" Yid asked, already turning toward the horses.

"To go where that fellow lives who likely got my plow."

Yid frowned. "Mincy, I have already just told you, I don't know where he lives, or even who he is."

Mincy frowned in return, took up a small rock from the yard, and tossed it underhand at the barn door. It hit, clattered to the ground, and rolled to a stop. "Yid," she finally asked when it had stopped moving, "when you rescued me, what sort of directions did you give the button?"

"You mean today? On the road?"

Mincy smiled. "That's right."

"Why, I told it to take me to you."

"Did you give it directions concerning where I was?"

"Not hardly."

"That's right," Mincy agreed. "You simply gave it general instructions. Now the point, Yid, is this. You didn't describe where the button was to take you, but *it* somehow knew. Right?"

"You mean the *button* knew?"

"That's correct."

Yid scratched his head. "Why, I reckon that's so."

"So do I. Now why can't we tell the button to take us to the man who was in front of you in that line? Or maybe to the *two* men. Didn't you tell me that there were always three, you and two others?"

"Tell the truth," Yid replied, scratching his elbow as he thought of it, "there always were until this afternoon when I got behind. Howsomever, you know we only saw one."

"I know we did. But maybe he was the second man there. Maybe some other fellow was there even earlier than him. Maybe *he* got the plow."

"That seems like a powerful lot of maybes."

"True, but it wouldn't be very hard to check them out, would it? Not with that button. Yid, we need the plow, and since we still have the button, this looks like our chance."

"I don't know, Mincy. I can't hardly..."

"Yid, please."

Looking at the sinking afternoon sun, Yid sighed. It seemed like the strangeness of this anniversary was never going to end. However, if the Go-Button could help them find the doggone plow, then why not give it another spin?

"All right," he said, grinning at Mincy's continued efforts to recruit his thinking time. "Give me your hand, honey-darlin'. Good. Now, Go-Button, we want to be taken to the man who stood in front of us in that line down in the Cove."

And they were.

Almost ...

PART FIVE

JOURNEY ONE

17

"Yid, is...is this what I think it is?"

Carefully Yid looked around him, his mind spinning with the enormity of the nightmare he was somehow still in the middle of.

"If... you mean the road we saw, the one that had the rainbow around it, then I reckon it is."

"But how did we get there? Or here? I mean, that wasn't even real. Was it?"

Yid took a deep breath, hoping to calm his pounding heart. What was it that he had told himself about fear, or about the bob tailed nag coming in first? Not hardly had he been right in either case. In fact, this experience didn't even look like the black with three stockings. More and more it was shaping up like the old left foot in Mincy's thunder-mug, for sure, and Yid didn't feel like getting a bowed tendon, nor shot for a broken leg, either.

"I truly wish I knew, Mincy," he replied slowly. "I've been more confused than a broken-legged man being taken for treatment to an insane asylum ever since my trip to the drummer a couple of days ago. And things haven't gotten any better since then."

For a moment neither spoke, and in the late afternoon the hillside was strangely quiet. The sounds of birds or insects were hushed and distant, the air was still, and even the dust of the road stirred hardly at all when Yid moved his foot across it.

Yet they were there, he and Mincy, wherever *there* was. He could see her, hear her, and even touch her, just as he could do with himself. So, much as he wanted to believe otherwise, he knew that this could hardly be a dream. Those sorts of things weren't part of dreams at all.

But it *was* a nightmare, of that he was certain.

"Law," he said, summoning his courage as best he could, "shall we see where the road goes?"

Without waiting for a reply, Yid stepped cautiously forward along the deeply rutted way, wondering as he did so why the Go-Button had brought them there when it had been instructed otherwise.

"Where do you suppose the man is who got our plow?" Mincy asked.

"I don't hardly know. I was just pondering the same puzzle. Maybe he's over that little ridge ahead of us. Shall we take a look?"

Mincy nodded, and so together the two walked up the small rise and over the top.

"Law, Mincy, look at the lake off there."

"It's big. Do you know where it is?"

"Not hardly. There are some houses down off thataway, though. Several of them. Do *you* recognize the place?"

"I don't think so," Mincy said nervously. "The rutted road means that a lot of wagons must go back and forth, but I don't think I've ever been here. I..."

"By jings," Yid suddenly breathed, "I know where we are, and it's just precisely where you said a little bit ago. That's Barton Flats off there. See? We're on the bar, probably this is Cedar Creek Wash, and down here below us is the old Battleground Cemetery. Which means that lake down yonder has buried old McCaleb's battleground, where he and Joe Skelton and the Mormon Kid and those other freighters and yahoos from Challis fought off all them Indians back in 1878.

"Over there," Yid continued, pointing, "is Lehman Butte and behind it the White Knob Mountains, down off thataway are the Narrows and the old rock Indian face, that canyon running back from the lake is Black Daisy Canyon, down south are Blaze and Taylor Canyons, and... Law, Mincy, somehow we got down past West's and Lehman's spreads, Whiskey Springs, the Big Turn and even the Elkhorn. How in blue blazes did we do that?

"And worse, where did that lake come from? Or those houses down off there below the Narrows? Mincy, tell you the truth, I'm shaking like a bobcat spitting buckshot. No matter what I said before, I'm scared."

"I know the feeling," Mincy breathed. "What...should we do?"

"Do?" Yid questioned. "I reckon we got two choices, honey-darlin'. The first is to sit down smack in the middle of this road, close our eyes, and hope the blamed thing will go away, entire. Or, we can hoof it down to those houses and see if some of those folks know which rotten apples have spoiled the barrel. Which would you prefer?"

For a long moment Mincy was silent, her eyes on the ground. Then, slowly, she raised her face and looked at her husband.

"Are...are you certain we have a choice?"

"Why wouldn't we?"

"No reason," Mincy answered quietly, "unless you consider that the road, the rutted one we've been on, is gone."

Looking quickly down, Yid discovered that the roadway had indeed vanished. Instead they were standing in the rock-strewn bottom of the dry stream bed called Cedar Creek.

"By jings, Mincy. We were on it until we crossed this little ridge. I..." Yid looked behind him, more baffled than ever. "Well, if that ain't something! Law, Mincy, I never felt so dumb and helpless in my entire mortal life. Look around us. We're not even near a ridge."

"Yid, let's go back. I don't like this."

Neither did Yid. Trouble was, like taking up the little black boxes earlier that day, he was feeling a curious need to push forward, to keep moving until he finally understood all that was happening. He tried to shut it out, to tell himself that he was crazy. But he couldn't. He knew, knew with a terrible certainty of however dubious origins, that the only way back for either of them was to press forward, ignoring the fear, ignoring...

"We've got to go down there," he said finally. "I don't hardly know why, but I feel it clear to my bones. If we're ever to get out of this nightmare, then we've got to see it through to the finish, whatever that means."

"Oh, Yid, are you serious?"

"As ever was."

"Then," Mincy said, taking a deep breath and doing her best to smile, "let us be moving forward."

With Mincy leading out, the two descended the rough creek bed, passed a very unusual fence, walked along beside a large metal pipe of some sort that was like nothing they had ever seen before, and came at last to a highway.

"You ever seen a road like that before?" Yid asked, breathing hard from keeping apace of his wife.

Silently Mincy shook her head.

"Me either. It's sort of shiny looking, and..."

Slowly Yid stepped out on it and stamped his foot. "Mincy, this feels like macadam, but I surely never saw any that looked like this. This has oil in it, or tar, and... By jings, Mincy, when in tunket did they get a road like this way up here?"

"Yid, look out!"

Yid turned, and to his horror he saw a huge wagon roaring toward him. Only there were no teams pulling it, and it was going terribly fast, much too fast for a wagon.

"Yiddddd!"

Spurred by Mincy's scream, and with a cry of his own, Yid dove for the side of the road. And his very cry was drowned by the terrible blast of the truck's air horn.

Trembling, Yid rolled over and watched as the huge object roared away down the highway toward the Narrows. Then, in amazement, he turned to stare at Mincy.

"What...what was that?" she asked.

"I haven't the least possible notion."

"Are you all right?"

"I reckon so," Yid replied as he picked himself up. "Wait a doggone minute, I do too know what that was. It must have been one of those new fangled horseless carriages everybody's talking about. I haven't ever seen one before, but I'd stake the farm and both horses that that's what it had to be."

"Someone at church said horseless carriages couldn't go as fast as a good horse," Mincy reminded him. "If that's one of them, then that man at church was surely wrong. I'd hate to see a horse going that fast."

"You're right as spring thaw. It would kill the poor horse."

"And the poor rider, if the horse ever stumbled."

Yid shook his head. "Can you hardly imagine being thrown at that speed?"

In awe Yid turned and looked after the almost invisible truck, and he said nothing further until it was out of sight. Then he turned back to Mincy.

"So now what?" he asked quietly.

"Uh...there's a house yonder, down near the river on the north end of the lake. Let's try there, and see if they've seen our plow."

"Are you up to this, honey-darlin'?"

"No," Mincy answered quietly, sincerely. "Trouble is, like you I don't think we have a choice."

Yid nodded solemnly, took his wife by the hand, and together they started down the roadway.

18

Why was it, Yid wondered as they walked along, that a man could tell a deserted dwelling from afar? What primal instinct surviving from a distant, hunted past let him know that the habitant was not at home, that the lair was empty, the cave abandoned, the hearth grown cold. He couldn't answer that question, not for sour apples he couldn't, but he knew, even as he and his wife moved toward the structure nestled in the distance, that it was empty. Further, he sensed that there had been trouble there, and the feeling worried him.

"Whoooeee," he exclaimed as they got closer, as much to calm himself as to express an opinion, "those are mighty fancy diggings."

"Maybe it's a small mansion," Mincy responded. "You ever see a mansion, Yid?"

"Just Brigham Young's old home, down in Salt Lake. But even then it wasn't like this one. This place is different."

"Maybe lots of folks live here. It looks big enough."

Yid looked at Mincy, wondering if maybe his feelings had been wrong. Had she seen something that he hadn't?

"Could be they do," he replied. Or at least, did. You see the plow anywhere about?"

"I don't."

"Neither do I. You want to try and 'hello' somebody out?"

"Try? You think nobody's at home?"

Yid shrugged. I don't. In fact, I've got a notion that nobody even lives here. Of course I might be wrong."

"You might be. I'll give a holler, just to see."

Mincy turned and put her hands around her mouth. "Hello the house?" she called. "Anybody to home?"

There was a brief echo, and then silence.

"Don't reckon they are," Yid said, opening the gate. "It appears I was right, for a change. Maybe we had ought to look around back, though. Could be they're out doing chores."

"Probably are. I know that's where we ought to be."

"Well," Yid muttered, "the calf will take care of the cow, and those horses can stand in harness for a spell longer. Come on, let's take a look-see. But be cautious as sin, Mincy. I've got a notion there's been trouble here. Bad trouble."

Carefully Yid and Mincy made their way around the side of the home. They found no one there, but they were astounded by what they did find.

"Mincy," Yid asked, staring at the first object that came into view, "you ever see a chair like that one?"

"I haven't. Looks kind of lonely, laying on its side like that."

"It does, but I didn't hardly mean that. Look at it. It's made of some sort of metal. Here, let me right it. There. You want to sit in it and try it out?"

"I...I don't think so."

Yid grinned. "Still not betting on the bob tailed nag, huh? Very well, I'll do it." Cautiously he seated himself, and then with a sigh he stretched back, and back even farther. "Well, lookee here. This chair rocks, and it doesn't even have rockers. By jings, these legs are springs, Mincy, like on the springbed wagon. Law. What I wouldn't give to have me a chair like this to set myself down in after a hard day's work."

"Yid, where are the outbuildings?"

Yid, truly enjoying the lawn chair, stood and looked around. "I don't rightly know," he muttered. "There are fields, sure enough. But where do these folks keep their livestock and their chickens? Or where is the privy?"

"I was wondering the same thing. I... Say, they've got a broken window there."

Yid nodded.

"My goodness," Mincy said, "look how *many* windows there are. I wonder..."

And without any further hesitation, she walked to the broken window and peered inside.

"Be careful, Mincy."

"I will. I... Yid?"

"See anything?"

"This is amazing. Come take a look."

Stepping up beside his wife, Yid gazed through the jagged hole in the glass.

"By Tophet," he breathed,   "what an incredulating sight!"

"What a mess, you mean. Look at all that filth and clutter. And do you see those holes in the walls? Yid, it looks like *animals* lived in there."

"Oh, it's some dirty," Yid agreed, "but Mincy, have you ever seen such spaciousness? Why, I'll wager we could get three or four cabins like ours in it. Just guessing, I'd say there are eight or maybe nine rooms under that one single roof.

"And lookee there. Those must be lanterns hanging from the ceilings, but I've never seen anything so fancy. And the walls? Mincy, even if they have holes in them, look how straight and smooth they are. And look at the floors. I mean under the clutter. I've never in all my born days seen such thick-looking carpeting. And look how it goes all the way to the walls. It'd be tougher'n old boot leather sweeping dirt under those rugs."

"Yes," Mincy agreed, "it does seem terribly elegant and

fancy. What would make folks treat such a fine mansion so poorly?"

"I don't hardly know. Maybe they just weren't raised proper.

"Well, if I'd had a say in it, Yid, I'd have told them off good. Folks like that, who treat such rare-fine things as though they are of no account, ought to be whupped good and then shot at sunrise. I just wish that..."

"Mincy," Yid whispered, "someone's here."

"Where?" Mincy asked, looking around inside the home.

"Not in there. Out here. By the corner to my right. I saw them, but I haven't looked carefully yet. Didn't want to spook them any by looking directly."

"Well, I'm not bashful," Mincy declared as she pulled her head back and looked.

To her surprise she saw a young girl standing in the deep brown grass a few yards away, staring back at her.

"H...hello," Mincy ventured.

"No one lives there anymore," the girl said, her voice sounding flat and empty.

Carefully Yid turned and studied the child. She might have been nine or ten, or maybe she was even eleven. Yid didn't have much experience in guessing the ages of children, and she was so slicked down with fineries that he couldn't have told anyway, at least not without a good look at her teeth.

Her hair was dark, however, almost the same color as Mincy's, and her eyes were the same unusual shade of blue. But what startled Yid most was the child's incredibly strange clothing. That and the way her eyes were painted.

He had never seen anyone paint their eyes, at least not anyone but a sporting lady he had seen once over at Gilmore. And that fact alone made him worry about the young girl. Was it possible that she was a woman of the night, he wondered? But no, she couldn't be. She was far and everlastingly away too young. But still, she was wearing ounces and ounces of gold jewelry, just like that whore in Gilmore had been wearing, and she also had some fancy earrings dangling down almost to her shoulders, just exactly like...

"Yid, look at how she is dressed."

Obediently Yid looked, and the girl's clothing bothered him just as much as her hair and painted face and jewelry. The clothing was bright, mighty bright, what there was of it. But there didn't seem to be very much. She had on a flame-red shirt that hung down hardly more than somewhat below her hips, and on her legs she wore what looked to be bright yellow long johns. Then she had on shoes that were hardly worth calling shoes at all, there was so little of them. They had mighty funny heels under them, too, high like Texas boots, only much, much more thin.

And those shoes, Yid realized with an embarrassed start, somehow made him look back at the young girl's legs.

Yid turned away in astonished, red-faced confusion, but Mincy certainly didn't.

"My heavens, child," she scolded, "you'll catch your death, out here in your underwear."

"My underwear? Look, lady, I don't like smart-mouths, even if they are big."

"Smart-mouths?"

"Yeah, like you. I just got this outfit over in Rexburg, and Mom paid plenty for it, too. So, what are you doing here?"

"We...we were just looking," Mincy stated uncertainly. "For our plow, I mean."

"Plow? You're *kidding* me. Do you think you're gonna find one of those in an empty kitchen?"

"Kitchen? This is a kitchen? But I don't..."

"Oh, come on, lady, I can tell a leech when I see one. You two are just looking for a free place to shack up. I know. Well, you won't be doing it in our house. I'll tell my daddy..."

"Your house?" Yid asked, turning back to the girl. "You live in this highfalutin shack?"

"It's not a shack," she said, and now her voice seemed to change, to harden a little more. "And I did live here, at least until the big fight. But Mom had to go to the hospital with a broken jaw, and when she got back, we both cleared out. I guess we'll stay out until the divorce is final."

"Oh," Mincy soothed, "I'm sorry."

"Yeah, sure you are. Look, lady, don't con me. The only ones around here who are sorry are the Bentons, and that's only because we can't afford to give them more than three hundred bucks a month rent."

"Three hundred..." Yid whispered in astonishment. "But..."

"Anyway, my Dad's mean, and he's big, too. Lot's bigger than you, lady. If he catches the two of you hanging around this place, he'll take you apart."

"But *why*?"

"Because it's his," the girl stated matter-of-factly. "Or at least that's what he claims. Why'd you think?"

"But...but we're only looking."

"Yeah, so you said. Listen, I gotta cruise. I..." Something seemed to halt the young girl, some thought that drew her to a stop.

"Say," she asked, glancing back, "you guys hungry?"

Yid looked at Mincy, and then he nodded that he was.

"By Tophet," he explained softly, "my tapeworm's been hollering for fodder for the past several hours, and I simply ain't had time to feed it proper. Why, my stomach's certain that my neck's been cut, and my belt buckle's been finished with knocking the lumps off my backbone for the past hour or more. Yes, missy, I am hungry."

Mincy giggled, and the girl looked quizzically at Yid, who gave her a lopsided grin in response.

"Well, you look it," the girl declared finally, smiling for the first time. "I never saw anyone so skinny. Maybe you're anorexic or something. You should probably check that out. Once a long time ago Mom took some other old men in and fed them. She said they were starving, and I'd say you fit the same bill. Maybe she'll do the same for you. I don't know. You'll have to ask her."

"And where do we find your mother?"

"Down the road a mile or so. Go past the Medicine Rock Ranch and Trout Haven, and we're a couple of places past that. The blue Camero is parked out in front. You can't miss it. Catch ya later."

And with that, the girl was gone.

19

"Yid, how on earth can you think of eating?"

Yid grinned. "Law, Mincy, I can't hardly recollect *ever* eating, it's been so long. Besides, where else would you want to look next?"

"Well," Mincy declared, "I don't rightly know. But I don't think we'll find our plow under that woman's dinner table."

"Maybe we will, and maybe we won't," Yid gently pushed. "But tell the truth, honey-darlin', it sure seems like the next likely place to go. You recollect how the little girl said we'd recognize her place?"

"Something blue. I suppose we'll know it when we see it. Yid, do you still think we are just north of the Narrows?"

Looking at the empty home, and at the discarded items strewn about the yard, Yid shook his head. "I don't know. Last time I was down the valley this way, there wasn't anything like this until I was almost to Houston. Of course that's been nigh onto a year, so you never know. I'd heard that folks were coming in to settle pretty regular. Mormon folks, mostly. Why? Have you decided on something?"

Mincy shook her head. "The mountains look the same,

Yid, and the river does, too. But that lake bothers me, and this house, with all its fancy fixings, doesn't make sense. Do...do you suppose that there might be another valley just like ours, only with different things in it?"

"And we stumbled into it, you mean?"

"That's right."

"Well, I wouldn't hardly think so, Mincy. But then, I wouldn't hardly think any of the rest of what we've seen today was possible, either. So I don't know. You might just be right. Question is, so what if you are?"

"I...I don't know. I guess I was thinking that if it was so, then we needed to find our way back to our own valley. The best place to do that, I think, would be back at our cabin, where we left it from. Maybe we ought to forget going south, and head home."

For a moment Yid stood silently, thinking. Mincy's evaluation impressed him, and he wondered if Amber could cogitate like that. Of course with the looks she had, maybe she wouldn't need any brains. And she did have looks, as even a blind man would have declared. Yid could see her clearly...

"Yid?"

Startled, Yid blinked and looked at his wife. "I...I don't think you're right, Mincy. I've ridden all over this country, and there isn't another valley like this, anywhere. No, I reckon we should go talk to that girl's mother. If it's a dead end, it'll only make a couple of miles difference, and we can still start home after that."

Gently Yid squeezed Mincy's waist. "You knew again, didn't you. You knew I was thinking of Amber Wiggins."

Silently Mincy nodded.

"Thank you for not pressing me about it. I...I... Well, doggone it, I don't know what's wrong with me. Wish I did, but I don't. I know I love you, and even if I never do learn to throw a rope on my thoughts and corral them up proper, it'll never change how I feel about you."

Yid turned then and walked around the empty house and out through the gate. Mincy followed, slowly, and while Yid waited, he noticed for the first time the electrical wires that were strung overhead.

"Mincy," he shouted, "take a look at that. They got electricity down here."

"Maybe it's a telegraph."

"I doubt it. That's supposed to come with the railroad, and that isn't due for at least another year. No, those are electrical power lines. Maybe that means they'll be stringing them up our way."

And then abruptly Yid stopped speaking.

"What is it?" Mincy asked.

"L...look, up there."

"What? What are you pointing at?"

"In the sky," Yid whispered. "Mincy, look at that...that... Law, woman, some poor fool's up there in a flying machine."

Somewhere off in the southeastern hills a coyote yammered with the crazed wildness which never fails to startle the oldest listener. Westward, disturbed in its stalking of birds down among the rushes along the river, a kit fox scolded back in his breed's sharply querulous manner. Before them, plaintively long- drawn-out, compellingly lonely, the cry of a lobo wolf came down from high up on the granite shoulder of Mount McCaleb. And then there was only the stir of the evening wind sneaking down out of the canyon to rustle the dry, soft curling grass that grew beside the road.

The lonely couple shivered and knew that the nightmare was real, and that its name was a home that wasn't home, a place that hadn't been and could never, in their own mortal lifetimes, ever be.

"Are you sure?" Mincy asked, her eyes drawn to the sky.

"Sure as skunks don't smell sweet. Men have been dreaming that impossible dream to fly like the birds for centuries, I reckon. And now look. Someone's gone and done it. Mincy, that means that...that we're..."

"That we're *what*?" Mincy whispered in fear. "Yid, was I right? Aren't we in...in our valley?"

Yid took a deep breath, for he didn't know how to answer his wife's question, not after coming to his own most recent conclusion. Nor was what he was thinking possible. It was just that, every daft and mind-snapping event of the past few hours considered, it was the only answer left to come to. And that being true, it left him and Mincy standing hock deep in the mucky sort of trouble that only came to pass in nightmares.

"Well, yes and...and no, not exactly," he finally stammered. "If I'm correct, it's our valley, right enough, and then again it ain't.

"Doggone it, Mincy, we've ridden the springbed over this way a couple of times. As you know full well, there isn't any road like this. Nor are there any houses like these, either. And you know for further certain sure there isn't any such outfit as a workable flying machine. Yet we just watched one go from horizon to horizon in hardly any time at all. I'm telling you something plumb crazy is going on. We've done some traveling, all right, but not to a different valley."

"You mean..."

"I mean this is still the Big Lost country, as ever was. Only I think we may be seeing things that haven't really happened yet. Does that make sense?"

"Not hardly, Yid. It frightens me and makes me feel like maybe I've lost my senses. Or I should say, we have lost our senses."

"Maybe we have, honey-darlin'. Maybe we have."

For a moment Yid stood silently, running his fingers through his thinning hair, his eyes on the strange pavement beneath his feet. Then, with excitement flashing across his face, he looked up at his wife.

"But I'll tell you what. I aim to find out where we are and what the blinking blue blazes is going on, and I aim to do it now. Are you with me?"

Taking a deep breath, Mincy did her best to smile. "I...I'm so scared I can hardly talk, Yid. But if that doesn't matter, then I suppose I am with you."

"Good," Yid grinned. "Give me your hand again, and let's go find that blue what-ever-it-was that the fierce-painted little girl told us about."

"But..aren't you nervous?" Mincy asked incredulously.

"You ain't just whistling 'The Yellow Rose of Texas,' I'm nervous," Yid growled happily. "Like the drummer said, I've been lusting, and now I feel fear. Fact is, Mincy, I ain't no ordinary coward. I'm most of three steps scarder'n all of the rest of that yellow-backed fraternity put together."

Yid took a deep breath and continued. "This place is a far piece from being where I want to be. But faint heart never won fair maiden, as they say. Let us leave be on our way. We'll win the brass ring yet."

Slowly Mincy held out her hand, and with a smile of comfort Yid took it. Then he held the button in his other hand.

"Go-Button," he ordered, "take us to the blue object that sits in front of the home where the girl lives who spoke to us a few moments ago."

"Gee," the little girl said as she looked up in surprise. "How'd you get here so fast?"

Yid and Mincy looked around them, trying to drink in all that they saw. The blue thing was some sort of wagon or stage, or at least it had wheels under it and seats inside. But the wheels were wide and low, the seats very padded, and the whole object was unusually shaped, not like any wagon or stage the couple had ever seen.

"What in tarnation is that?" Yid asked, pointing at it.

"That? Oh, just Mom's old car. It's a piece of junk."

Yid nodded soberly, though he doubted the girl's evaluation. Casting his eyes further, he looked at the house itself, which was not unlike the one they had just come from. This one seemed a little smaller, but it was just as amazing. In the early evening, light streamed from every window, electrical wires ran overhead to connect it to a pole out in the road, and noise seemed literally to emanate from it. Altogether it was more than either Yid or Mincy could take in, at least in one eyeful.

"So how did you get here so fast?" the girl repeated.

"With the Go-Button," Yid replied honestly as he continued to roam his eyes over the place. "Have you asked your mother about chuck? I ain't certain why, but I feel hungry

enough to eat a saddle blanket. Yes sir, give me a chance to
pad out my belly, and I'll sure enough do the job up right."

The girl once again cocked her head and stared at Yid.
Finally she turned from him to Mincy. "Is he for real?" she
asked.

"What?"

"I asked if he was for real. He talks so funny that half the
time I don't know what he's saying."

Mincy laughed. "Honey, he's talked like that ever since
I met him, and I love it. In fact, you get him going and
you'll like to die laughing, he's that funny. But translated,
what he wants to know is if your mother still intends to
feed him."

"Are you kidding? How should I know? I just barely got
off my bike. Give me a minute, will you, and I'll find out.
Uh...what'd he mean, 'Go-Button'?"

"This," Yid said, pulling his button out of his shirt-front
pocket. "She's the genuine article, too. You tell 'er where
you want to go, and bang, you're sure enough there."

The girl looked at the button, then at Yid, and then at
Mincy. Suddenly she grinned. "What do you take me for?"
she asked scornfully. "A sponge? I'm not gonna buy that
garbage."

"Buy what?" Yid asked, surprised. "I'm not hardly selling anything, leastwise not unless it's the one-way ticket I
must've bought to come here. Happen you're buying that
hot little item, I'll swap you straight across for a ticket back
again. And what the ring-tailed devil is garbage? I don't
savvy your lingo at all, young lady."

The girl looked up at Yid askance. "Gee but you're
weird," she declared. "Lady, is he wacko or something?"

"I...I don't know," Mincy answered. "What does wacko
mean?"

"Oh, sit down," the girl declared in disgust. "I told you
already, you can't sponge me. I wasn't born yesterday, you
know. Mom won't let you stay in our old house, and I
guarantee it, no matter whether you act crazy or not. So cut
the act and stop talking funny."

"By jings," Yid declared, "that's sure the pot calling the kettle black. You call my chin-music funny, but I never in all my born days heard such passing strange lingo as yours. Course a friend of mine talks strange when he tells about this old catawampus who comes rackin' into town and orates as how he's got more troubles than old lady Levine the day following the one when she passed away and went down instead of up. This old idiot proceeds to fool around about town until he's knocking about like a blind bear in a bramble patch. He tries to make it appear he's tough as tripe and lets out a yell that'd drive a wolf to suicide. So he's standing on the high gallery of the Silver Spoon Saloon orating again when the city marshal swoops down on 'im like forty hen-hawks on a settin' quail, and he pronto gets as harmless as a pet rabbit. He starts to bowing and bending to the law like a pig over a cracked nut, but he loses his balance and falls down the steps, bounding along like a barrel rolling downhill. Once he hits bottom, he begins feeling all over his carcass for broken bones, and when he don't find any, he heaves such a sigh they could feel the draft fifty miles away. Now that feller did talk funny, though not hardly worse than you."

The girl, absolutely astounded, suddenly started to giggle. "She was right," she snickered. "You're funny. Can you do that again? Talk fast and silly, I mean?"

"I don't hardly reckon I could," Yid declared soberly. "Fact is, the only man I ever heard of who could, other than my friend that I just mentioned, had a mouth big enough to plop a cantaloupe into. Folks called him Lame Johnny, on account of he never done nothing else but talk, so they figured he must be lame. But he was full of verbal lather as a shavin' mug, and was most of the time using words that run eight to the pound. Truth of the matter is, he talked so fast you could smell sulphur burning. Then one night some hombre caught him stealing a horse, and the jig was up. Lame Johnny climbed the Golden Stairs on a tight-stretched rope, and his mortal remains were shortly carted off to Boot Hill. On his board they carved this message:

"Lame Johnny"
Stranger, pass gently over this soil.
If he opens his mouth, you're gone, by hoil.

Yid grinned. "He's the only other fast and silly talker I ever heard of."

The girl giggled again. "I like you," she said then. "You may be crazy, but you're funny crazy. Let's go see the old lady."

"You're mother is old?" Yid asked, surprised.

The girl once again eyed him with one eyebrow raised high above the other. Then, with a shake of her head she turned toward the house.

Suddenly from around the corner a small dog charged headlong. It was barking ferociously, and was obviously determined to protect the girl from Yid and Mincy. Mincy stepped back in alarm, but Yid simply put his thumbs in his ears and bent to the ground so that his face was nearly on a level with the courageous dog's. Fluttering his long fingers, he emitted a perfect imitation of an enraged tomcat, complete with hissing spit, into the astounded cur's face. The animal screeched wildly, reversed itself in mid-attack, and again disappeared around the side of the house.

The girl laughed outright, took Yid's hand in hers, and from that moment both Yid and Mincy were accepted.

20

"Mom," the little girl called a moment later as she led her new friends through the back door, "I found a couple of people looking around the old house. You wanna talk to them? They're real funny."

"Why should I want to talk to them?" a woman shouted from another room. "And what do you mean, they're funny? Are they still there?"

"No, I..."

"Well, it's a good thing for them. The county sheriff patrols that place, and so does your father. Either of them catches anyone messing around, and they're in real trouble."

"That's what I told them," the little girl replied. "Mom, the man says he's hungry, and I told him that maybe we could feed him."

"You *what?*"

"Feed him. You know, like you used to when those old men came by when we lived down in Rigby."

"Oh, Carol," the woman complained as she came to the bedroom door, "You know I don't have time to... Oh! Who are you?"

"These are the people I caught," the girl called Carol replied proudly.

"Howdy, ma'am," Yid said, sounding as friendly as he possibly could.

"H...hello," the woman responded, trying to recover from her surprise. "What did you want at the house?"

"We were looking for our plow."

"Your *what*?"

"That's what I said when they told me that," Carol added. "Can you believe it? I think they're playing crazy or something, but the man is really funny, too. He talks weird, and you should have seen what he just did with Rags."

"Rags? Your dog?"

"Uhhuh. It was so cool. Rags started barking, and this guy stooped way down and snarled just like an old cat. You should have seen Rags run. He's funny, and I..."

"Carol," her mother interrupted, looking behind her and out the window as if she expected something or someone to be there, "I'm awfully busy. Tell me tomorrow, all right?"

Turning directly toward Yid and Mincy, the woman immediately dismissed them. "I'm sorry, but I'm sure you understand. Carol is just a little girl, and she doesn't..."

"Ma'am," Yid said, stepping forward and interrupting her, "my wife and I lost our plow, and it's important as Christmas is to a kid that we find it. This is where we were brought when we asked to be taken to the man who had it, so I reckon it's got to be around here somewhere. If we might just take a look-see around?"

"Who brought you?"

"I...uh..."

"Hitch hiked, did you. How come the guy thought we had it?"

"Guy?" Yid asked, trying to follow the woman's strange thinking.

"That's right, the man who gave you the ride."

Yid looked helplessly at his wife. "I...I don't..."

"Oh, never mind," the woman sighed as she turned back into the bedroom. "I'm not anywhere near ready for tonight, and I'm totally out of time. Carol, if these people want to look around outside for their plow, then that's fine with me."

"Can I feed them?"

"If they'll settle for a slice of bread and butter, then you can get it for them. I wish I had time to fix a meal, but tonight is the wrong night for that. Now please excuse me."

Carol looked up at Yid and Mincy. "You interested?"

"I'm not very hungry," Mincy stated, "but if he is..."

"I surely am," Yid declared.

"Okay, come on in the kitchen and let's do it."

Carol led Yid and Mincy down the hall and into the kitchen, and it was one of the most interesting walks the couple had ever taken. They started with surprise as the girl flipped on the brilliant lights, they stared in amazement at the appliances, and neither of them could keep their eyes off the digital clock on the microwave oven or the digital radio on the counter. The entire room was filled with fascinating things, and both were quite speechless as they gazed around.

"All we've got is white bread," Carol said as she opened the refrigerator and took out the margarine. "Do you want anything on it?"

"What...what do you mean?" Yid asked, his voice reflecting his concern and confusion.

"I mean jam, or maybe honey. I think we have some honey. I know we have strawberry and grape jam."

"Well, I..."

"You sure you don't want one?" Carol asked Mincy.

"No, thank you. I don't think so."

Carol smiled. "Sure you do. I'll fix one grape and one strawberry, and you can take your pick. Mom's got a hot date with Daddy tonight. They're split up, like I said, but Mom's really trying to put things back together. I don't know if I want that, though, because Daddy can be so mean. How did you learn to sound like a cat, Mister?"

"I reckon I just learned it," Yid answered. "I heard a cat once, and practiced a little. It wasn't altogether hard."

"Can you do other sounds?"

"I reckon so."

"Do some, will you? Please?"

Yid looked at the girl and smiled. In spite of the eye paint and the funny clothes, he found himself liking her.

"All right," he grinned. "We have an old cow back home, and when she's happy she sounds like this."

Yid then put his hands around his mouth, and Carol was treated to a near perfect rendition of a lowing cow. That was followed by the bellow a cow makes when it wants to be milked, which was followed by a horse nicker, and so it went.

"Wow," Carol declared over and over while she busied herself with fixing the sandwiches. And still Yid and Mincy continued to experience surprises. When Carol turned on the microwave oven to defrost the frozen jam, they were startled enough to step backward. And they almost fled the room when the garbage disposal was turned on a moment or so later.

"All right," Carol said as she turned to face them, "two jam sandwiches. I should have put peanut butter on them, but I didn't think of it. Take your pick, and I hope it helps."

Slowly Yid reached out and took up one of the sandwiches. At first he nibbled just a little, and then with a smile he took a larger bite. Seeing that, Mincy took the other sandwich, and soon she too was enjoying the fruits of a modern supermarket.

"What did you call these preserves?" Mincy asked.

"Which?"

"These fruit preserves. What did you call them?"

"Oh, that's just jam. So where are you from?"

"Idaho," Yid answered without thinking.

"*This* is Idaho," the girl replied sarcastically, "and I know you aren't from around here. You dress too funny, and I never in my life heard anybody talk like you."

Yid and Mincy looked at each other, and both almost started to laugh. As with her speech, how could anyone, especially anyone wearing such a ridiculous costume as the girl was wearing, accuse them of dressing funny?

"Listen, little sister," Yid declared, his soft voice going even lower and softer, "are you recommending that we had ought to dress and speak like you?"

"Well, you do look out of place, sort of, but I think your clothes are cool, real cool. Where do you buy them? I mean, maybe Mom could take me there, too. I really like your shirt, especially that flap with all the buttons. My friends would *die* if I came to school in a shirt like that."

"You'd wear a man's shirt?" Mincy asked, astonished.

"You bet I would. Nobody cares any more whether or not a shirt is a man's or woman's shirt. Now where'd you get it?"

"I sewed it," Yid replied quietly.

"You *what?*" Mincy asked, staring at her husband and ignoring the little girl. "You sewed that shirt? But I thought you said you bought it at the co-op."

"I didn't hardly want you to know. I did it when you were asleep."

Mincy was dumbfounded, and it showed. "Yid, when will you ever stop surprising me? That is a beautiful shirt."

Yid nodded agreeably.

"Well if that doesn't beat all. I meant to ask you before, but I forgot. Why haven't you ever told me that you were a tailor?"

Miserably Yid answered. "It didn't hardly seem like the sort of job a real man would have."

Now Mincy laughed outright. "I declare, sweetheart. You do have some of the strangest notions I ever heard of."

"I think it's really cool that he can sew," Carol declared. "I wish I could. Do you have another shirt like that?"

"One more, but it's home."

"Gee, that's too bad. Bet I could have talked Mom into buying it from you."

Carol grew quiet, and Yid and Mincy slowly finished their sandwiches, their eyes meanwhile never ceasing from the examination they were giving their strange surroundings.

"Carol," Mincy then asked, changing the subject, "what's this city called?"

"City?" Carol questioned. "What city?"

"Why, this one, with all the homes."

"This isn't a city. It's just a town, with 540 people in it. It's called Mackay, but we don't hardly even live in it. The town doesn't really start for another couple of miles down the road."

"Mackay?" Yid asked as he chewed. "I haven't ever heard of a town called Mackay."

"My teacher says it was built at the end of the railroad," Carol responded without much enthusiasm. "It's a real old town. It's funny you haven't ever heard of it. You must have come in from the north."

"The railroad, huh," Yid muttered, shaking his head in confusion. "Old town, my thundermugged left foot. I know for a certain fact that the railroad won't get into this valley for another year, maybe two. And I know just as doggone well that Houston is supposed to be the railhead. And by Tophet, Houston is a whale of a lot further down the valley than this burg. Providing, that is, that this burg is even here, which I happen to know it ain't! Law! Something smelly as last year's spoiled potatoes is sure enough going on."

"You sure?" Mincy asked.

Yid shrugged. "Yes, and no. Who's sure of *anything* any more? But I'll bet, honey-darlin', that we ain't in the middle of our September 2, 1899, anniversary any longer. Fact is..."

"What are you two whispering about?" Carol interrupted.

"Nothing. These are very good preserves," Mincy said as she licked her fingers.

"Yeah, I like the strawberry best, too. So what are your names?"

"Mine's Yi..."

"Carol?" the girl's mother called from the other room "Carol, will you *please* answer me?"

"What, Mom?"

"Call Aunt Viv and ask if I can borrow a pair of nylons from her."

"Aw, Mom."

"Do it. And hurry."

Pulling a face, Carol lifted the reciever of the wall phone and dialed her aunt's number while Yid and Mincy watched in confused silence. They had no idea what the object in Carol's hand was, and could not imagine what she was doing.

"Hello?" Carol spoke while Yid and Mincy gaped in amazement. "Aunt Viv, this is Carol. Hi. Yeah, just fine. Mom wants to know if you can lend her some pantyhose. Yeah, she's a klutz, all right. What? Oh, gee, aren't you coming by or something? Well, I guess I'll have to come over on the bike. Yeah. See you later."

With another face, Carol hung up the telephone. "Gee, now I gotta ride all the way over to Aunt Viv's."

"What is that thing?" Yid asked, pointing to the telephone.

"This? The telephone?"

"That's a telephone?"

Carol raised her eyebrows suspiciously. "Yeah. Don't they have them where you live?"

Yid shuddered. "N...not yet. A toll line is supposed to be in by next year or the year after. But I never saw a telephone that looked like that before."

"Yeah, they do have a lot of different styles. One of these days Mom's going to get me a Mickey Mouse one. Either that or a fancy white and gold one. Sure wish you had a car. I'd get you to take me to Aunt Viv's house."

Yid looked at Mincy and slowly held out his button. Mincy only shrugged, so Yid turned to the girl.

"You want a ride, we'll be purely delighted to give you one."

"But how?" the girl asked suspiciously.

"I'll show you. You want us to take you?"

"Sure, if I don't have to ride that dumb bike. Mom," Carol then yelled, "I'm going to Aunt Viv's to get your stupid pantyhose. Back in a jiff."

Reaching out, Yid took hold of Carol's hand. For a moment Carol looked at him, questioning. But Yid smiled at her and almost instantly she relaxed. Mincy then took the girl's other hand. Yid, still holding the button, told it to take them to Carol's Aunt Viv.

"M...my goodness!" a woman sputtered as she looked up from polishing her nails, "Carol, I didn't even hear you knock."

She stared at the three, who had so mysteriously appeared in her bedroom. She looked from one to the other, and let her gaze finally rest on Carol, whom apparently she hoped would explain a few things to her. But Carol was just as surprised as was her aunt. She'd had no idea at all that they had even moved, let alone gone all the way to her aunt's. Yet here she was right in Viv's bedroom.

"I...I..."

"Carol, it's polite to knock before you go into someone's bedroom, especially if you have guests. Hasn't your mother taught you that?"

"Gee, I'm sorry, Aunt Viv. I didn't know..."

"You should be. I just hope you never do it again. Well, aren't you going to introduce me to these people? I don't have all night to sit here gaping, you know."

"I...I... Well, this is Aunt Viv, you guys. And... I guess I don't know these people's names. Say, Mister, how did you do that?"

"Do what?" Viv asked quickly, looking from Yid to Mincy and back to Carol.

"Gee, Aunt Viv, you should have seen it. One minute we were standing in our kitchen, holding hands, sort of, and the next minute we were here. It's like a miracle!"

"Uhhuh," the woman declared as she glanced at her nails to see that they were drying properly. "That's nice, Carol, real nice. *Joey*, for the hundredth time, will you *please* turn down that TV. Listen, I'm sorry, but I didn't catch your names."

"Uh...I'm Yi..."

"*Joey*! Turn that TV down right now. I can hardly hear myself think."

"It sounds like someone's hurt in there," Mincy suddenly said as she tried to see into the darkened room beyond. "Hadn't you ought to go see?"

"Hurt? I don't..."

"By tunket," Yid agreed, turning toward the same dark-ened room. "My wife is right. Listen to that fearsome scream. And... by jings, someone is shooting."

Both Carol and Viv looked hard at them. Then Viv erupted to her feet, turned and stormed into the darkened living room.

"Joey!" she shouted while Yid and Mincy quickly fol-lowed. "I told you to turn down that TV."

"Yid," Mincy breathed, "look."

"I...I reckon I *am*, Mincy."

"Do you see...the box?"

"With the little people in it? I sure enough see it, but..."

"My goodness, Yid, it's the true 'little people', the lepre-chauns that you Irish folks are always speaking of. It *must* be them."

"By Tophet, sure and it is," Yid agreed, just as surprised by the reality as was his wife. "But I allow... Ma'am, how do you keep them penned up in such a terrible small box?"

"What?" Viv asked as she looked up from her disobedi-ent son.

"The leprechauns you have in your box, them as have come from Ireland. How do you keep them from escaping away and wrecking havoc upon your home and farm? It's gosh-awful powerful they are, and I can't help wondering how you ever threw such a dandy loop on them."

"But...but..."

"Aunt Viv," Carol suddenly interrupted as she stared up at Yid's face, "they talk sort of funny, but I *think* they mean the TV."

Viv stopped in surprise. "Is *that* what you mean?" she asked incredulously, pointing at the television.

"Right as religion," Yid stated. "You see, ma'am, we've heard a mort about those wee elfins, but we thought it mostly yarns and such. Leastwise we did until we saw your amazing box cage."

"Those aren't little people or leprechauns," Viv declared with disgust. "That's a TV, and those are only images. You know that as well as I do.

"Now what do you want of me, and why do you have my niece..."

"Oh, glory be," Yid whispered in sudden alarm, his mind already shutting off the woman's unimportant prat- tlings, "that one has a gun again. Look out, the rest of you. By jings, look out."

Viv looked at Carol, who only shrugged. Quickly then, and with absolute disgust, she turned off the television. Of course it went immediately blank, leaving Yid and Mincy in astonished silence and Joey complaining loudly.

"Uh, Carol," Viv then said as she moved quickly back into the bedroom, "here's the pantyhose for your mother. Why don't you let *me* take you home? I have to go right by there anyway."

"Gee, Aunt Viv, you said that you weren't..."

"Carol, I said that I would take you home. Now don't argue with me!"

"Oh, you don't hardly need to do that," Yid responded softly. "We brought her. We'll be more thrilled than belly- filled baby robins to get her back again."

"You *what*?" the woman asked, startled by Yid's unusual speech.

"I said that..."

"No," the woman stated suddenly, emphatically. "No thank you. I will do it. And I think that you had both better leave."

"But..."

"Mercy," Viv muttered to herself, "now is one of the few times when I wish I had a husband. I mean it, you two. Get out of here. Now."

"You don't have a husband either?" Mincy asked in as- tonishment.

"No, I don't! Now please..."

"But you have children."

"Aunt Viv got a divorce just like Mom's getting," Carol declared with smug satisfaction.

"Carol!"

"Well, it's true, and Mom says it runs in the family. All three of yours and Daddy's brothers are divorced, you are divorced, and Aunt Cee, your only other sister, is getting ready to be divorced, too. She's found a man she likes a lot better than poor old Uncle Welby. I feel sorry for him."

Viv was flustered, for she did not particularly relish the idea of the two very suspicious strangers knowing so much about her and the family she was part of.

"You're *all* divorced?" Yid asked in surprise.

"So what?" Viv responded. "Now I asked you two to leave, and..."

"But *why*?"

"Why should you leave?" Viv asked with amazement.

"No! Why are you all divorced?"

"I don't think that's any of your business."

Sadly Yid nodded his head. "I...I reckon you're right. I just...well, we've never known so many divorced people before. So I was purely wondering why all you folks did it."

Viv stared at Yid and Mincy. Then she shook her head and sat back down on the edge of her bed. "Oh, what the heck? I've told everybody else, so why not tell you? I got a divorce because I was a real jerk."

"A jerk?" Mincy asked, not understanding.

"Yeah, a jerk. You know, wild, unfaithful, *stupid*. My husband took off and left me, and I don't blame him. Looking back, I can hardly comprehend how dumb I was. Thank the Good Lord there is such a thing as repentance, because I have paid the price, and I have repented. But oh, the damage I did before I learned."

"You didn't do any damage, Aunt Viv. You shouldn't talk like that."

Tenderly the woman looked up at the girl. "Carol, I'm glad you're young, so you don't have to see things clearly. But if I don't even mention the pain my behavior caused my husband or myself, then that still leaves poor little Joey, who is being ruined because he doesn't have a father here any longer.

"In addition to that, think of what your dad is doing to you kids, acting the shameful way he does. Does that help you to feel good about yourself? No, I think your mother is right, Carol. *Something* has surely messed up your dad's and my family."

"Well," Carol said proudly, "Mom and Daddy are getting together tonight, after I get back with her pantyhose. I'll just betcha that after tonight my dad comes back home."

Gently Viv reached out and hugged Carol to her. "I hope he does, honey. I really do. It would be a real shame for him to walk away from a daughter as sweet as you.

"I'm sorry," Viv then said, looking up at Yid and Mincy. "Like I said, I feel so awful about my stupidity that I can't stop talking about it. Maybe I'm trying to keep others from being so out of it. I don't know. Anyway, I apologize for bending your ears.

"Now Carol, hadn't we better be getting that hose to your mother?"

"Oh, yeah! She'll be waiting."

"We'll be going, too," Yid declared as he took Mincy's hand. With his eyes then he signalled Mincy to take Carol's hand, and after a quick, questioning look Mincy did so.

"Good-bye, Carol," Mincy said as if she were taking leave of the girl. "It was nice..."

And at that instant Yid gave orders to his button to be back at Carol's home.

21

"Wh...wh..."

"Did you bring what your mother asked for?" Mincy asked the dumfounded girl as she stepped away from her.

"Yeah, but..."

"Then maybe you had better take it to her."

Carol stood still, stubbornly refusing to move. "But how did you *do* that? Were we really there? At Aunt Viv's, I mean?"

"We were," Yid replied, "but..."

Yid was interrupted by the clamoring ring of the telephone, which caused him to duck down with surprise. Carol looked at him, shook her head, and lifted the receiver.

"Hello? Oh, Hi, Aunt Viv. Yeah, it's me, Carol. Honest. Well, I don't... Honest, Aunt Viv, we were... Oh, all right, just a sec. Mom? Aunt Viv wants to talk to you."

For a moment she held the telephone against her ear, and then slowly she placed it back in the cradle. "Aunt Viv doesn't think I was really there," she said quietly. "I don't think I do, either."

"Then where did you get the hose there in your hand?" Mincy asked quietly.

"Yeah," Carol agreed, looking down at the pantyhose. "I got these *somewhere*."

"Isn't that what your mother asked you to get?" Yid asked.

"Sure it is. But gosh, I don't understand."

"Nor do we," Yid said as he placed his hand on the girl's shoulder. "All we know is that we are here, wherever *here* is. You see, Miss Carol, the drummer gave us this Go-Button I showed you, and it takes us where we tell it to take us. Or at least it did until we got that crazy Future-Compass. Then it just took us to the wide, rutted road instead of to my wife's plow, like we had asked. We walked here from that rutted road, and we are still looking for the lost plow."

Slowly Carol nodded as if she understood. "Who *are* you guys?"

Yid sighed deeply. "Who we are, Miss Carol, is a couple of poor, lost fools who wish with all their hearts that they were home; who are not even certain, any more, that they have a home to be at."

"You don't have a home? I thought everybody had a home."

Yid smiled and squeezed the girl's shoulder. "They had surely ought to, Miss Carol, but I don't reckon everyone does. 'The foxes have holes, and the birds of the air have nests; but the son of man hath not where to lay his head.'"

"Huh?" Carol asked, confused.

The little tailor-turned-farmer paused, his thin face lined with fatigue, his wide eyes dark with the longings and regrets that were beginning to bother him.

"That's from Matthew," he said quietly. "Eight and twenty."

"Carol," her mother called from her bedroom, "What's going on? I thought I told you to go to Viv's. And what on earth is Viv so upset about?"

"I don't know, Mom. But I went there, and now I'm back."

"You're back? But Viv just told me that she was sick, and she didn't think you had better come over."

"Sick?"

"That's what she said. Apparently she had this crazy dream about you appearing and disappearing in her bedroom. I hope she hasn't got the flu. Last time she had it she was out of her head for three days.

"But Carol, I've *got* to have those pantyhose. Now who can we call?"

"Mom, I have them right here."

Astonished, Carol's mother walked into the kitchen. "But how..."

"Mom, I told you I went to Aunt Viv's and got them."

"But Viv just told me that she..." Suddenly the woman looked at Yid and Mincy, and she smiled with understanding. "Oh, so that's how you did it. These people gave you a ride."

Carol looked up at Yid and Mincy and winked. "Yeah, Mom, I guess you could say that."

"Well," the woman declared to Yid and Mincy, "thank you for helping my daughter. That was very thoughtful of you, though I will tell you flat out that I don't like the idea of my daughter being in a car with strangers, especially ones who speed. So no more rides, please.

"Now like I said, I'm in a terrible hurry so you'll have to excuse me. Maybe we can visit some other time. Carol, will you please clean up the kitchen. I'll likely be too late to do it when I get home."

Carol groaned, but her mother paid no attention. She merely walked back into the bedroom, shouting continued instructions as she did so.

"Mom can't get over him," Carol explained quietly, ignoring her mother's distant voice. "Aunt Viv was right. Sometimes Daddy is a real jerk. But he doesn't have to be. Mom says when they first got married he was really nice. She thinks maybe it was an act all along, but she really loves him so she keeps giving him more chances. I guess I don't blame her, but I sure wish she'd stay home now and then to be with me. I wish they both would, so them and my brothers and I could play games and stuff. I guess maybe they don't like *me* anymore. At least, that's how they act. How come everybody has to go and fall in love with other people all the time? I think it stinks."

Feeling guilty, Yid looked at the floor. "I...I don't hardly know," he replied quietly. "I reckon that maybe sometimes two people just sort of drift apart like two old snow-blind cows in a blizzard. They can't even tell it's happening until it's too late.

"But Miss Carol, I don't think it was you that could have caused whatever happened between your Ma and Pa, I surely don't. Why, you're pretty as a hid-up fawn on a bright spring morning, all shy but raring to go. And law, Miss Carol, you've got a smile that would light a lamp wick, it is that bright. Except for my wife here, I never saw the sun rise any brighter in a person than it does in you. I tell you truly, you can't be shadowed by any other flower on the whole mountain, and that's a fact. So I ask, how could you ever on this green earth cause such a thing as a blanket-splitting?"

"Gee, mister," Carol said slowly, "you might talk funny, but you sure say nice things. I don't..."

"Oh, *no!*" Carol's mother suddenly shouted in anger from the bedroom. "That miserable, no-good..."

"Mom," Carol cried in alarm, "what is it?"

"Carol, you stay inside. You hear me? If George has the nerve to bring that hussy out here with him then I'm going to..."

And without finishing, Carol's mother stormed out the front door.

"Oh, no," Carol whispered as she ran into the living room. "Oh, no."

"Carol, what..."

"It's Daddy," the girl cried as she reached the window. "Oh, Daddy, why did you have to bring *her* with you?"

"What is it?" Yid asked as he hurried up to the girl. "Is something wrong?"

"Is water wet?" Carol snapped as she did her best to hold back her tears. "I'll say there's something wrong. Daddy's here in his pickup truck, but he's got that stupid Ruthie with him, and... Oh, Daddy."

Yid and Mincy stared out the window and watched as a man climbed out of what must have been called a pickup truck. He was big — big enough, Yid thought, to hunt bears with a switch. His hair was dark, almost exactly like young Carol's. And he surely did look upset.

The woman who was with him, a smallish woman with piled-up blonde hair, remained watching from the pickup.

"George," Carol's mother stormed angrily, her voice coming in through the still open door, "I told you to stay away if you were going to hang around with the likes of her. What's the matter with you, anyway? You said you were coming out to see me."

She was cut short by the man called George, who growled something unintelligible. Then he reached out and, to Yid's and Mincy's horror, smacked Carol's mother with his open hand.

"Shut up," he thundered. "I'm here to see my daughter, not you. Why should I want to see you?"

"Because when you called you said..." Suddenly the woman stood straight with anger. "You jerk!" she stormed. "You unmitigated jerk! You know I have a court order. And now that you hit me, so help me, I'm going to use it."

"Oh, get out of my way."

"I won't," the woman responded bravely as she held her stinging face with her hand. "You can't see Carol! I've told you that a hundred times, and if you hit me again I'll go straight in and call the cops. Then we'll watch you try to knock a few of them around."

"Why, you dirty, sneaking little..."

"George?"

George turned and watched as the blonde woman slid out of the pickup. She was small, but Yid, who had come to appreciate such things, decided instantly that her size was perfectly ample. And it was well and embarrassingly displayed, beyond that.

"George," she smiled as she minced up to the big man, "she isn't worth it. And neither is the little brat. I told you

already, just give the lawyers a chance with them and
you'll end up with custody and everything else. Just
because you didn't get your tires and other parts today
doesn't mean the whole world has fallen apart."

"Yeah," the man growled, "maybe not. But I lost that job
I was counting on, and I can tell you I *needed* it."

"It won't even matter, George. You've still got the land
and that's what counts. Now leave her alone, and let the
lawyers have a go at her. I guarantee that you'll win the
whole package."

George leered at her. "Does that package include you?"
he sniggered.

Carol's mother laughed. "It would serve you right if it
did!"

"Why, you..." George growled, raising his hand at his
former wife again.

"You try it," his estranged wife snarled back. "I dare
you. Touch me once more and I'll hit you with the biggest
lawsuit you ever saw. And I'll tie up all that precious
property you're so proud of, too. Then we'll see how fast
you can sell it."

"That does it," George thundered as he pushed the
blonde behind him and turned back upon his estranged
wife. "That's the last straw. Sarah, so help me, if you even
think of trying to stop my development, you'll never see
the brat again. Yeah. That's it. You won't, and that's a
natural promise."

With a screech of instinctive motherly rage, the woman
leaped against the huge chest of the man called George,
hitting and raking with her nails. Surprised, George took a
step back, and then with an oath he grabbed her by the hair
and yanked her away. Finally, methodically, he began
slapping her.

"By Tophet!" Yid shouted as he stepped through the
door, "you can't do that to a woman."

"Says who?" the big man roared as he continued his
vicious slapping. "Just try and stop me."

"Stop that," Mincy shouted then, following Yid from the
house.

George, finally seeing Yid and Mincy standing on the

walk, slowly lowered his hand. "Who're you?"

"We're the ones who are telling you to stop," Mincy declared authoritatively. "Now let go of that woman and be gone, or by heaven I will personally clean your meathouse. I'll not abide a man who strikes a woman, especially a man as big as you. Now get."

Glowering, George lowered his arm, and then with a laugh he struck his wife again. The woman sobbed with pain, and Mincy started toward him. But then, before she could take more than a step or two, Yid hurried past her and up to the surprised man.

"Excuse me, Mister," he said softly, disarmingly, and in the same instant leaped and struck George a raking, closed-fist blow across his nose and cheekbones. The blow knocked George, bleeding, back into the blonde woman, who shrieked with surprise.

It was not a hard blow, but it was unexpected on all counts, and George simply stood then, holding his hand against his face, staring.

Yid, who had stumbled after his brave but foolhardy strike and had fallen awkwardly to the ground, also stared, for he knew that the fat was in the fire. Now it was put up or shut up, and he'd already laid his thin and only ace, face up, on the man's nose.

In the scant second of interim before the man would surely tear him apart, Yid cast about for an idea. Then, knowing that whatever he did next would likely also be the last thing he ever did, he rolled in under the stunned man. Then with his legs he lashed out and, astoundingly, threw the big man to the ground.

Instantly George was back on his feet, his eyes bulging, his teeth bared, his face swollen with anger and Yid's blow. He growled out a string of curses that would have, as Yid thought, peeled the hide off a Gila Monster, and then he stepped toward the still prostrate Yid, swinging a clumsy, reaching blow at the smaller man. But somehow Yid found his feet and came up inside of George's arm's length in a desperate move, and wonder of all wonders accidentally brought his skull against George's chin with a crack that split the bigger man's mouth and sharded four of his front teeth.

Finally, before the pain-dazed George could react further, Yid ducked away. Quickly he seized Carol's astonished mother, who was nowhere near as astonished as he was, and dragged her back next to the dumb-staring Mincy.

Nor could the big woman who was Yid's wife bring her mind to grasp what she had just seen. Yid Francom, *her* Yid Francom, had just stood up to, and soundly pounded, the hulking bully George. Why, it couldn't have been him! Not Yid. Not in a million or so years could she imagine him doing such a thing.

She could quite easily imagine a twenty- fourth of July howling blizzard on the Sonoran desert, and it wasn't inconceivable to conjure up the image of a beached blue whale on the banks of Big Lost River. She could even picture the followers of Chief Big Foot coming back to life at Wounded Knee and getting elected to Congress by complete and unanimous popular vote. But Yid actually fighting a huge, inhuman brute like George whoever-he-was? No sir, she couldn't hardly bring herself to imagine it. The stretch was just too much for her poor mind to make.

Trouble was, her peace-loving, gentle Yid had done it, and she had seen it. Now she had, somehow, to come to grips with what she had seen.

"It appears you're not welcome here," Yid stated at last, his voice low and quivering, his chest still heaving. "Was I you, I'd do what my wife said and get."

"Why you..."

"George," the blonde woman pleaded, restraining him with her hand, "they're trained fighters, both of them. Can't you see that? And that big mamma on the walk hasn't even started yet. I have a feeling that you don't want to face her at all. Now let's go. There's always another day."

"I'll be back," George growled through his bloody mouth and hand. "Nobody does that to me. Nobody. And I'm coming after the brat, too. You hear me, Sarah?"

Turning then, he shoved his blonde escort ahead of him toward the truck. Not bothering to help her climb in, he stormed around, entered the other side, slammed the door, and with a roar of the engine he sprayed gravel and was away.

"Th...thanks," the woman called Sarah gasped.

"You're welcome," Yid answered, still wondering at what had happened. "There aren't many who dare stand up to my wife when she gets riled. That fellow's doggone lucky he left when he did. If she had gone after him..."

"Yid," Mincy whispered as she excitedly grabbed Yid's arm, "the *plow*! Did you see it? In the back of that wagon thing? He...George, I mean, has my plow."

Yid stared after the departing pickup. "He does? Are you sure?"

"I saw it, I tell you. Now come on."

Feeling like he was in a dream, Yid touched the Go-Button in his pocket and gave the order.

And they were taken, certain sure enough, but not to George and his pickup load of a brand new 1899 McCormick Farm Implement plow. No sir. Not by a humming long, smooth-bore rifle shot. Instead he and Mincy were standing once again on the rutted road, the one with the rainbow light glowing eerily around it.

And suddenly, both of them were trembling like aspen leaves in a high south wind.

PART SIX

JOURNEY TWO

22

The moon hung quartered in the early dark sky, luminous and misty and bathing the vast land in soft and muted light. Even the rutted road seemed less rough, less formidable. Yet that did little to comfort the two travelers, the large but compellingly sweet woman and her husband, the prone-to-enjoy-fantasizing tailor-turned-farmer known as Yid Francom.

"Yid," Mincy whispered in fear as she clutched Yid's hand, "how did we get onto this road again?"

"I don't know," he replied, looking around. "Law, Mincy, I'm so weak I'd need to lean against a post just to spit. By jings but I feel awful."

"You're sick?"

"All of a sudden I am."

"Well, let's sit for a few minutes and see if you feel better."

They did on a nearby bank of earth, and the silence between them was not an uncomfortable thing. Yid was thankful for that, for he truly didn't feel like talking at all.

But by jings, what had he just seen? Was that what had laid him so low? Had the realization of what Carol's father was like, or of what her aunt Viv had been like before she had repented, affected him so much that he was ill? As Yid thought about it, he couldn't help but conclude that it was so. And the reason, stated with plainness and simplicity, was that both Viv and George had reminded him of himself.

But was that what *he* was like? Was it? Did his fantasizing dreams, which he found so harmless and enjoyable, appear that sickening and disgusting to others? Was that what so upset Mincy? Was it possible that she saw him like he had seen George?

Now that Yid thought of it, he was dumbfounded that it might very well be so. And that single realization, the understanding that his lustful dreams could turn him into a sorry specimen such as George, or even later into an agonizing soul such as Viv, jolted him more than any other thought he had ever had. It literally made his stomach turn, it was that bad.

Slowly Yid shook his head. Might that also have been why Christ had enjoined so strenuously against looking upon others with lustful thoughts? Yid had never seen any sense in that portion of the Sermon on the Mount. He had been unable to see what harm a man's errant dreams could possibly do. But now, seeing what a few years of that sort of thinking had made of George or his poor sister, Yid was suddenly frightened.

No, he was worse than frightened. Yid Francom was shaken clear to his toenails.

"M...Mincy?" he finally asked, trying to shut his mind of the uncomfortable ideas which seemed to have developed there.

"Yes, sweetheart?"

"I sure enough gave the Go-Button proper orders."

"What?"

"We weren't supposed to come here, I mean. I gave the button orders to go after that plow."

"But we came *here*," Mincy declared, almost pleading.

Yid nodded. "We certain as sow bugs camp under buffalo chips did. But for the life of me, Mincy, I can't explain why. It's enough to give a body the fluttering fantods."

"I'm frightened, too," she breathed.

"Amen and amen," Yid agreed.

Again he cast his gaze upon the moonlit landscape. "It's the same place where we were before, though, except that now it's dark. I'm certain of it. Same rutted and well-traveled road, same mahogany trees coming down almost to it, same brown dead-looking grass, same low ridge up there ahead of us. Sure as Admiral Dewey took Manila we are in the same place as we were...well, whenever it was that we were here earlier."

"Well," Mincy exclaimed, shivering a little, "to tell the truth, I am glad to be away from that other place."

"Me, too. I'd hate like blazes to run into that George feller again."

Mincy looked at her diminutive husband. "Yes," she said quietly, "I'd imagine."

For a moment neither spoke, and then Mincy once again broke the silence. "How'd you do that, Yid?"

"Do what?"

"You know. How did you know how to... I mean, well, I never saw you whup anything before. Not ever. And I was proud of you as could be. But how did you..."

Mincy was having obvious problems bringing her question to a boil, and Yid wasn't certain that he wanted to help her out. After all, he had mightily enjoyed realizing that he had properly beaten that man. It had given him more than a passing good feeling. Trouble was, it had also been accidental. The odds against him ever doing such a thing again, or even trying for that matter, were about equal to the odds against an army mule being agreeable. Doggone it, much as he wanted to do it, he couldn't be taking credit for that fight.

"Mostly," he admitted, looking away,"It was accidental."

"The fighting, maybe," Mincy agreed. "Least that's how I figured it after it happened. What I want to know, is how you went after that George feller in the first place?"

"I don't rightly know," Yid admitted. "He made me

angry, of course, but it sort of happened before I realized what I was about. It was like picking up those little black boxes all over again. I just couldn't help myself.

"Once into it , though, I was running plumb yellow. Fact is, my craw was so shrunck up it wouldn't have chambered a single piece of pea gravel."

Mincy smiled. "You have an interesting way of running scared, swetheart. Most folks fly the other way; but you went right at him. I didn't have the least notion that you were frightened. But truthfully, I am most proud that you had the courage to do the right thing, hard as it was."

Yid looked at his wife, and suddenly it was in him to tell her what he had just thought of, to maybe enlist her help if she was still willing to give it.

"I was scared, all right," Yid stated quietly, sincerely, "but not so scared as I am right now."

"What?"

"That man George, Mincy. I looked at him, and I swear, I felt as though I was looking in a mirror. It like to made me sick, it was so awful. Why, Sarah getting beaten was the meanest thing I ever saw. And that poor little Miss Carol like to broke my heart, she seemed so miserable. But the worst of all was the look in that man's face. Like he was dead to anything that was important or real. The way he leered at Ruthie, the things he said... By jings, Mincy, he had a soul that was black as a lobo's side-hill cave, and it came to me, just as I hit him, that he got it from doing exactly what I have been doing."

Yid paused, breathing deeply, seeking courage. "And that's why I'm scared. I don't want to end up like he has."

From Mincy came a slight, almost imperceptible intake of breath, and Yid looked at her in the darkness, wondering.

"Honey-darlin'," he said softly, reachingly, "I wish things would be back like they were. I've just got to get control so they can be. More than anything in all the world, I don't want to end up like that feller back there."

Out of the darkness then came what sounded a little like a choked sob, and Yid's heart felt as though it would break.

The pain *had* been there, the pain and the disgust and the sickening feelings. He had caused them in his wife just as surely as George had caused them in him.

"I *mean* it, Mincy," he continued, softly, desperately. "I know I've hurt you considerably, but I'll do better. I promise you that."

"Sweetheart," Mincy said brokenly, "I waited a long time to hear you say this. But are you sure?"

"I am," Yid affirmed. "If that woman Viv can change, then so can I."

"Oh, Yid," Mincy cried as she threw her arms around her husband's neck. "I'm so happy for you, for us. I know that so many things will be better for us now. All it took was you really wanting to, and now that you do..."

Mincy placed her head on her husband's shoulder, felt his arms go around her, and she knew that she was finally happy.

Neither of them spoke, and around them the mountain night returned the complement of velvet stillness. Mincy had never listened to such a big quiet. Not in her entire life had she been so close to actually feeling the presence of her Maker. There was something in the black wine of the air, the buttressed peaks ragged against the encircling skyline, the lantern-bright wink and glitter of the stars and gleaming of the moon, the scent of sage and fall-dry grass that lined the road, the strength of man-arm held round her that put a woman more in mind of her God than all the words, sermons and warnings she had ever heard preached.

Funny. Yid was always talking about the big quiet, him with his wonderful, colloquial grammar. "It's wondrous quiet," he'd say, pointing off to Dickey Peak. "Man can hear himself think up behind there. Fact is, once the morning was so quiet, I heard the sun come up. That was the morning I knew God had made that mountain. Tell the truth, Mincy, that was the morning I knew God had made *me*."

Mincy thought of Yid again, and her heart felt like it would burst. He had changed, just like she had prayed that he could, and would. Somehow all of this craziness had happened in response to her fervent but almost hopeless prayers, strange events which even yet she didn't understand. But they had caused her husband to see his actions for what they were, and so that had surely been answers to her prayers.

She rejoiced in that, she rejoiced in her husband, and it wasn't long before the experience of that briefly held breath of a September night, seven thousand feet up in central Idaho, became a revelation to the big-boned, faithful woman. Not a regular revelation, actually, but one that got the job done, nevertheless.

Nothing in her previous experience, nothing in the fringe-living ways of her parents and ancestors, had prepared her for her overwhelming contact that night with the love and personal compassion of her Creator. Twenty-five years a farm girl, even being baptized had sort of converted but not hardly convinced her. This was her virginal realization that the Lord had actually created the earth and all that dwelt thereon, and that He held all things in the palm of His hand. It was an exhilarating, yet terribly sobering, discovery.

Again her thoughts turned to Yid, and impulsively she turned to him and kissed him on the cheek. Then she snuggled more closely against him and contemplated further the good news. Yid was hers again. The Lord had heard her cries, and her husband had been shown himself as he would become, had been jolted thoroughly by the terribly realistic vision.

Around them the night came gently to life. At first it was the enquiring friendliness of a small tufted owl, calling *tah-hoo? tah-hoo?* from its perch in a mahogany up the hill. Then it was the chittering flutter-about of several curious, sharp-eared mountain bats that had not yet gone into hibernation. Next it was the bright peering of two field mice from a hummock of grass, undecided as to what the people might be, but determined to welcome their arrival into their quiet lives, regardless. And lastly it was the big-eyed, ear-forward stare of a small kit fox who appeared from nowhere to stand listening and watching from the far side of the rutted highway.

"H...hello," Mincy whispered timidly.

At the sound of her voice, the mice vanished back into the grass, the bats skittered away, and the owl left the skeletal tree and floated silently off into the night. But the fox remained motionless in the moonlight, its huge eyes wide upon her, and Mincy wondered at that.

"He's something, ain't he," Yid said quietly.

Mincy nodded. "Puts me in mind of you," she replied.

Yid laughed outright, and the fox, startled, turned and vanished into the darkness.

"Why me?"

"I don't know," Mincy answered. "Maybe it's his eyes, big and curious and warm and loving."

"Probably his ears," Yid argued, grinning. "Mine always did sort of poke out."

Mincy giggled. "No, it was his eyes, sweetheart. They surely do put me in mind of yours."

Yid hugged her tightly against him, and he couldn't recollect ever feeling so happy. Mincy was warm against him, so warm that his whole soul was filled with the joy of it, and it was heady, wonderful. In fact, her warmth made him think of the night he had been in Amber's cabin, when the incredibly fetching widow-woman had placed her hand upon his arm.

"By Tophet," he growled fiercely as he released his wife and rose abruptly to his feet, "by everlastingly Tophet!"

"Yid, what is it?"

"It...It... Oh, nuts! It's hopeless, that's what it is. I've got no control, and it's foolishness to try to make either one of us believe otherwise. Now stand up, and I'll take you home."

Mincy, dazed by her husband's startling actions, rose to her feet to stand beside him. "I...I don't understand, Yid? What..."

"It's nothing, by tunket. Now hang on while I use this blamed button. Button, take Mincy and me to our cabin."

Then they waited

23

"What happened?"

Yid shook his head. "I don't reckon anything did. Blasted button. Here. Let me give it another try."

He did, but still nothing changed. They remained exactly where they had been all along.

"Well," Yid growled, frustrated beyond belief, "if the doggone button won't do it, then by jings we'll walk."

"Yid," Mincy cried as she struggled to keep up, "what happened?"

"You don't know?"

Mincy stared at him. "Know? How would I? Oh, Yid, not her again."

"That's right. With all I saw, I still haven't changed. It's enough to gag a maggot, the way I'm so weak. But I'm not going to let it hurt you any longer, Mincy. I just won't do that to you. That's why I'm clearing out. It's the best I can do for you, so you won't have to be sick to death every time you look at me."

"But sweetheart..."

"I mean it, Mincy. I'm just no good. Clear to the core I'm filled with lust, and I can't ask you to carry such a burden any longer. No, I'll be leaving, and you can at least be at peace until you can find somebody else, somebody who will be more worthy of you."

"Peace?" Mincy cried as sudden tears coursed down her cheeks. "Peace? How can I be at peace when the man I love, more than I love life itself, is leaving me? Yid, don't do this. Please. Think of all we've been through."

"By jings, Mincy, what we've been through ain't real. Not flying machines, not Mister Bell's fancy telephones, not those sorts of fast horseless carriages, not those blinding-bright electric lights, none of it. I know it ain't. Why, even in the Montgomery-Ward cataloge I haven't seen fooforah like we saw tonight. And those houses, law! Did *you* ever even imagine anything like that?"

"I... I... No, but..."

"Well, there she is, roped and tied and ready for the iron. I know in some things I haven't been far enough around the teacup to find the handle, but for a certain fact, I know this. You and I have just been to, and come back from, some-place that isn't."

Yid's words hung solemn and ominous in the chill night air. Somewhere far off a nightbird cried out, and Mincy, her tears still flowing, shivered, not altogether from the cold.

"You're saying?" she whimpered plaintively.

"I'm saying," Yid answered slowly, "that that Future-Compass thing did more than show us a couple of roads, and that by somewhat. Mincy, it took us there, too. Like I said, we've been someplace that isn't, at least not yet. And we went there for a reason. Law, Mincy, even allowing that I ain't altogether stricken with the brights, I ain't so dumb that I can't take a hint when it's thrown in my face."

Mincy stared at Yid, trying to understand what all this had to do with him deciding to leave her.

"Worse than that," Yid went on, his voice low and scrap-ing like a burro with a bad cold, "we're back on that same future sort of road. Mincy, you and I are standing in a road that doesn't even exist."

"But...but what hint..."

"I mean, Mincy, that we were taken to the future, or at least we were shown it. Whichever, I saw just exactly what I'm going to be like, given a little more time. I know I am, I can't change because I've tried and it doesn't work, and I won't put you through the misery and sorrow that's going to happen to me because of it. That wouldn't hardly be fair, not to either of us. That's why I'm quitting, clearing out."

"Yid, please don't."

"I've got to, Mincy. Maybe I'm being more nervy than a busted tooth, but it's how I've got it figured. Ever since I started contemplating for more than a passing minute the assets and uncommon attributes of Amber Wiggins, things have gone straight downhill. The old drummer stopped smiling and being friendly and started sending me those warning messages, the plow kept breaking, I lost my place in line, we got that infernal thread and button and compass, we've been to somewhere that ain't, I met that George feller and got a good look at the hell he created for everyone around him, and... well, you get the picture. You and I are somewhere that we hadn't ought to be, it's my fault that we're here, and I reckon I've learned what I'm supposed to learn from it."

"I...I don't think I can stand this," Mincy cried. "You're deciding the wrong thing, Yid. You also saw Viv, saw that she could change — had changed. How do you know it isn't her that you're supposed to learn from?"

"Like I already told you, because I've tried to change, and I *can't*."

"Oh, sweetheart, this isn't right."

"Neither's what I've been doing."

"I know that," Mincy declared. "But that's no sign to give up. Anybody can change. *Anybody*. That's what repentance is all about, Yid. Changing. The Lord said through Isaiah: 'Though your sins be as scarlet, they will be white as snow.' Sweetheart, Christ was wounded for these very transgressions and iniquities that you are suffering with. All you need to do is turn to Him for help, and then put them behind you."

"I can't do it," Yid stated flatly. "How can I turn to the

Lord when I'm so blasted full of filth and guilt? I can't even pray anymore. Law, Mincy, if *you* get sick at the sight of me, then think what God must feel like.

"No, if any changing *ever* takes place, I've got to do it myself. Only, I've tried, and it can't be done. That's why I'm taking my miserable self out of your life. There's no point in both of us suffering."

At that Mincy straightened her shoulders. "Yid Francom, don't you go knuckling under on me. Things may be bleak, but they aren't entirely dark. We're still together, and providing we stay that way, and lean on the Lord, we'll work our way out of whatever this is all about."

Yid didn't respond, wouldn't respond even to Mincy's continued pleadings. Instead he started walking along the rutted road, leaving Mincy with no choice but to follow him. Without speaking further she did, and within minutes the two had crossed over a little ridge .

With an explanation of surprise, Mincy took Yid's arm.

"Look," she said excitedly, "we're home."

Yid stopped and looked across the moonlight-washed valley. "By jings, I do think you're right. I wonder how we got here so quick?"

"I'm sure I don't know," Mincy said, smiling. "But I do know I am eternally thankful to be home."

"And home it is," Yid declared with a grin of his own. "If my memory hasn't altogether departed, that wash ahead is Arentson Gulch. And there beyond it is Willow Creek Summit. Our cabin will be off down there beyond the hill. Yes ma'am, we're truly home. Or at least, you are."

Defiantly Mincy stared Yid down. "No, Yid," she stated emphatically, "*we* are. You and I are going to conquer this thing together. After that, everything will be fine."

Without waiting for her husband to reply, Mincy left the rutted road and made her way down the hill toward the wash. Yid followed slowly, and moments later they crossed it and started up the slope toward their cabin.

Only, where the cabin should have been, to Mincy's

complete bewilderment, was a moon-bright spot that showed no evidence of a cabin ever having been there.

"Yid, where is it?" Mincy whispered frantically. "Where is our home? Or the barn, or the corrals, or the out-buildings? *Yid, what is happening?*"

Sighing with discouragement, Yid sat down on a low rock. "I don't know, Mincy, except that I allow that we're still someplace that isn't. By *jings* but I'm tired of this."

Mincy gagged with sudden nausea as she looked back at the cabin-less site. "I think I must be going crazy," she gasped. "Everything is here! The hills, the valley, the wash, the summit. But where is our home? Where?"

"Mincy, honey-darlin'," Yid said, quickly rising and going to her, "are you all right?"

Bleakly Mincy shook her head, brushing away her tears as she did so. "Y...Yid, I'm s...sick and scared, and I d...don't know what to do n...next. And with you leaving...I can't... Oh, sweetheart, I th...think I've gone insane."

Mincy was sick again, and Yid, kneeling beside her feeling awful about what was happening but helping as well as he could, suddenly knew what he had to do. "Like we con-cluded before," he growled in his funny-buzzing voice, "could be we're both crazy."

Then, standing up, he took Mincy's arm in a grip that felt to the woman like the closing jaws on a number 6 lynx trap. "Now," he muttered, "you haven't noticed, but there is a building of sorts, a round building, off thataway. Shall we see what it is doing out there in the pasture? Or find out who in blue blazes put the road through there? As we have both freely admitted, honey-darlin', neither of us knows much about what's going on. But as sure as glass breaks, this isn't over. And until it is, I'm going to hang onto it like an old-time Indian to a whiskey jug. By jings, I'm not leaving you or this farm until the both of us understand what is going on."

"You mean..."

Yid grinned ruefully. "I mean, I wouldn't leave you in a

mess like this, honey-darlin'. Not ever. I love you too much to do that. So for now, at least, I'm staying!"

Mincy, thrilled beyond words, threw her arms around her husband and squeezed. Yid blanched as his ribs and spine popped and cracked, but then he smiled. Law, but Mincy was a woman! A woman, and then some.

Finally released, Yid took Mincy's hand and stepped out, and soon the two people moved across what had been the back edge of their property.

And stopped abruptly, staring around them.

"It's *daylight*," Mincy gasped.

"It sure as sulphur smells bad is," Yid agreed, just as surprised.

"But...but..."

"Here, Mincy, step backward."

Together they did, and within two steps were standing once again in moon-bright darkness, with no sign of daylight anywhere about.

"Now that's mighty interesting," Yid muttered.

"Incredible," Mincy whispered. "Yid, this can't be real."

"Of course it isn't," Yid agreed quietly. "Not any more than anything else we've seen."

"But I...I..."

In the darkness Yid smiled reassuringly. "Mincy, don't you fret yourself about this. I've got a feeling that it'll be all right. I also think we're getting perilously close to the base of this keg. And you should know that I aim to keep digging until I get past the staves and hit bung-end bottom."

Taking two steps forward again, Yid once more found himself bathed in noonday brightness. Shaking his head and grinning, he reached back and pulled Mincy forward with him.

"Amazing," Mincy whispered, looking around.

"It is, and stupendous to boot. And more so because it can't be seen until we're in it. Have you noticed that there ain't...isn't a sun up there?"

"But how can that be? It's surely warm enough."

"Yeah, like maybe noonday July or August warm. But in all that brightness there's no sun that I can see."

"Yid, look at this."

Yid, by then a step behind his wife, stopped as suddenly as she did, looking down. "Mincy," he said enthusiastically, "it's all been plowed under. The sagebrush is gone and the whole farm is under cultivation."

"I know. Look at all this grain, and... My gracious, Yid, how can grain be growing at this season?"

"I...I don't hardly know, Mincy."

"And look at this...this material that the grain is growing out of. Yid, I can't even see the soil. One of the men I worked for always said that the soil was the thing, and that when a man lost sight of the soil, then he was doomed to destruction. How can we see the soil if it is covered with this stuff?"

Yid shook his head, and then with firm step he led off down the slope.

Everywhere the ground was covered with the strange fabric. Yet they quickly discovered that it was not all exactly the same. Some of it was red, some was yellow, some was green, some was buff, and some was a pale violet in color. The rest, in very small patches, were a variety of other shades and colors.

In one spot, as Yid knelt to examine it, he found that it was laid out in long strips, each less than a foot wide, but hundreds of yards long. The plants were growing from those fabric strips in exactly uniform locations, giving the whole the look of a perfectly groomed garden.

The other surprise was that in some strips the plants had reached the age to be harvested, while in others they were only just emerging from the strips. There seemed to be no pattern to that, though Yid was certain that there would be one if he could only find it.

"Yid, what are those?"

Looking up, Yid saw that Mincy was pointing toward tiny objects that floated above them in the air. Not more than an inch or so across, they had small wires protruding from them, making them look, as he remarked to Mincy, somewhat like flying baby porcupines.

"I didn't notice them before," Mincy said thoughtfully,

"but there sure are a lot of them."

"Yeah, maybe more'n we can see. You reckon they're watching us?"

"Those boxes? I can't imagine how. Do you see any people yet?"

"No, but you can bet there'll be somebody around. I... By jings, Mincy, look over here."

"What? I don't see..."

"Mincy, it's raining."

"Raining?"

"Sure as there ain't no sun it is. Look at this. Right here, above the *corn*? By Tophet, this is a regular truck garden! Law, there are even mellons. Who ever imagined that such things could be grown at this altitude, and in September, to boot?"

"This can't be real."

"You're right as rhubarb pie," Yid affirmed. "Trouble is, we're both in the middle of it, and for the life of me I don't know what that can possibly mean. And cast your eyes at this little rain shower. Impossible, wouldn't you say? I would, for a Big Lost country fact. But I still see it plain. I don't see any clouds, but look at it rain. You can see the water falling in small drops all along these rows. It isn't happening anywhere else, but right there it's wet enough to bog a snipe."

Mincy stared. "I see it," she whispered, "but I certainly don't understand it."

"Nor me either. But seeing is believing, so they say. Can you hardly figure what they have done with our farm?"

"I can't. My goodness, look at how tall that corn is down at the far end. I've never seen it grown that high."

Yid stared in amazement. "Mincy, those stalks must be fifteen feet tall. The few stalks of corn we got last year hardly grew four feet."

"They did better than us, for a fact. And Yid, that corn's hardly started to tassel yet. And just look at how many ears are growing on those stalks."

"What kind of corn *is* this?" Yid breathed as he gently

touched the plants. "By jings, Mincy, there must be twenty, thirty ears per stalk."

"Or more. Yid, those ears are growing like triplets — three ears from the same place. I've never seen corn or anything else grow like this."

Picking their way across their farm, or rather what had been made of it, observing and examining as they went, Yid and Mincy at last approached the strange building. It was not large, hardly more than thirty or thirty-five feet across, and it looked like two deep-hewn bowls stacked bottom up to bottom down of each other. The structure was windowless and doorless, and appeared to be metal except that it did not ring out like metal when Yid tapped it. More than anything else, in fact, it reminded him of the strange metal that the drummer's wagon had been made of.

Oh, and one other thing? The structure was floating a few feet above the ground, and was anchored by a single small cable that hung loosely below it.

"What do you think it is?" Mincy whispered as she followed Yid around the structure, gazing upward.

"I ain't got the foggiest notion. If I could see inside, then maybe..."

"Hey, you two? What are you doing here?"

Spinning, Yid and Mincy stared in surprise as a woman strode toward them. "Don't you know that this is a no-trespassing area?" she asked harshly.

"A *what*?" Yid asked.

"A food-producing area. It's sterile, of course, and you could contaminate it by just breathing. Besides, you don't even have your shields operational. That's crazy. There are Raiders everywhere, and Neighbors, too. Any one of them would hazer you in an instant. Now who let you in here?"

"Nobody, ma'am," Yid drawled easily. "We came by shanks pony."

"What?"

"He means," Mincy clarified, "that we walked."

The woman frowned. "You walked? But you couldn't

have! The automatic hazers destroy any living thing that
walks or flys through the barrier. Nobody..."

"Carol?"

Now the woman spun about to face the trees from which
she had just emerged, and for the first time both Yid and
Mincy noticed that there were trees, tall, leafy trees, growing on their farm.

Under the trees a man stood watching them, a man who
had not been present only seconds before.

"Hello, darling," he said, stepping forward. "You having trouble here?"

"No trouble. Just a little surprise."

"For me, too. I thought you said we would be alone, that
no one ever came here."

"No one does. But these two clonks somehow got
through the barrier."

"Are they Raiders, or Neighbors?"

"Neither, I think. Their shields aren't even operational."

"You're joking. Don't they know the danger?"

"I warned them."

"Well, who cares about clonks, anyway? I'm worried
about my own skin, and yours. Now get rid of them. I
don't have much time, you know. Adelia is growing suspicious, and she just might try to follow me."

"Malcom," the woman pleaded, "I'm trying." She then
turned to face Yid and Mincy again. "Listen, both of you.
Just take your Go-Buttons and get yourselves back to
wherever it was that you came from. It's dangerous here,
and I won't accept responsibility for you. So please, use
your buttons and be gone."

Yid stared at the woman. "You know about our Go-
Button? By jings, we've been closer with that information
than the satin over a cancan dancer's seat. How's come
you know?"

But the woman did not answer. Instead she was looking
at them rather strangely, obviously thinking.

"Have we met before?" she finally asked.

"Carol," the man shouted angrily from behind her. "I
mean it. You get rid of those two, or I'm gone."

"Malcom," she pleaded, turning to look at him. "I can't just pick them up and throw them out through the barrier. Besides, I think I know these people."

"That does it," the man stormed. "I risk my marriage *and* my job to meet with you, and what do I get? A quakahoo."

"A quakahoo?" Carol stormed. "Listen, you thread-brained wupp, do you think *my* marriage is getting any better because of you? You told me that you could help me."

"Which marriage is that?" the man asked sarcastically. "The sixth or the seventh?"

"Why, you..."

"You need help, that's for sure," the man called Malcom declared. "You and your entire family. Between the bunch of you, you've had more marriages than I can count. You're all crazy."

"Malcom, you can't talk like that. You can't. It isn't true, not like what you are saying. I just thought that maybe you and me could, well, maybe if things worked out, I wouldn't mind being married to you."

At this the man laughed. "*Married*? Carol, I already *am* married, and quite happily, too. Did you forget that?"

"But you came here."

"Sure I did," the man grinned as he took hold of the single button that was secured to his shimmering shirt. "After the come-on you gave, who wouldn't have? I thought you wanted to have a little fun, just like you did with Shelby and Norman last week. But never mind. I can find prettier fun somewhere else, and she won't be crazy, either."

With that the man disappeared, and the woman stood silently, staring after him. Then with a fury she turned upon Yid and Mincy.

"You!" she raged. "Who do you think you are, fouling up the best chance I've had in ten lousy years?"

"But...but..."

"Go on. Get out of here. I'm sick of the sight of you."

"But, ma'am..."

"Yid," Mincy whispered, interrupting him.

"What in tarnation do you want?" Yid snapped, upset by how the woman was treating them.

"Yid, have you looked at her?"

Yid glanced at his wife, but did not notice the unusual expression on her face. "Looked at her? Of course, I've looked at her. I'm looking at her right now. I..."

"Lady," the woman called Carol stormed, "I don't know what you're trying to program, but you can cancel it right now. I want you off this property."

"Carol," Mincy asked quickly, taking a step forward, "you thought we looked familiar. Maybe we did meet, once."

"I don't care, not even a little. Now take your buttons..."

"Were you ever taken on a magic ride, Carol? When you were a little girl? For instance, might you have been taken by two people to your Aunt Viv's home to get some pantyhose for your mother so she could step out with your father?"

Now the woman stared at the two people.

"You were maybe ten years old," Mincy continued earnestly, "or eleven. That day your father, a man named George, stopped at your home. He was with a blonde woman named Ruthie, and he slapped your mother around something awful. But two people, a man and a woman, stopped him. Or at least the man stopped him. Do you remember, Carol?"

"I do, I think."

"Wait a minute," a confused Yid said to his wife. "Are you cogitating up a proposal that not more than a few hours ago we were with this here woman when she was a little girl?"

"It's *your* theory," Mincy replied quietly.

"Well," Yid breathed, "just thinkin' on the ramifications of that thought makes me feel like I've been struck with a stroke. The whole idea is plumb astounding and incredulous."

Yid then peered more closely at the woman, still shaking his head in wonderment. "And you really think, honey-darlin', that this is the same Carol that caught us looking through the broken window of her father's home, and who took us home for sandwiches, and whose dog Rags and me had us a regular spitting and growling match?"

"That's it!" Carol shouted excitedly, interrupting him. "You're the couple. And... Oh, good grief! You had a Go-Button then, didn't you? That's how you got me to Aunt Viv's that night for... was it *really* pantyhose that Mom sent me for? It's been so many years that I can't remember."

"We can," Yid declared soberly. "In fact, the whole episode is so bright and fresh a memory that it seems like it was only this afternoon. But you're right as rain in the monsoon season on both counts, Miss Carol, and had ought to get the brass ring for your efforts. We had us a Go-Button, and we took you to your aunt's house for that pantyhose stuff, and by jings, we were glad to do it."

Carol grinned. "Yes, you're the man, all right. I've never heard another soul talk as funny as you did, and I doubt that I ever will again. But how did you get it? The button, I mean. I know they've only been readily available for the past three years. Did you have a prototype or something? Were they working on them way back then? I mean, that has to have been back in, well, I think 1988, wasn't it?"

"We're not certain," Mincy answered, watching Yid as she did so. "The button was given to us. We don't know where the drummer got it."

"Well," Carol smiled, "never mind. It can't possibly matter. How did you get here tonight? And why don't you look any older? I can't see that you've aged at all."

"We hide our ages tolerably well," Yid said easily. "Besides which, we are mighty happy to see you again, ma'am."

"Thank you," Carol replied with another smile.

Yid looked keenly at the woman, who was obviously in her early to mid thirties. Yet it was definitely her; the Carol they had known as a child. As Yid muttered to Mincy, there was no mistaking the trail of those pony tracks, at all.

"What about that Malcom feller?" Yid then asked sympathetically. "It appears that we sort of cut him out of the herd and hazed him off."

"It wasn't the most convenient time for you to show up," the woman agreed. "But it was probably for the best. Uh... why don't we go to my home? You can meet my two daughters, and I can patch out a bite to eat. Just take your button..."

"Can't do 'er, ma'am," Yid said sadly. "Our button appears to have thrown a shoe."

"What?"

"It's broken," Mincy translated quickly.

"Well, they aren't too difficult to repair. Let me take it, and I'll see what I can do. Then I'll take you home, and we can visit all we want. Obviously I have a free evening, and my husband certainly won't be interrupting us."

24

Quickly Carol took the button and popped it open. "My goodness," she exclaimed as she studied it, "this must be the very earliest model. See how the circuitry in the core is burned?"

"Burned?"

"Yes, only one primary function. But wait a minute. This one even has a time slice, where you can go back and forth in time. Did you know that? I don't think I've ever seen one of these, they are so rare. The manufacturers got rid of them in a hurry, within months after they came out. People were trying to change their histories, and *everything* was getting messed up. Does anyone know that you have this?"

"Well, you do."

Carol grinned. "Then you should be safe. If anyone else finds out, they'll no doubt confiscate it. Come on. Let's go inside the monilab, and I'll see if my brother has any spare cores."

Carol held out her hand against the side of the structure, and instantly the wall folded in upon itself, just as the wall of the drummer's wagon had folded in upon itself so long, it seemed, before.

"There," she declared as she stepped up an ascending ramp and through the opening, "now let's see if I can find anything in this mess."

Yid and Mincy followed her and found themselves in a room that seemed open and spacious, pleasantly cooled, and illuminated by many large, square, lantern-like objects that surrounded them. They were staring at these when Carol stepped back to Yid and handed him his Go-Button.

"I'm sorry," she said sincerely, "but my brother has no parts that fit this particular button. However, I'd say that your problem was in the de-molecularizing circuitry; some sort of line-grem, I think they call it. Those old units went out quite often. I remember my first one nearly drove me crazy. I..."

"Oh, no! Ralph, what..."

Yid and Mincy looked at Carol's horrified expression, and then at the large, round wheels at which she was staring.

"What are they?" Mincy asked, touching them carefully.

"Truck tires," the woman answered hoarsely, the fear in her voice palpable. "*New* truck tires. But...but..."

"What in thunderation is it?" Yid asked. "You look mighty peaked, ma'am."

"If you knew the trouble my brother was in," she whispered, "you'd look 'peaked' too. Oh, Ralph..."

"Ma'am, he ain't even here. How can he be in trouble?"

"It's those tires," the woman responded, still staring. "He's not supposed to have them. No one has used tires since the big quake ten years ago when the world's ground transportation system was destroyed. But six years ago, or maybe five, right after Go-Buttons were developed, someone found that the material in these tires collected and absorbed hazer beams, completely nullifying them. Raiders got onto that in a hurry, and for a time nothing could stop them in their destruction.

"Finally the various governments got together, the people united behind them, and a worldwide sweep was made to gather all tires made of this material, and destroy them. Since then it has been illegal to own any sort of pre-quake tire at all, and Neighbors and all other police and protection groups are authorized to treat all who do as public enemies."

"Seems like mighty harsh judgment," Yid responded, not understanding at all what the woman had just told him, but trying nonetheless to be sociable.

"It *is* harsh," Carol continued. "But if you understood the incredible cruelty, wickedness and corruption that is perpetrated by the Raiders upon virtually every other facet of society on the earth, then you would also understand the harshness of our retaliation."

"Well, you're most likely right. Uh...who are the Raiders, or the Neighbors, for that matter?"

Carol looked at Yid as if he might be a little beyond help. "You really don't know?"

"Neither of us do," Mincy responded, taking her husband's arm.

"That's hard to believe. How can anybody not know of the Raiders?"

"I reckon we've been some protected," Yid said simply.

"Yes," Carol said as she looked at them, "I daresay. Well, the Raiders are people who banded together after the quake to live at the expense of others. They take secret oaths to protect each other, and they stop at nothing to get what they want. They are like vultures, constantly preying on what they consider to be the carcass of society."

"They sound like regular varmints," affirmed Yid. "Why don't you hunt them down and put them out of your misery?"

"They are much too powerful for that. But we are working on it, and those who aren't Raiders are also getting stronger. Maybe one day..."

Yid looked back at the tires. "So what are you going to do about these?"

"I...I don't know. Talk to Ralph, I suppose. How he ever found these, or where, is beyond me. I haven't even *seen* any since the big sweep. You know, it's funny, but I remember when my father would have given almost anything for a set of tires like these."

"By jings," Yid agreed, "so do I. Didn't he say that he lost his job on account of he couldn't get any? He got discouraged, and that's why he brought that woman out to see you and your mother instead of coming alone."

Slowly Carol nodded. "Yes, I remember now. Strange, isn't it, how things happen..."

She grew silent, her thoughts far in the past, and Yid and Mincy looked at each other.

"Carol, ma'am, what *is* this place we're in?"

The woman, her reverie instantly broken, laughed. "You don't know that either?"

Yid shook his head, as did Mincy.

"I surely would like to know where you've been for the past twenty-one years or so."

"Ma'am," Yid replied laconically, "with that there question you have not just stepped into any plain old ordinary cowchip of a mystery. No siree, you have lit with both brogans right square in the middle of the granddaddy pasture flapjack of them all."

"Colorful," Mincy grinned, looking at her husband, "and very accurate. Truth is, Miss Carol, we don't know."

"You don't know what?"

"Where we've been."

For a moment there was no sound in the structure save the quiet hum of the machines. Then, with a shake of her head, the woman called Carol turned away and began speaking. And as she did both Yid and Mincy were given to understand that she was saying one thing so that she could avoid delving into another.

"This is the environmental control center for Ralph's farm. It's small because he can't really afford a large operation. And frankly, it is totally obsolete. I don't understand how he makes a living at it, especially now that his income is being deducted into so many families. He's helping the rest of us, you know. He's the only one left who can."

Yid and Mincy looked quickly at each other, but neither responded.

"So, what do all these fancy doodads accomplish?" Yid finally asked.

Again the woman laughed nervously. "Actually, I'm not much good at explaining it. These monitors are the database for everything on the farm. Even the ceiling is a high-resolution display, just like the ones we used to have in our homes, before Sensavision came along.

"The whole system here can be voice-activated, but at the moment the visi-checkers are monitoring..."

"Visi-checkers?"

"Yes, perhaps you saw them — small objects that patrol above the crops?"

"Porky-hogs," declared Yid. "Baby porcupines."

"Y...es," Carol agreed hesitantly. "Uh...well, the visi-checkers monitor all the environmental factors on the farm. They tell the computers in here to produce exactly the required amount of heat or light or moisture, on a twenty-four hour basis, to any given crop-roll, and the plants respond accordingly."

Yid shook his head. "Ma'am, you don't make no more sense than Nellie Bly and her newspaper racing against that fictional Phileas Fogg feller to get around the world in less than eighty days."

"What?"

"Let me elucidate more plainly. The wife and I are farmers, and we know somewhat of farming. But you're using long-handled words here that don't make no more sense than... Oh, never mind. I reckon we're both just plain old fools."

"I...I...," Carol stammered, uncertain how to proceed. "Uh...I'm trying my best."

"And you are doing a dandy job," Yid agreed. "It's only that we're likely both balmier than we look. But you go ahead, and we'll do our best to spur in and ride 'er out."

"Very well, I'll keep trying. This monitor here, for instance, deals with the crops obtaining light and heat. The computers activate a molecular agitator, and the resulting mass movement along the particular, assigned, band of molecules creates local atmospheric friction, a simple phenomenon that produces both heat and light. I don't know the principle by which it is so well contained, but it is, and it works."

"Clear as Mississippi mud," Yid affirmed.

"Yes...I...I'm not very good at explaining."

"It isn't you," Mincy declared. "We just, well, we came from back in..."

"We were wondering about that little bitty rainstorm we saw out there," Yid stated, temporarily preventing his wife from explaining. "Can you tell us about that particular and peculiar atmospheric phenomenon?"

Carol smiled. "I can try," she said hopefully. "To produce rain, a molecular digitizer of ions is activated, which digitizes or spaces electrically charged, sub-microscopic particles that are insta-spread above the crop to be watered. Those digitized ions, electronically agitated, collect and unite hydrogen and oxygen molecules at a high rate of speed, and the resulting water precipitates directly beneath that particular belt of ionized particles. In other words, almost instant, and very localized, rain."

Yid stared at her, and the quiet in the room got so deep-still that when he let out his long-held breath, it sounded like he'd shot off a canon in the cemetery at four o'clock of a Good Friday morning.

Mincy jumped, but Yid paid no attention to her. "Miss Carol," he drawled fiercely, "you do, and you'll for certain have to clean it up."

"What do you mean?"

Smiling, Mincy reached out and took Carol's hand. "He's being funny, Miss Carol. He didn't mean anything by it. But all of this is so incredible that, well, we feel like our brains are spinning."

"Oh, this is nothing. It isn't even really fun to watch. I like to be here when the peds do the harvesting. That is fun."

"Peds?"

"You know, tripedambulatory robots. But not like we used to think of robots when I was a kid. These are hardly more than laser-operated baskets with arms, but they move so fast and harvest so efficiently that it is difficult for the eye to even follow them. Ralph keeps two or three peds on

alert so that the visi-checkers can signal them when a particular crop is perfect for harvest. In just moments they get
it all done, and then other peds take the crop and get it
packaged in huge sealed bins. Then each corner is tied with
a small length of anti-gravity thread, and the crop is ready
for shipment."

Yid and Mincy looked with sudden understanding at
each other. "We had some of that awful anti-gravity
thread," Mincy stated. "My husband sewed my blouse
with it. And he sewed that Go-Button on with it, too."

"Oh, no," Carol groaned. "Why did you ever do that?"

"We didn't know any better. After it was used, neither of
us could do a single thing except float around. Even after
I got the blouse off, I still floated."

"I know," Carol sympathized. "The effects spread, and
can last for days. That's why the thread is not for human
use. Didn't you read the warning?"

"Warning?" Yid gasped. "You mean about repentance,
or lusting?"

"What?" Carol responded blankly. "I don't understand."

"Never mind," Yid quickly told her, for some reason
feeling vastly relieved. "I did see a 'Use with caution' note.
So taking such free and generous advice into account, I
stitched us up with caution."

"The note meant much more than that," Carol replied,
smiling. "The thread was designed to save energy, which
was awfully critical in the two or three years following the
big quake. With that anti-gravity thread we can take things
that weigh literally megatons, put a bit of it on them, and
move them around with infinitesimally small expenditures
of energy."

"The big quake? You keep talking about that, but neither
of us have ever heard of it."

"But how can that be?" Carol responded. "It occurred in
ninety-nine. How could you have missed it?"

"I reckon we must have been asleep."

"Nobody slept through that. It was too awful, too long-
lasting. People all over the earth were killed, millions of

them, and for a time most who survived thought that society was doomed. There were diseases and infectious plagues, and... oh, it was simply awful. But mankind survived, at least some of us — though the way things are going we could destroy what's left of humanity at any time. And neither of you knew of it?"

"Not hardly."

"My goodness, that is amazing."

"To us, too," Mincy said. "What happened after the quake?"

"Well, from that time on, men began to divide into two groups, the Raiders and the rest of us, Neighbors and what have you. And though so much of our technology was destroyed, people in our group continue to have the most incredible ideas, and they have developed the most amazing devices that you can imagine. That's when the Go-Buttons were developed, for instance."

"What were they for?" Yid asked.

Carol smiled patiently. "Highways were totally destroyed, petroleum fuels were impossible to obtain, communications were wiped out, and it looked as though society was finished. Then someone came up with these great little buttons to provide personal transportation, and suddenly everything was even more advanced than before. Now the buttons are far more powerful than the one you have, and can be activated simply by thought. Of course that makes the wars harder to fight, too, and the Raiders nearly impossible to control.

"That's why the barriers and shields were invented, and the print-activated structures like this monilab. People cannot pass through any of them with their Go-Buttons. One more little hedge against the Raiders."

Yid and Mincy stared at her, and then again around the domed room. Never had they seen or heard such things, never had they even imagined that such things might exist. But suddenly, without even realizing what they were doing, they had come to this place.

"Miss Carol," Yid asked, his voice almost trembling with apprehension, "may I ask you a question that's likely going to sound more foolish than anything we've yet asked?"

Carol smiled. "Certainly. And I won't laugh, either."

"Good. What year is it?"

"Year?"

"Uh-huh. Right now. Today. What year are *we* living in?"

"Why, 2009, of course," Carol answered, at the same time looking at Yid with a strange expression on her face. "September 2, 2009. Or at least it will be until midnight."

Yid gulped and looked at Mincy. "I knew it," he breathed. "What did I tell you, honey-darlin'? Sure as Joe Pulitzer's gone blind from writing all those newspaper articles, we've gone to somewhere that ain't, at least yet."

"But how can this be?" Mincy asked. "I don't... Yid, why is all this happening to us? I've got to know."

"What is it?" Carol asked, interrupting Mincy. "Why are you both so concerned about the time?"

"Because September second is our anniversary," Yid answered slowly, "and we can't hardly seem to get shut of it. This doggone particular day sort of keeps humming along for everlastingly ever, twisting in and out like a Navajo weaver's prayer rug. But 2009 is the true and actual year? If that don't ring all the bells in St. Mary's Cathedral, then I doubt that anything ever will."

Perplexed, Carol shook her head. "What on earth are you *talking* about?"

Miss Carol," Yid said in response, "I reckon you had ought to sit down, happen you can find a chair. We'll answer your questions, but the answers may knock you over."

Carol backed up a step, and then shook her head. "Just tell me. I don't need to sit down."

"You want to do the honors?" Yid asked his wife.

Mincy shook her head, so Yid turned back to Carol. "Ma'am, when my wife and I left our log home this morning to take a trip to the Cove down on the Big Lost River, it was September 2, 1899."

"Wh...what?"

"That's right, Carol," Mincy affirmed. "I mark each day

on my calendar, and this morning it was September 2, 1899. We've been married three years today, so I had ought to know."

"But...but...," Carol stammered, "that can't be. I know you had to use your Go-Button to get here, and they didn't have anything like them until 2004."

"Miss Carol," Yid gently interrupted, "we *did* use the Go-Button. It was given to us, accidental-like, we think, by the old drummer down at the Cove."

"He's right," Mincy agreed. "I was there and saw it."

Carol stared. "This is incredible. You are actually *from* 1899? You didn't go there from our century first?"

"No, ma'am. We're both of us boneyard, broomtail, nineteenth century Big Lost Country natives, for a simple fact."

Suddenly Carol smiled with anticipation. "If that's so, then what was it like then? I mean, can you tell me?"

"You truly want to know?" Yid asked in surprise.

"Oh, I do! I used to *love* reading history. And books of any kind. But nobody prints books anymore, and the old ones are getting harder to find. Well, anyway, if you could tell me something about your day, I would love to hear it."

Yid grinned. "I reckon I can tell you a little, then. Life in the Big Lost is mostly dirt and hard work and not enough sleep nor education either, providing you were not born with a silver spoon in your mouth. And I allow that no one in the valley that I know of happened to be so sorrowfully fortunate.

"And the valley is remote, too. Why, there ain't hardly any more than half a dozen ranches and farms up to our end of the valley, three or four thousand cows to go on them, two or three dozen cowboys and homesteading dirt farmers to stir up the soil and sit company with those cows, and maybe half a hundred families bunched up in the mining towns down to the South. It is a high-far and wolf-lonely place, and Big Lost Country is as good a name for it as any man is going to invent.

"Why, the place is so remote that not even the Postal

Department knows where it is, all mail for the Big Lost being simply sent to Arco stamped 'Please Forward'. As with the U.S. Mails, so with the freight line passengers who ride freight because there aren't any stages. Them sorry people who set out for the Big Lost are simply forwarded and deposited, care of General Delivery, on the downhill side of Whiskey Springs. After that it is up to them to get to where they might be going.

"Outside of the valley, and of course last I heard, William McKinley is president of these United States, Admiral Dewey won the Spanish American War just a year past, and last week I heard tell that another war is shaping up down in Africa, with the Boor folks. The Salmon River Railroad Company is building a line from Blackfoot all the way up here to the Big Lost, and they figure to put the terminal at Houston or nearby. I also heard that the Oregon Short Line is figuring on running it.

"Hereabouts once again, John Lehman is settled in his new log home since his other one burned to the ground last fall; last I heard, Old Joe Skelton was still taking nourishment and occasional spirits through his neck-funnel where the steer gored him; the Big Slough down by Joe Dickey's is being used as pasture by all the cattlemen in the valley this winter..."

"Except us," Mincy interrupted proudly. "We've raised enough feed to care for our own."

"Now doggone it," Yid growled at his wife, "you want me to tell Miss Carol the history of the Big Lost country for 1899 and thereabouts, or don't you? Happen you do, then stop making your interruptions."

Mincy grinned at him, and then turned to Carol. "I love to listen to him talk, don't you?"

Carol nodded, smiling.

"Of course, Mincy continued, "he's never had much schooling and can't help it if he gets a few words wrong. Fact is, he's likely not much of a history student, either."

"Why now I reckon that's so," admitted the accused Yid Francom soberly. "I've always mainly had an interest in what makes us tick in our own times, so to speak. Fact is,

I agree with old Voltaire. He figured history was a waste of time. Allowed it was nothing more than a written-down register of the crimes, follies, misfortunes and general all-around tomfooleries of mankind. Now there's a man makes sense to me. Who wants to stomp around kicking up yesterday's dust when we got more than enough of today's to choke on? Happen, that is, that we can figure out exactly where today is."

Mincy took a revised and wondering look at her husband. For all his cowboy idiom and stuttering shyness, she had learned something else about him, something in addition to his ability to sew. One could not entirely dismiss as uneducated a man who could mix vintage Voltaire with Big Lost River country gossip. Where had he learned all that, she wondered? She had never seen him reading Voltaire, or much of anything else, for that matter. Of course, neither had she seen him tailoring any new shirts, but now she knew for a fact that he'd done both.

So where or when...

"Like I was saying," Yid continued, "Joe Dickey's figuring on making him a post office down at his ranch come spring. Folks are talking up building a bridge across the Big Lost River so they don't have to ford all the time and get the womens' skirts wet, newcomers are settling thick as blowflies in the meetinghouse window of a Sunday morning down west of the Slough. And a week or so back, Maude and Ella Pearson from down to Moore told me that Ben, their father, is closing Nosebag up for good."

"Nosebag?"

"Yeah, the feed station for the teams hauling north to Challis and Salmon. The buildings are down thataway about a mile, in the bottom. Or they were there once, I mean. When it was operating, nosebag was our closest and only neighbors. They fed the stock there to get em' primed for going over the top, which was called Willow Creek Summit. Reckon they'll have to carry their own feed, now."

"Or else *we'll* provide it," Mincy said quietly.

"That's correct," Yid agreed. "There is always that possibility, providing we can get the land ready and the seed in the ground."

"But what do you *do*? I mean, what is, or was, it like, living then?"

"Like?" Yid declared, waxing eloquent again. "Law, Miss Carol, it's about the most wonderful thing a man could hope he could ever have, it's so lovely and beautiful. Why, Dickey Mountain right here is part of the Pahsimerois, which are part and parcel of the Lost Creek Range. When it hits it proper, the sun turns that old mountain to gold, pure heavenly treasure, and we can enjoy it every blessed day of our lives.

"That peak off to the Southeast there, beyond Doublesprings Pass and above Thousand Springs and Al West's ranch and stage station, is one of the highest peaks in Idaho. One of these days they'll measure it and name it..."

"Borah," Carol interrupted. "You're talking about Mount Borah, and you are right. It is the highest peak in Idaho."

"Why, that's a dandy name," Yid breathed. "Mount Borah. I like that. Then beyond that is Leatherman Peak, where the Killions and Jim Pence found and buried old Henry Leatherman's body a few years back.

"Then off there to the west, way beyond those hills, are the Pioneer Mountains. Beyond them are ranges like the Sawtooths, and it is almost like all this gorgeous wilderness will never quit."

"Wilderness? You mean it was uninhabited?"

Yid shook his head. "Not hardly, ma'am. It was inhabited, just not by men. Last spring Peaches and I took a fishing trip into the Pioneers, and what I saw can explain it better than anything else I could say.

"It was warm and the air was heady with the scent of pine. The streams sang from the runoff of the dwindling snowpack, and grass was springing yellow-green from every bed of moist soil we crossed. Each ambush of rocky crevice, or gnarled root, waylaid the trail with bursts of flower fire; Indian Paintbrush of red, orange and white, lupines of blue, larkspur of darker blue, yellow buttercup and glacier lily, harebell, crocusses and a dozen more sprayed the mountains. As far toward any point of the compass as I could cast my eyes, there was nothing but beauty, bounty and birds singing. I'll tell you, Miss Carol, I love every gorgeous ridge and rocky draw of this far-flung land. It's so lovely that it takes my breath away, and living in it is like living in the Lord's Garden of Eden."

"But for a woman," Mincy said gently, "the beauty comes not so much from what's about her, as from who she shares it with. Because I share my life with a man like Yid, I am happy and more than content. He is such..."

Mincy was interrupted, and violently, too, by a sudden explosion that sent the floating monilab rocking wildly back and forth, bobbing, as Yid might have said, like a cork on the Big Lost River at flood time.

And one look at Carol's face told both Yid and Mincy they were in very serious trouble.

25

"Jumping blue blazes," Yid growled as he clung to the floor of the crazily pitching monilab, "what in thunderation was that?"

Mincy, clinging to a metal rail of some sort, shook her head in wide-eyed ignorance. But Carol, just beyond Mincy and holding fast to the same rail, did know. Yid could tell it by the whiteness of her skin and by the fear that seemed to be pulsating in her eyes.

"Miss Carol?" he asked.

"Raiders," she whispered hollowly. "Either Raiders or Neighbors, and it won't matter which."

"Why?" Mincy questioned.

"Because either way, we're *dead*! That's the law, and...and... oh, I should have known."

"Hang it all," Yid growled, "known what?"

"That they would come. You don't have shields, and Ralph's visi-checkers sent that information out long ago. It was picked up either by the Raiders or the Neighbors, and now it's too late to do anything about it. Why didn't I think of that?"

Yid and Mincy looked at each other. "Yid," Mincy whispered, "why don't..."

But suddenly the monilab was rocked by another blast.

"Look," Carol whispered frantically as she pointed to a wildly spinning object high on the wall, "the monilab shield is going! It can't take more than another hit or two. It's too old and weak! Oh, we're going to go up."

"Then save yourself," Yid shouted at her. "Miss Carol, use your Go-Button and get out of here."

"I can't," Carol replied with a sob. "Once a hazer has locked in it will follow my particular body-pattern heat circuitry no matter how far away I take myself."

"What in double deuce is a hazer?" Yid growled.

"A heat laser," she replied with empty voice. "I don't know much about them, but I know the beams follow heat and destabilize molecular structures that put the heat out. I saw a man get hit once, and his entire arm literally vanished. The molecules of his arm simply destructured, and the man was dead of shock within minutes."

Again Yid and Mincy looked at each other.

"So why are they shooting at us?" Mincy asked. "We've done nothing wrong."

"But you have. You've penetrated a barrier without a shield and without authorization. The only ones who do that are Raiders. That's why... Oh, no!"

"What is it?"

"It's the *tires*! I left that door open without thinking, and the visi-checkers must have picked up and sent out information concerning those tires, too. I'll bet that's why... Oh, we're all going to be killed. I know we are."

Yid looked from Carol to the tires and back again. "Wait just a doggone minute," he growled. "Did you say that tires drew those hazer things?"

"Drew? I don't know what you mean. I..."

"What in tunket do tires do to hazers?" Yid pressed impatiently.

"Something in them acts as a shield," Carol responded. "They gather in hazer beams and somehow stop them from penetrating."

"That's enough, ma'am," Yid said, putting his hand up. "Now you two give me maybe half a minute, and then come after me on the run. I'm going to..."

And the monilab was rocked wickedly by a third explosion.

"Yid?" Mincy whispered, "don't..."

"Not now, honey-darlin'. Those buzzards up there have me madder'n twenty-nine hornets fighting over a dead grasshopper, and I ain't going to sit around this here skyboat thing and perish. Not without a fight, I ain't."

"But what are you going to do?"

"I don't know, at least not the particulars. But my basic idea would likely make a ghost turn pale, it'll be that chancy. Probably I'd have a better chance of tracking weanling mice across flat rocks. Nonetheless, it's all I've got, so it'll have to do."

"So what is it?"

Yid grinned wickedly, like he was having a great and wonderful time at someone else's expense. Which most likely, come to think of it, he was.

"I'm going to take two of them tires and run to the left," he answered, "down toward the little butte. Give me thirty seconds or so, and then each of you take a tire, put it around your necks, and head right, down toward Arentson Gulch. And run like teased snakes, the both of you. I'll meet you in the gulch within thirty minutes."

"And if you don't?" Mincy asked.

"Well now, honey-darlin', don't you go asking fool questions like that. I'll be there, and that's an ironclad promise. By the way, Miss Carol, can you turn off those visi-checker outfits?"

"I think so."

"Then do it. Right now." With that, Yid scrambled to his feet, put his arms through two tires, lifted them gruntingly to his shoulders, and leaped from the pitching monilab.

For an instant nothing happened, and the small man, with more courage and not much more sense than Custer's bugler blowing the second charge at the Battle of the Little Big Horn, ducked and began his staggering run across the farm.

Suddenly there was a blinding flash, and the tire-heavy Yid found himself rolling across the ground. For a moment he lay still, trying to decide which part of him was missing. But then he noticed a small, glistening hole in the side of one of the tires, and his heart leaped with hope.

"Yeah!" he shouted in defiance at the blinding sky. "Try that again, you misbegotten whelps of impacted sidewinders. By Tophet, folks who'll shoot an unarmed man ought to have their gizzards cut out and roasted over a hot fire. Or their ears cut off and strung up for baby monkeys to swing on. They'd ought to be sat down hard and read to from the book, and that by piles and piles more than somewhat."

Scrambling to his feet, Yid shouted another taunt at the unseen foe and took off running again, moving, as he would have said, like a turpentined cat. Another blast came, and then a third and a fourth and a fifth, and each time Yid was hurt no worse than the tumbling on the ground gave him.

At last, out of breath and bruised but still unhurt, he reached the side of the small rocky outcropping that he and Mincy had called Little Butte. Pausing, he gave thought to what he was going to do next. He had hoped to leave one of the tires as a sort of decoy, but now he realized that that wouldn't work at all. It would only lay on the ground, stationary, while he moved off with the other. Any tinhorn alive would know which one was him. Of course he could always climb the side of the butte and roll one of the tires off, but that wouldn't give him more than one or two hundred feet at the most.

No, he was going to have to come up with some other plan. Trouble was, there wasn't...

Another hazer blast sliced through the boulder under which Yid was crouched, and he was sent tumbling again. This time, however, he smacked his head on a small rock, and when he staggered to his feet it was all he could do to keep his balance.

"By jings," he muttered as he swayed back and forth, "I feel worse than a calf with the slobbers. The way they keep on shooting, them fellers must be packing enough hardware to give them kidney sores."

Pausing, Yid squinted skyward, trying to see who was attempting all the damage. "Listen, you yahoos," he shouted in total frustration, "the rule of gun-fighting in the Old West is, if you can't get the job done with five rounds, it's time to pull your freight. Now vamoose!

"Law! That there rock..."

And suddenly Yid realized that something had moved across his blurry field of vision.

Rubbing his eyes, he saw an odd-looking creature maybe fifty feet away apparently eating from one of the rows of crops. Yid couldn't tell exactly what sort of animal it was, but it didn't hardly matter, either. An idea had come to him, and he was instantly determined to carry it out. That is, he was if he could just throw a rope of some sort on the critter and hold it down for a minute or two while he did.

Staggering toward it, Yid did his best to move quietly. But that wasn't easy, what with two big tires over his shoulders and someone blasting away at him from goodness knew where up above. Yet he was amazed, as he progressed forward, that the critter paid him no mind. It didn't bolt and run, it didn't even turn its head to watch, and that surprised the small man, who continued his body-pounding course toward it.

"Whoa," he called out softly as he staggered nearer. "Whoa, there."

But still the critter didn't bolt. It just sort of whirred at the row of crops without paying Yid the least bit of attention.

Suddenly, however, it was no longer in front of Yid. Instead it had moved four or five feet down the row so fast that Yid hadn't even seen it happen. Now it was whirring contentedly at *those* vegetables, and it still hadn't heard him.

Yid rubbed his eyes, and finally realized just exactly

what sort of "critter" he had been chasing.

"Tarnation," he muttered in surprise, "that there is one of those tripeda... Well, leastwise it's one of those 'ped' machines that Miss Carol mentioned, the kind what moves mighty fast and harvests the crops for her brother."

Yid grinned at his discovery, and stepping up behind the metallic creature, he eased one of his two tires toward the pointed top. But just as he reached it, the machine zipped to another spot a few feet further on.

"Whoa there, dagnab it," Yid shouted. "Now don't you go getting your tail in the air, you mangy crowbait hunk of boiler iron. I ain't going to do no more than throw a rubber-tire harness on your shoulders."

Finally Yid reached the machine again, and with a satisfied chuckle he slipped the tire up and over the pointed top.

Instantly the whirring movement stopped, and Yid stepped back just as it began again, only in the anxious whining of high gear. The ped whirred and chugged and strained every bolt and rivet and weld joint that held it together. But whir and grind as it would, it could not free the arms that had been doing the picking, the arms that the tire had instantly pinned down.

Then, almost as if it were alive, the metal critter spouted a belch of smoke or steam from its straining gears, spun about two or three times, and then like a streak was gone up the row.

Yid stared in amazement as it halted some dozen yards away, spun some more, took a direct hit from the unseen hazer, a hit that didn't seem to faze it hardly at all, and then it was off to another part of the farm on its frantic course.

Another bolt from the hazer chased it down, and then another and another, and suddenly Yid realized that the beams were no longer coming at him.

"By jings," he grinned widely, "them fellers on the cow-ard-side of that hazer ain't altogether bright. That'll learn 'em, and learn 'em good, providing they ever discover their error."

In cautious good humor Yid turned toward the distant gulch, and moving slowly, he worked his feeling-proud way toward it. And all the while, the poor, tire-harnessed ped was zinging this way and that on the farm, taking constant hits from the hazer and doing its best to ignore them and return to that for which it had been programmed — the harvesting of twenty-first century crops.

26

"Do you think he'll make it?" Carol whispered as she and Mincy huddled in the darkened recess of Arentson Gulch.

The large woman was silent for a moment, thinking. "He'll make it," she finally whispered back. "He's neither very big nor very strong, but that doesn't seem to matter. He's smart, and besides that, he's too good a man not to make it."

"It is so obvious that you love each other."

Mincy took a deep breath and sighed. "I've never loved anybody in my life like I love him. I tell you, Carol, he's the most unusual person I've ever known. When the Good Lord poured that man out, it was a terrible thin and watery mix. But when he broke open the mold, someone mighty special had set up inside. Every day that fact becomes more evident to me."

"I see it, too," Carol agreed. "Your husband has something about him that almost shines."

"Yes," Mincy affirmed, "he does."

"And I have decided that the way he talks isn't funny," Carol concluded. "And it isn't even cute. Instead, it is very,

very poetic. It makes me want to get to know him better, to listen and listen until my whole soul has been filled with the understanding of him. Does that make any sense?"

Mincy nodded. "It does, for he gives me the same yearnings, though I have never thought of it quite like you just expressed it. But I think you must be a poet yourself, Carol."

"No, I'm not. I would like to have been, but my life has gone so many other directions. No, I will have to be content to obtain my poetry by listening to the rare people on this earth who are like your husband. For surely somewhere there must be a few more that are like him."

"I hope so," Mincy said softly. "But truthfully, I doubt it."

"And so do I," Carol responded sadly.

Both women were silent then, thinking their own deep thoughts, and wondering.

Around them the night was still as death. In the distance, however, frequent concussions could be heard, concussions caused by the hazer splitting through the barrier that surrounded the farm. The two women listened to those explosions, huddled closer together, and wondered if the small man who had diverted fire from them would ever escape and find his way to their hiding place.

"I wish I hadn't called him a clonk," Carol suddenly said, staring out into the night.

"Is that a bad thing?"

"Not bad, really. It just means worthless. After the quake so many things that had seemed important became useless. Anything that fell into that category became a clonk. I think it came from the sound things made as they were being thrown out. Now the term is used derisively, of course, for people.

"Listen," Carol whispered suddenly, "I think the hazer has stopped. Oh, no, what if your husband has been killed."

"I don't die *that* easy," a quiet voice growled from just a few feet away, startling both women. "Now come on. When those fellers on the blister end of that hazer find out they didn't get me, they're likely to be madder'n old Ben Pearson the day he discovered all his water barrels had leaked dry during the ride back to Nosebag. And that was some mad, I can tell you."

"Oh, my goodness," Carol started to cry out, thoroughly surprised at Yid's sudden appearance.

"Hold 'er down there, Miss Carol," Yid ordered as he looked behind him toward the farm, "before I have to grab your nostrils and pinch you quiet. We've fooled 'em for the moment, but I'm not hankering to send out any verbal announcements concerning our whereabouts."

"I'm sorry. You surprised me, though, and I didn't..."

"Didn't mean to, ma'am. I reckon I was too busy hiding from them fellers to consider sending up a smoke signal for you."

With a hand sign for the women to follow, Yid then melted into the darkness up-gulch, and he was as loud about his going as an owl's shadow scraping across creek-bank scrabble rock. Still, it was likely one of the few times when a shadow had cast a shadow in near moon dark. Or rather, two shadows. Behind Yid, Mincy and Carol picked their way almost as cautiously forward, understanding that a noise as big as a cricket's cough might very well cost them their lives.

Slowly and carefully they moved, yet steadily, and Yid didn't stop again until the three stood beneath the mahoganies at the side of the rutted road.

"Where are we?" Carol gasped, out of breath from the forced climb.

"Four hours and a half, maybe five, from your home...I mean, where you lived when you were a child," Yid told her. "Happen you still live near there, I think we can follow this road and get you back."

"Good, because I do. Actually I live less than a mile from the old place. What road is this?"

"The rutted one the Future-Compass showed us," Mincy answered. "It's the one we always seem to come to. We followed it to get here tonight."

"Do you think those Neighbors will come after us?"

Carol asked fearfully, staring down into the darkness where her brother farmed.

"They might," Yid affirmed. "It's mighty hard to tell. But I've a notion we had ought to be moving out, no matter."

"But why don't I use my Go-Button?"

"Law, Miss Carol, I didn't even think of that."

Carol smiled. "I understand. But now that I've thought about it for a few seconds, I'll not use it. The hazers might detect our body movement, and then all you have done will be for nothing. Please, sir, lead out, and we will follow."

Yid stepped ahead then, and quickly the two women fell in behind him, their course southeast along the side of the mountain.

"How did you get away?" Mincy asked as they walked.

"Luck, more than anything else," Yid responded. "Just about like that fight with George, I reckon. I caught up with one of those ped outfits..."

"You mean a tripedambulatory robot?" Carol questioned, sounding surprised. "But how could you catch one of them?"

"That wasn't hard at all, Miss Carol. The thing was busier with its harvesting than a prairie dog after a rainstorm, and while I allow I made more noise than a snorting stallion in a herd of lonesome mares, the doggone thing never even spooked. I figured after I caught it that it was sure enough took with the denses. Still, what it didn't know about moving fast and furious you could have painted on the head of a pin with a barn brush. By Tophet, I said to myself as I saw it scamper, that critter could certainly galvanate. It'd do fine for what I needed, short of somthing else with good sense."

"So what did you do with it?"

"Not much. Just harnessed it with one of those tires. I figured it would move around some, maybe confuse the hazer. I didn't count on causing the poor ped no strangulating fit. But like my wife has told me time and again, you place your money on the bobtailed nag or the bay, and the black's likely going to come out of the herd and win the race every time. Nothing's dependable at all."

Mincy and Carol looked at each other, totally confused.

"What I mean to say is, that ped critter was all gurgle and no guts. It didn't take to that tire hardly at all. Instead it started spinning and whining worse than old Rick Laing down to Arco doing the Virginnie Reel with his arthritis acting up, and the next I knew, the poor iron critter was all over that farm trying to get shut of the tire. Worse, the hazer was blasting away at it, and I decided it was time I took my leave. That's about when I had my idea."

"Which idea is that?" Mincy asked, smiling at Carol's amazed expression. "And sweetheart, say it plain for Carol, if you possibly can."

"Oh, I can say it plain," Yid grinned. "You see, me running drew fire from that hazer every minute or so. Yet the ped, moving faster than a red-tailed hawk diving after his first dinner in a week, drew fire every few seconds. That got me to thinking about what Miss Carol had said, about the hazer being able to follow even a Go-Button, and it came to me that speed was the ticket to our getting out of this mixed-up version of Buffalo Bill's Wild West Show. Or maybe I should say, lack of same.

"Which, dear ladies," Yid concluded, "is why we're walking along this rutted road of ours, and not running."

"Do you mean to say that a hazer won't track down something that's going slow?" Carol asked, absolutely amazed by the reasoning of the man she was following.

"Don't mean to say anything of the sort, Miss Carol. Nothing's ironclad in this vision my wife and I are having. But so far, so good. Nonetheless, I ain't about to go throwing away this black rubber-tire collar I've taken to wearing. High fashion or not, I'm adorning my neck with it anyhow. I'd recommend the two of you continue to do the same."

Yid then stepped out ahead of the women, obviously watching for trouble, and in the darkness behind him Mincy nodded. "See what I mean, Carol? Yid is a man who would see the sun with his head in a charcoal sack during an eclipse. Somehow, no matter how dark things get, no matter how you think he's been beaten down, he always comes out on top."

And Mincy meant what she said, too. The longer she watched her husband, the less she felt like she knew him. In one moment he looked sissy as skim milk. The next, he acted gritty as pork chops rolled in sand. Cock her head one way and he seemed so helpless he couldn't drive nails in a snowbank. Cock it the other and it appeared he might, as her father used to say, haul hell right out of its shuck. That was why most folks wouldn't bet either way on him in a tight election. But Mincy would, and she knew it. And Yid would win, for there was no other way that things could possibly go. He was simply too good a man not to.

What did she care if he wasn't the valley's greatest farmer? What did she care further if he hardly knew a whiffletree from a wagon tongue or a whey-belly bull from a bred and swelling heifer? Such things hardly mattered. What did matter was that he was a good man and a dear husband. And that was why she wasn't giving up on him. Not now. Not ever. It didn't matter that he was as out of place behind a plow as a Missouri mule sitting down for a visit in the parlor. He was something far and away above the ordinary, and knowing that gave her more courage and determination than she would ever have supposed she could muster.

"He certainly is something special," she concluded with a sigh.

"I'd give *anything* if my husband was like him," Carol declared then, her voice a lot louder than she had meant it to be.

But Yid somehow had heard her, and as it turned out the damage was instantly done.

"You...you're married right now?" he asked, turning back in surprise. "But I thought ... Well, I heard you tell that Malcom feller that you wanted him and you to..., to..."

Carol scowled defensively at the man. "I said married, not happy. I'd get out of my marriage in a minute if the right man came along. My husband is an absolute binary-brain in every sense of the word, and I want out."

"Binary-brain?"

"That's right. He only thinks of two things; eating and ionized adventures. I don't think he's been out of bed in two years. He just lays and eats and experiences. It's a real quakahoo."

"But," Yid protested as he planted himself in front of the woman, stopping them all, "why should whatever you are talking about make you want to split the blanket?"

"Wait until we get home," Carol answered. "Then you'll understand. My first husband installed a molecular ion digitizer. You know, one that turns our whole bedroom into an ion chamber. Well, maybe you wouldn't know, but it has grids on the floor and ceiling, and life-sized images fill our bedroom twenty-four hours a day. They call it Sensavision. I call it brainless escape. Tobe, my third husband, can imagine up anything he wants to see with the brain-wave activator, and he not only sees and hears it, but he *feels* and *smells* it, too. In form-filled living color. In other words, it might as well be real, except that it isn't. And that's the problem. It is simple, brainless escapism.

"For instance, Tobe's main interest is African safaris and nineteenth century Indian warfare. Can you imagine that a grown man would spend his life playing games like that? And he doesn't even have them right, because he's never taken time to study the history of such things. But that's what he does. And he thinks he is a very strong and competent individual because he always imagines himself the victor.

"To tell the truth, I don't know why I married him in the first place. One of my two daughters wanted a father, I suppose, and I sort of stumbled onto him after my second marriage dissolved in a severe case of boredom. Now this one is ready to die the same death, and the girls *still* don't have a father. I just can't seem to..."

Carol suddenly buried her face in her hands, and Mincy hesitantly put her arm around her.

"There, there," she soothed while she tried to console the smaller woman. "It'll be all right."

"Oh, how can it be all right?" Carol cried. "When I was little I wanted a daddy, and I never got one. All my father ever wanted to do was play around with any and every woman he could find. He never cared about anyone but himself. He was totally selfish.

"I hated that, and now here I am, exactly the same way. I... I blame others for the failure of my marriages, but you know who is really at fault? I am. Me. Sweet little Carol."

Sobbing, the woman swiped angrily at her eyes, oblivious of the two who stood helplessly by.

"We're sorry," Mincy said, caressing the woman's silky hair with her big hand. "We surely are."

"So am I," Carol wept. "Every time I'm with another man, I'm sorry. I hate myself for it, just like I hated my father. But what does that change? I can't stop. I tell my girls that it won't happen again, and I might just as well be blowing smoke against the wind. I just can't seem to make my thoughts do what I want them to. I start letting them wander, because what I imagine about a man feels better than any reality I've ever known. And the next thing I know, I have let myself and my children down."

Yid and Mincy stared at each other in surprise.

"And you know what is crazy?" the woman continued. "My father used to tell Mother and my brothers and I exactly the same thing, all the time, before the divorce. Empty promises. I even saw him make the same promises after, with his next wife, and then with his last one, the one that finally murdered him.

"Two of my three brothers have the same trouble. Wandering eyes or lusting — whatever you want to call it. They get caught up in that trap, and it changes them. It changed me, I can tell you that. I'm so miserable I can hardly stand it, and I don't even know where to turn any longer.

"But lusting leads to more serious problems. Or at least it has for my one brother and I. The other who can't control his thoughts is still in the fighting- and- arguing stage with his wife. That poor soul is constantly being wounded because she feels so betrayed. And I don't blame her for feeling that way, either. People who make commitments ought to be true to them, no matter what.

"My brothers and I have even talked about trying to

stop. Or at least John, who is the youngest, has talked about it. Loren won't discuss things with us, but I know that he feels the same. They're just like me, both of them. They want to stop hurting themselves and their families, only they just can't seem to get it done. And even poor Ralph, who has never chased around, has never even had problems with wandering eyes, is miserable with worrying about the rest of us.

"It's almost as though we *inherited* this...this selfishness, this longing all the time for other peoples' bodies."

Yid shot a guilty look at Mincy, but said nothing. And neither, strangely, did she.

"And oh, my poor little girls," Carol continued. "What kind of a life are they going to have? Am I passing these tendencies toward misery on to them? I'm terrified to raise them to adulthood, and I don't know what to do about it."

"But maybe they'll be different?" Yid said with hope sounding in his voice .

Carol literally sneered. "Don't you believe it. I told you about my brother Loren? Well, his oldest son is already on the same course that he followed, and Loren is being emotionally destroyed, just watching his boy. He knows that it started with his own Senavision and the erotic images he used to visualize, and that knowledge nearly kills him. Loren has mostly stopped that now, but the boy saw those images once and was instantly hooked. It's such a sad thing. Now he might just as well be dead."

"But how can that be?" Yid asked, trying desperately to understand, and trying just as desperately to stop the mind-throbbing images that were assailing him.

"Because *no one* can ever find an intimate reality that can match the imagination," Carol responded bitterly. "It can't be done, and so people who let themselves get caught up in such fantasizing literally shrivel up and die in the filth of their own minds, waiting for their lusts to become reality. Tragically. few seem to learn, and the soul-destroying epidemic is growing. Human vultures in our society have turned living one's imaginations into a veritable science, a destructive science that no one knows the end of, even yet.

"Loren's son is caught up in that very trap. He's twenty-one years old, and except for his Sensavision he has stopped trying to find a meaningful life for himself. It has become a habit that he cannot break. Loren has told him how he is trying to change, but the boy just can't see that it matters. Even pure, righteous Ralph has tried to talk to him but the boy just won't listen. He is becoming exactly like my husband; a sensory participating vegetable. I just wish that..."

"But doesn't anybody ever change?" Mincy asked plaintively.

Carol looked up. "Oh, sure. My Aunt Viv changed, and when she was killed in the big quake she died a happy woman. Her son, Joey, is a good man, too. I love him. He has the sweetest wife and children. And Ralph says that he has changed, too, though I don't think he ever had much of a problem. There are others in the family who seem happy, too. But there are so many who *aren't*.

"Oh, what's the use? My father left all of us but Ralph in such a mess. Why should I expect my life to be any better than it is?"

"Because any of us can expect anything he wants to expect out of life," Mincy affirmed as she looked at Yid. "Anything. All we need to do is repent of the things that hold us back, and whatever we desire in righteousness will be ours."

For a moment Yid looked longingly at her, and Mincy thought, hoped, ached, that he would agree. But then the moment passed, and she saw the light go once again out of her husband's eyes.

"That isn't always true," he said quietly as he finally looked away. "Sometimes things happen that are bigger than us, and all we can do is take our lumps from them and move on. We can't always have what we expect or even want to have."

Mincy gazed at Yid with a look that would have melted a quartz outcropping. Trouble was, no quartz outcroppings were around, and Yid didn't seem in any way meltable.

Seeing that, Mincy too looked away in sorrow. A moment passed in silence, and then another. No one spoke, yet no one moved, and it seemed to Mincy as if Yid were waiting, thinking, trying to decide.

"Dear God," she pleaded silently, "please let him see that it is wrong to give up."

"Your Aunt Viv died happy?" Yid asked suddenly.

"Oh, I should say. She was very much at peace with herself."

"And she had had... problems?"

"Yes, at least from what I've heard. But she put them behind her, repented was the word she used, too. Just like your wife, here."

"But how?" Yid asked in anguish. "How did she do it? And how did your brother Ralph keep from being eaten alive by this lusting after others?"

Carol looked at him, a little surprised by his vehemence. "I don't know," she responded finally after a long pause. "He tried to tell me once, but I wasn't really interested, I guess. I know he must have had a method or something, though, for I've certainly never been able to control *my* thinking just because I wanted to. I've tried, but it never works."

"Nor with me, either," Yid declared, "I've tried, the Lord knows I've tried. But I reckon it's like Mincy says— I just don't want to change bad enough. Even with what I've been shown, I don't. That doesn't make much sense to me, but it must be right. Only, you'd think if a man saw something as spine-chilling awful as what I saw in your father's face, he'd perk up like a baby robin expecting dinner. But no, by jings, that ain't the case with yours truly. Not by a long shot. Law, if only the Good Lord would make things clearer for me, then maybe..."

Yid didn't finish his sentence, but instead turned and started down the road again. It was then that he stumbled over an outcropping of rock and crashed into a clump of tall brush.

"What the?"

"The rutted road," Mincy cried out, looking around her,

"it's gone again."

Unable to grasp the meaning of Mincy's statement, Yid extricated himself from the brush, scrambled to his feet, and looked around. But it was as his wife had said. The rutted road, the one they had been standing in the middle of only moments, perhaps seconds, before, was nowhere to be seen. Instead they were gathered on the barren rocky hillside, while the moon, lowering in the west, was giving them less light than ever.

"By jings," Yid said as he brushed himself off, "this here deal is about as confusing as a short dog running twin rabbits through tall oats. Kind of reminds me of Marsh and Jim Madison's 'horse tradin' deals, down to Antelope. Nobody ever knew who was getting whose animals. Come on, we'd better be making tracks."

But Yid was interrupted by an arc of light that sizzled into existence directly above him. As he blinked his eyes against the sudden, blinding glare, an empty, hollow-sounding voice stopped him cold.

"Stand still!" the voice thundered from above and be-hind them. "Do not move, or you will all be hazed."

27

For an instant no one did so. But then Yid, overcoming his shock and deciding finally that he had had enough from the crazy vision he and Mincy were in and some to spare, moved.

"By Tophet!" he thundered, starting forward. "I'm sick clean to my eyebrows of anti-gravity thread and Go-Buttons and Future Compasses and hazers and peds and crazy folks who think they can blast away innocent pedestrians and bystanders without hardly no more than a by-your-leave. Now get out of my way."

"Cease and desist," the voice warned. "Halt. This is your last warning. You will be fired upon..."

"Blast away then," Yid shouted defiantly as he gripped his tire collar. "I've had me a middling hard day, and a long one to boot, and I'm feeling sociable as an ulcerated back tooth. Worse, any more I just don't hardly care what happens. So I give you yahoos fair warning, I won't take kindly to no tinhorn idiots..."

"No, Mister," Carol cried in alarm, "don't do it. They'll kill you. Let me talk to them."

Instantly Yid put his arm out to stop the woman. "Miss Carol," he ordered, "I speak from experience. Messing with these sidewinders is about as safe as kicking a loaded polecat, as I have already discovered. They're touchier than a teased snake, and meaner'n a hunger-struck wart-hog. Now stand back, and leave me a little elbow room to have at these Philistines with my black, rubber-tire jaw-bone."

And Yid was knocked rolling by the first hazer blast.

"By tunket," he growled as he staggered to his feet and started forward again, "that does it. *Now* I'm mad enough to kick a razorback hog barefooted. You fellers just shot down the wrong hombre, 'cause I'm up and coming at you like a bad cold, and you won't never stop me."

For the second time Yid was knocked rolling by a hazer blast. But this time, when he came to a stop, he didn't move.

"Yid," Mincy cried out. "Yid, are you all right?"

But the small man lay where he had fallen.

Mincy, seeing her husband lying death-still, gave a low cry, and then she herself turned toward the unseen voice and the menacing hazer. Quickly and in terrible silence she moved forward, and if Yid had been able to see the expression on her face he would have warned the poor men who stood in the darkness behind the hazer that it would have been safer, and that by far more than somewhat, to go pulling the sucking cubs off an old sow bear than to face his wife in a knuckle-to-chin showdown such as she obviously had in mind. But Yid was not able to warn the men, Carol had no idea that she needed to, and so Mincy's attack proceeded forth unrestricted.

Her tire-collar took a direct hit from the hazer, then a second and a third. But where such scoring hits had knocked the smaller Yid rolling, the deadly explosions served only to make Mincy stand taller, and to growl more menacingly.

She may once have learned to talk like she had been to school, all right. And her fine speech may have reflected an adopted high culture and religious principles that she cherished. But behind that hard-earned but veneer-thin surface, Mincy and her forbearers were high-up and way-back mountain people. A fire-headed, hard-eyed, hog-poor lot, they had for generations, right up until Mincy's father had deemed it wise to move north between two suns, made their clannish way acting as New Mexican receivers for Old Mexican beef products, imported in the original longhorned, hair-covered containers. Terms of delivery were damp from the Rio Grande, conditions of import, nocturnal.

To any who were foolish enough to try and show them the legal and moral error of their ways, they had replied with fists, teeth, feet, heads, knives, guns, and whatever other items that could be brought into service as weapons. They feared neither man nor beast, and the devil himself would likely have fled a-running had he met one or all of Mincy's ancestry, or her as well if she was riled, in that same dark of night on a deserted Big Lost country road.

But then the devil is cunning-smart and knows when to take his chances and when not to. The men with the hazer weren't, and didn't. And poor Yid was no longer able to warn them.

The first any of them knew they might be in danger was also the last that two of them knew anything at all, at least for a while. They were already down and out. Mincy had simply walked over the light-emitting weapon as if it had ceased to function, which it shortly did. Then she grabbed the two men by the sides of their heads, and with hardly any effort cracked their skulls together.

With them knocked cold enough to skate on and her eyes adjusting already to the dark, Mincy saw the hands of the two others jerking fearfully toward their Go-Buttons. Faster, as Yid might have said, than chain lightening with a link snapped, Mincy reached out with both hands, ripped the respective buttons from the men's shimmery shirts, and gave the small, round objects growled directions to take themselves to New Orleans and dance together in the next Mardi Gras.

Being obedient, the buttons were once and instantly

gone, and then with a snarl of anger and contempt Mincy turned upon the two remaining wide-eyed men.

"Shoot *my* husband, will you?" she snarled as she grabbed one of the men and raised him above her head. "Why, I ought to tear you in half."

Spinning once, twice, and three times, Mincy hunched her shoulders, flexed the muscles in her back and arms, and let the man fly. And fly he did, for perhaps a dozen feet, to where he dropped like a belly-shot elk into the waiting, bone-hard limbs of a mountain mahogany.

The tree shook to its roots when the big man landed; two of the lower, larger limbs were sheared right off, and the man himself became so enmeshed in the resulting splintered debris that, later on, it took the combined efforts of himself and two of his three friends to extract him.

Without even watching to see where the man might fall, Mincy turned back and, with doubled fist, brought in a looping uppercut that traveled all the way from somewhere down near her large but finely turned ankles. That last and only man, staring open-mouthed and fear-trembling at the ferocious leviathan before him, never even saw her fist coming. First there was her snarling exclamation, then there was a sudden, explosion in his brain. Following that, his teeth snapped together like a trapped weasel's, his feet left the ground simultaneously and altogether, and when he came to earth a few yards away he was sleeping like a baby.

Well, what followed was the biggest quiet, as Yid would surely have said, since that painted-up sporting lady down to Gilmore had showed up for church on Easter Sunday morning. And seeing that the lady in question hadn't heard a preacher, worn a hat, or been seen abroad in daylight for six years, that was some quiet.

"Are...are you hurt?" the astounded Carol finally called.

"Not hardly," Mincy answered, prodding with her toe one of the groaning men.

"Did you... *kill* them?"

Mincy looked up at the woman. "Kill them? Of course not. Like my poor, sweet husband might say, they're too ganted up to kill. Wouldn't hardly have been fair. He would say, and I couldn't say it better, that the poor souls had put up a fight like they'd all been wintered through on prickly pear and catalogue paper. Wasn't hardly even a battle. I...

"Oh, mercy! I most forgot about Yid. Is he...is he..."

"He's sitting up," Carol responded enthusiastically. "He has a large lump where he thumped his head against a rock, but he'll be fine."

Mincy breathed a sigh of relief, and then hurried to Yid's diminutive side. This wasn't over yet, she vowed. As long as there was breath in her body, she wouldn't let this wonderful man get away from her, or from himself, either, for that matter.

28

"Ralph?" Carol cried moments later as she bent to exam
ine one of the fallen men. "Oh, my gracious, this is my
brother Ralph."

Mincy, looking up from where she sat with her arms
around Yid, nodded. "Shake him a little," she instructed.
"That usually works with sleeping rattlesnakes. Maybe it
will bring *him* out of it, too."

Overhead the arcing light continued to glow, and in the
artificial daylight Mincy looked back to Yid. "How's your
head, sweetheart?"

"If it means that you'll keep holding me," he mumbled,
"then I reckon it's awful."

"That's what I thought," Mincy said as she squeezed
him. "Now don't you worry..."

"He's waking up!" Carol called excitedly from beside her
brother's thrashing form. "Ralph, it's me. Can you hear
me?"

"Oh, C...Carol," the man groaned as he opened his eyes,
"not you again."

"Ralph, what are you doing here?"

"We...we got the message that my monilab door had been opened, and that someone without a shield was inside. Carol, how many times have you promised me that you wouldn't go to the farm with your so-called 'friends' any more?"

"But Ralph, I didn't..."

Groggily the man sat up, holding the side of his head. "Don't lie to me," he mumbled. "I saw the man's image on my barrier penetration corder. Now why don't you... Agh...this hurts. What hit me, anyway?"

"She did," Carol replied, pointing toward Mincy.

"She? A *woman*? But how did she get past the hazer... Hold it. *Hold it.* There were only two images on that corder, and there are three of you. How did you manage that?"

Carol shrugged her shoulders. "I don't know, Ralph. I went to the farm, yes, but not to meet these people. They were already inside the barrier when I got there."

Ralph looked from his sister to the unusually dressed couple. Then quickly he turned back to his sister. "Give me the hazer, Carol. Hurry."

"But..."

"Do it. I've got to blast them."

"Ralph, no. These people are friends. They saved my life."

The man snorted. "Friends? Carol, whoever else they are, they are *not* friends. They've developed a new penetration device, can't you see that? It's the only way they could have broken through the barrier. Give them another chance and they'll steal me blind. Then they'll be turned loose and nothing in the whole world will be safe from them. No sir, I'm de-molecularizing them right this instant, just like the law says I must."

"Mister," Yid moaned as he held his hand to his own double-thumped head, "I think your saddle is slipping somewhat. We didn't penetrate anything more than a little privacy. That was our farm once, and we walked onto it, looking for our old home. No hazers blasted us, no peds chased us down, nothing. Not at least until you buzzards came along. The place was quiet as a recent-fed baby with its thumb in its mouth. We just ambled in through your so-called barrier, no trouble at all."

"Oh, no," the man groaned, "just what I need. Quaka-hoos."

"If that means daft," Mincy declared, "then maybe we are. We've surely wondered about that ourselves. But what my husband says is true. We walked from up on the side of the mountain, across Arentson Gulch."

"But *nobody* walks anymore."

"We did."

Carefully Ralph looked Mincy over. "Is she serious?" he asked his sister.

"You should know, Ralph. You're the one with the sore head. I'd call that very serious."

Ralph rubbed his head and nodded in agreement. "Well, they surely must have had *some* device that would allow them through."

Carol nodded. "They have a Go-Button, but it's an early model, totally obsolete, and I think nonfunctioning. Other than that, I have seen no device on them at all. And you should know that I ran into them maybe twenty years ago, when I was eleven. They came to the house, and they had a Go-Button even then."

"Impossible."

"Maybe, but they had it. They even used it to take me to Aunt Viv's and back home again."

Suddenly Ralph grinned with understanding. "Does their button, by any chance, have a time slice in it?"

"It does," Carol replied.

"Then that explains it. These people are Raiders. They're in a warp, and they just keep moving wherever in time they want to go, in any direction. Barriers apparently mean nothing under those conditions. They come and go at will, taking what they want as they travel. It must be the ultimate hiding place for them."

"We're not Raiders," Yid growled, "and we can't go to anywhere we want to. At first we could, but then the drummer gave us that doggone Future-Compass, and..."

Ralph's head came up with a jerk. "What?" he asked, his voice suddenly strained. "What did you say?"

Sadly Yid shook his head. "Mister, was I you, I'd have your ear canals examined for beans, cockroaches or other nefarious obstructions. They seem a might choked up. Now listen carefully while I repeat myself. I said that the drummer gave us a Future-Compass. That was when we turned in the antigravity thread, trying to get back our plow. We finally figured out how to use the thing, and..."

Slowly the man called Ralph pulled himself to his feet. "You...you have actually *seen* a Future-Compass?" he whispered.

"Sure as skunk oil makes poor perfume we have. Saw it and used it, too. Leastwise I *think* that's how we got here."

There was a moment's silence on the mountain, and Ralph stood staring at Yid, his breath coming in drawn, ragged gulps.

"Ralph," Carol asked, concerned, "what is it?"

Ignoring his sister, Ralph suddenly stepped forward and grabbed Yid by the shirt. "Describe it to me," he ordered. "Everything."

For a moment Yid simply stared at the larger man. Then he looked down at the hands that were entwined in his shirt, lifting him to his toes. And finally he looked back up into Ralph's glaring eyes.

"Happen you don't let go of me immediate," Yid drawled, his voice hardly louder than a whisper, "I'm going to be all over you like a heavy sweat. Or like..."

"Or like *me*," Mincy declared from behind him, stepping forward. "You might recollect *me*, Mister Ralph? And how I come down on folks like you who mess with my husband? Was I you, I'd let him loose pronto."

The man looked at Mincy, blinked two or three times, and then quickly released Yid's shirt.

"I...I'm sorry," he said, stepping back. "I don't know what got into me. I only wanted to know."

"By jings," Yid muttered, "some folks act like they never got past the flyleaf of the first grade primer on manners. Mister, you ever heard of asking nice?"

Ralph looked up, and slowly nodded. "You're right, and I apologize. Could you please describe this compass to me? I mean, would you mind?"

Yid looked at Mincy, grinned, and then turned back. "Now that's asking nice, and I appreciate it, Mister Ralph. What's more, I don't reckon that describing the Future-Compass would hurt us any. Do you, honeydarlin'?"

Mincy smiled and shook her head. "It's round," Yid then said, using his hands to illustrate, "maybe six inches across, golden in color, and curiously ornate. It also has colored stones that for all we know might be diamonds and rubies and sapphires and such. They are scattered about on it, and if they are pushed down in the proper order..."

"What do you mean, 'proper order'?"

"One after the other, like naming in order the colors in a rainbow. At least that's how we did it when we saw the vision of the roads."

Obviously shaken, Ralph turned away. "They surely must have one," he muttered. "They surely must. Oh, if I could only get my hands on one of them. If only I could."

"Ralph," Carol said as she placed her arm about her brother's waist, "what is it?"

"I...I... Oh, never mind. I just..."

"Ralph, talk to me. Please? John and I talk a lot, and it helps to share, it really does."

Ralph stared out into the darkness, silent. The three other men who had been vanquished by Mincy's blows staggered into the light, found that they weren't seriously hurt, gathered up the damaged hazer, and without saying anything at all departed together using the single Go-Button that remained between them.

The mountain was empty then, save for the arcing light and the four people who stood within its glare. Finally Ralph sat down upon a rock, sighed, and spoke.

"It... isn't that much, really. I...I just want so badly to help."

Carol was instantly beside her brother. "Ralph, you already help us so much. You shouldn't expect to do any more."

"If I don't do it, Carol, then who will?"

"I...I didn't mean..."

"I know, I know. None of us mean it, and that's the problem. Carol, look at us. Have you ever seen a more miserable family? Our lives have no value, Loren is losing his children as fast as they get old enough to think for themselves, and John is going to lose his wife if he doesn't change. You'll lose your daughters, too, one of these days, just like you lost your husband, unless we can somehow turn this thing around."

Carol stared, amazed. "But Ralph, you aren't caught up in all this. You should be happy."

"Happy, Carol? How can I be happy when I watch my brothers and sister, people I love, destroying themselves and their children because of weaknesses they can't overcome? Yes, I am at peace about my own life, but I am the oldest brother, Carol, and I have some family responsibilities that go beyond my own wife and children. How can I be happy when I see what you and John and Loren have done or are doing? Nor will I be happy until I can somehow help the three of you and your families find the same peace I have found."

"Oh, Ralph, that isn't fair."

"And do you call how you are living fair? To yourself? To your daughters? Look at yourself, Carol, really look. There you were, just a few years ago, a lovely, intelligent woman with two beautiful daughters and an excellent husband. But did you appreciate and value what you had and were? Hardly. Instead for some crazy reason you went chasing after other men, worthless men who gave nothing and took everything. Now you have a broken family, no integrity, no sense of personal worth, no respect, nothing but a deep and poorly hidden misery."

The man took a deep breath. "Tell me, Carol," he asked quietly as his eyes searched his sister's, "am I wrong?"

Silently, the woman shook her head.

"And you're not alone," Ralph continued, sighing under the weight of his burden. "It's almost like we've all been cursed. Carol, if it doesn't have to be that way, then *why is it?*"

"I don't know." the woman responded tragically. "But Ralph, it isn't so with you."

"Oh, no?" Ralph declared with anguish in his voice. "I had to change, Carol. You bet I did, and I thank God above for the forgiveness He has granted me. But what about Loren's boy, who is just where I was at one time? Loren's given up trying to help him, but how can I, when I know so much more than Loren does? I see that boy's potential just as clearly as I see his destruction, and I keep hoping, and aching, and praying. Carol, you can't know how constantly I pray to God that He will show me how to help him. But so far, nothing.

"Do you want to know why I've wanted a Future-Compass so badly? Because it's the only thing I can think of that will help get all your lives straightened out. And God above knows we all need some kind of special help. Maybe if I can show all of you your futures, even more clearly than I saw my own before I finally repented, then you'll wake up to what you are doing to yourselves."

"Mister," Yid declared emphatically, "it won't do any good. I was shown *my* future, and it's awful. But that hasn't helped me change a thing."

"But *why?*"

"By jings, I don't hardly know. I reckon I'm just all gurgle and no guts, like that ped outfit of yours. I just haven't been able to make my promises, to myself and others, stick."

"Mercy," Ralph sighed. "To them that have little shall be given much, I suppose. All right, man, listen carefully. The only reason you haven't changed is because you haven't *wanted* to"

"So I've been told," Yid mumbled. "Trouble is, I don't believe it. Not any more."

"Well, you'd better believe it, because it is true. No man will make real changes in his life until he is willing to pay the price, until he absolutely, more than any other thing in

all the world, wants to change. Then, with very little difficulty at all, he will."

"I can't hardly believe that."

"Which lack of faith," Ralph said quietly, "is the rest of
the reason that you haven't changed. You've lost the Spirit,
don't you see? That's why you are denying your faith.
And now you've become paralyzed into not repenting by
the fear that you can't repent. What a tragedy!"

Yid stared at the man, his eyes wide with surprise.
"How...how do you know those things, I mean about losing
the Spirit, or denying the faith, or fearing?"

"How?" Ralph asked, shaking his head with impatience.
"Because they are in the scriptures. Those three issues
comprise a solemn promise that the Lord makes to all
those who get caught up in the mental web of lusting. As
I said, and I am only repeating what the Lord has already
said many times Himself, such people will lose the Spirit,
deny the faith, and fear. Man, you should understand that
by now, considering what you have been shown. What
good has that Future-Compass done you? You haven't
learned a thing."

"By Tophet," Yid declared, "I've sure as sowbelly tastes
good tried. But that Future-Compass doesn't altogether
make sense."

"Of course it does. A Future-Compass is exactly what it
says it is. It shows the way of the user's future. You make
a decision, and then in proper order activate the compass
and use your Go-Button, and you will be shown the actual
results, the exact consequences, of the decision you made."

"I know all that," Yid stated. "Trouble is, it wasn't
enough. I saw those things, tried to change but couldn't,
and so we keep coming back to that same rutted road."

Instantly Ralph was attentive. "Rutted? You didn't say
anything about that."

"I reckon I forgot," Yid said, wiping at his forehead in ex-
haustion. "One of the roads the compass showed us was
wide and rutted with use; the other was narrow and covered with grass. We were on the rutted road both times,
and I don't know what it means."

Ralph nodded with satisfaction. "I do. It is perfectly clear to me. You made one decision and were shown the consequences; you did nothing about what you were shown, which is also a decision, and so you are being shown *further* consequences. And the reason you are on the rutted road is because each of your decisions is the same one that would be made by most other people in similar circumstances."

"Well, I reckon you sure must be right," Yid declared sadly.

"I am. Now, may I ask why are you here?"

Yid shook his head. "That's another bronc that's throwed us. I've learned the horrors I was shown, all right, and since I can't change, I had intended on depositing my wife back home, where she could maybe find a little happiness without me and my misery. Only we can't seem to find our way back."

There was a deep silence, broken only by the distant but steady hum of insects and the occasional call of a night bird.

"I...I'm sorry, Mincy," Yid finally declared as he looked up into the face of his teary wife. "I really am. If I could only change, then I would. I mean that with all my heart."

With a low moan, Mincy turned away from her husband and covered her face with her hands.

"Mincy..."

"No, Yid, no. I can't bear to see you quitting."

Softly Mincy broke into sobs, and in anguish Yid looked out over the lovely Big Lost River valley, his eyes unseeing, his heart heavy with defeat. And neither he nor Mincy noticed the sudden interest on the faces of Ralph and his sister Carol.

The man was right, and Yid knew it. Further, what he had done, the lustful things he had thought and dreamed and hoped for, made him totally unworthy of his wife's loyalty and affections. In perfect candor, he knew that he could expect nothing else from her. And now that he had been shown the misery that those sorts of decisions had brought into the lives of others, he also knew what he, himself, had to look forward to. And he could never, not in all eternity, subject his honey-darlin' Mincy to the kind of pain that George had inflicted upon his wife and lovely daughter .

"I...I reckon," he muttered disconsolately, "that we had ought to saddle up and point our mounts back down the hill."

In agony Mincy's sobs increased. "Oh," she wailed, "if...if only we could go back to that old drummer. We could give him back the Go-Button and the compass, and maybe then we could..., could..."

29

"Excuse me," Ralph interrupted, his voice filled with more excitement. "Did you say that you got your button from a drummer?"

"Y...yes," Mincy quavered, her emotions still running rampant.

"Isn't a drummer a salesman?"

"One and the same."

"A drummer is a salesman?" Carol asked in surprise.

"This kind was," Ralph replied, turning to his sister. "They called them that back in the nineteenth and early twentieth centuries. I think the name came about because people who sold for a living, had to go out and drum up business rather than waiting for it to come to them. Now we call people of that same trade dispentitions, for they need some very particular technical training in order to competently dispense products."

Quickly then the man turned back to Yid and Mincy. "Listen to me, carefully. Was your drummer old, and white-haired?"

"Sure as Hosteller's Bitters ain't sweet," Yid answered slowly, suspiciously.

"And did you meet him at the Cove, down off Swensen Butte?"

Ralph's voice was filled with rapid-running excitement, and both Yid and Mincy wondered at it.

"Right again," Yid declared. "But so what?"

"Please tell me all you can about him."

Yid nodded. "All right. He always unhooked his wagon at the Cove, though I don't know where he pastured his teams. There was a line of three men that waited for him to open up, and for some reason I always felt like I had to be first. And I was, too, until this morning, or maybe it was yesterday morning, when this terrible mist developed. Then Mincy and I got lost, and...and..."

"It was you!" Ralph cried out, almost in ecstasy. "It was *you!*"

"Wh...what was me?"

"Who got out of line."

Now Yid and Mincy both stared. "Y...you were there?"

"Of course I was there." Ralph declared. "Only I always had to be last. For years I worked to become a better man, and finally I was given my invitation to see the dispention. After that, whenever I needed something that would help my life to become better, I had only to go to the Cove, stand last in line, and ask. The wall in his module would part, He would be there waiting, and I could obtain whatever it was that I needed."

Yid was stunned. In fact, he could say absolutely nothing, and for Yid Francom, that was some surprise.

"But more than anything else," Ralph went on, "I have wanted a Future-Compass to help my family. I had even spoken with the dispention about it, and he had promised that I would have one.

"Then came yesterday, when at last I was to pick it up, plus the original Go-Button to use with it, the one with the time slice feature. I was also to get a spool of antigravity thread for my farm. I went to the Cove and found it filled with a terrible, suffocating mist."

Again Mincy grabbed Yid's arm, but this time Yid paid her no mind. Instead he listened intently to the man called

Ralph, and as he listened, he felt as if his head would literally explode with the pressure of trying to understand.

"You...you mean to stand there unashamed," Yid sputtered, "and tell me without hardly no lie-blush at all that I was standing in line with a feller who was most of a hundred years away from even being born yet?"

"I suppose I am. Though the thought staggers me almost as much as it does you."

"Well by jings if that don't beat all the lies and tall-tale yarns I ever heard spun. Law, man, go on. I reckon you had ought to finish your story."

Ralph nodded. "I staggered around in the mist," he continued, "and finally came upon the dispentition's module. Only, it *wasn't* a module. It was an obsolete truck, a van, I remember them being called, and it was selling automotive parts. Nor was I last in line anymore. In fact, I feared that I had come first, until I saw a man, a very angry man, disappearing off into the fog ahead of me. But there was only one man, not two, and I can't tell you how I worried about that."

"You don't need to tell me," Yid breathed. "I reckon I already know."

Ralph nodded in understanding. "The dispentition wouldn't speak with me, and when I asked for the compass he had promised, he closed the window to the van and I found myself alone with some obsolete truck parts and an illegal set of tires."

"*That's* where you got the tires?" Carol asked in surprise.

"Of course. Didn't you notice that they were new? I brought them to the farm, did my best to secure them in my monilab, and then went to notify the authorities that they were there. We were coming after them when the visi-checkers notified us of your presence and we began blasting."

"That part I reckon I know all about," Yid affirmed.

"Yes, I imagine. What you don't know is how my life has literally fallen apart in the few hours since I got those tires. Personally I have struggled more than ever before, Loren's son has completely stopped listening to me, both John and

Carol here have gone off the deep end again...

"And when we did not get our plow," Yid interrupted, "our lives went through the same terrible unraveling, precise and exact."

"And was the third man," Carol asked quickly and without any hesitation, "our father?"

"What?" Ralph asked in surprise.

"Of course," Yid declared, finally tying the entire package together. "Only he wasn't the third man, not originally. Now that I think on it, he had to be second. I needed the plow, he needed the tires and the parts, and you, Mister Ralph, needed the thread, the button and the compass. But somehow I got lost in that infernal mist that came from goodness knows where."

Suddenly Yid's eyes opened wide. "By tunket, I do so know. That mist was caused by my own ignorance, my own selfishness, my own mistakes and sins. A man can't hardly see clear if his heart ain't right."

"That's correct," Ralph agreed. "It is called losing the Spirit."

"Why sure enough, that's so. The Holy Writ says it, too, and fairly often. Still, that was *my* problem, not yours or your father's. Why did the two of you have to suffer because of *my* blindness and evil doings?"

Carol and Ralph looked at each other, and with a slight smile, Ralph nodded.

"Don't either of you know?" Carol asked as she stepped up to stand between Yid and Mincy. "Have you not looked at us, and seen?"

"What?" Yid muttered, his voice sounding strained. "I don't..."

Carol smiled and took hold of the couple's arms. "Your name is Yid, right? And yours is Mincy?"

"That's correct."

"And you told me that you homesteaded this farm?"

"Bingo again."

"And your last name is Francom?"

Yid stared. "Who in tarnation told you *that*?"

Now Carol's smiling composure broke, and tears filled her eyes as she held tightly to the arms of the couple who had travelled so far to meet her.

"N...nobody," she declared, letting her tears fall freely, "because nobody needed to. Grandfather and Grandmother, the name Francom is also our last name, and my oldest daughter is named Mincy. After you, Grandmother."

"And Loren's oldest son," Ralph added quietly, speaking to the stunned couple, "the one who is struggling so desperately to control his thoughts, is named Yid, after you, sir."

Both Yid and Mincy stared, dumfounded, as the thunderbolt of understanding jolted through them.

"But...but how can that be?" Mincy whispered. "We have no children."

Ralph looked at her in surprise. "But...but..."

"Ralph," Carol said then, "they told me they came from 1899."

"Oh," he breathed with relief, "that explains it. I've just been completing a family history, and if our records are correct a son will be born to you on May 3 of the year 1900.

"But unless your decisions are altered and you get off the rutted road of popular but wicked decisions, your son will do as you have done. Then you and he will become, through his sons George and Mac, the miserable and unhappy people you see standing before you tonight."

"He *has* to?"

"No, but he did *choose* to. We have the records of it."

"But...but," Yid stammered, "why are we allowed to know all this?"

Ralph smiled. "Obviously, because what you have seen doesn't have to be so. Both of you must have been very good people, for the dispention gave you direct access to him. And he must have known you could change or you would never have been given the Go-Button and the Future-Compass and granted the privilege of using them."

"The dispentition?"

"Yes, or as you call him, the drummer."

"Law! How can that old man..."

Ralph's shocked expression stopped Yid, and he stared silently, until the man finally broke the heavy silence.

"You don't know?" Ralph asked softly. "You've never felt compelled to remove your shoes?"

Thunderstruck and altogether embarrassed, Yid could do no more than stare at his equally shocked and red-faced wife. "By jings," he muttered in dismay, "oh, by mortified jings, are you meaning to say that Mincy and I were standing in the presence of...of..."

"Yes," Ralph replied reverently, "it is Him, or at least one who represents Him."

Silently Yid shook his head. "And *He* thinks I can change? Truly He does?"

"He *knows* you can! But as I said, there is a price."

"Which is?" Yid whispered fearfully.

"The willingness to give up even the little things, those hardly noticeable sins that seem so unimportant and so pleasant to cling to. And most of us *do* cling to our few favorite sins, you know. We see ourselves as good people with a few little problems that He will likely overlook, and in that manner we deceive only ourselves. He *can't* overlook them, because He is a God of law and must obey all He gives to us. That is why He once described the gate as straight, and the way narrow. No intentional deviation into sin, no matter how slight, is allowed."

"But..."

"There is one other thing, dear Grandfather. You must be humble enough to go to Him at the beginning, now, not later, and ask him to remove the burden of this from you, through His suffering."

"And that is all?"

"That, and then enduring to the end with the same untarnished and undimmed determination. Which means, I think, asking, as quickly as they occur, to be forgiven of the accidental errors you will naturally make. All of us have unwanted actors and actresses on the stages of our minds. The sin comes when we applaud their performances and call for encores. To be free of that sin, we have only to push our unwanted thoughts off the stages of our minds, immediately.

"If you can do these few things, then not only will you and Grandmother be blessed, but *our* very lives will be altered."

"I still don't understand," Yid declared, shaking his head. "Why should what I do have such mortal-hard results on you folks all these many years after me?"

"I read once," Ralph replied in answer, "where the ancient Amish people of eastern Pennsylvania had a saying, 'Siss in blut.' Translated, it means, 'in the blood.' That isn't quite right, but it's close.

"Actually, we have learned that our decisions, our very ways of living, affect the molecular structures of our bodies. Specifically, genes in a precise region of human chromosome eleven pick up, and pass on to our offspring, our attitudes, strengths, and *weaknesses*."

"You're saying," Yid muttered with slow but coming understanding, "that not alone blue eyes and bald heads and pigeon-toed feet..."

"Exactly," Ralph concluded. "In exciting, terrible reality, our children and their children after them, can become *everything* that we are, physically, mentally, morally and spiritually."

"They become every exact thing?" Yid asked in thunderstruck dumbfoundedness.

"Not quite," Ralph explained patiently. "I said 'can become.' They inherit only the *tendencies* to become everything that we were. We each have our agency. But the wonderful or awful tendencies to accomplish great and marvelous things or to make the same soul-stumbling and unrepented-of mistakes again and again are passed along from one generation to the next."

"Unrepented-of," Yid questioned. "Wait just a minute. Are you saying that if a feller repents, and really changes from his wicked ways, then the Lord somehow wipes those things out so they won't be passed along to posterity?"

Ralph smiled at the hope in Yid's voice. "I'm not saying

it, sir. The Lord did. He shed His precious blood in Gethsemane to pay for all sins. When we hand ours back to Him through true repentance, then He has promised that He will remember them no more. Not in us, not in our children or their children. But if a man or woman does *not* repent..."

"But why?" Yid interrupted again, feeling frustrated. "That just doesn't seem fair. Why does He allow the unrepented-of sins of fools like me to be passed along to innocent folks like yourselves?"

"I can't answer your question any better than Moses did," Ralph replied, smiling slightly and taking Carol's hand. "And he didn't exactly say why, either. He just said it was so, and that we had better be aware of it.

"You may read the Lord's statement yourselves in Exodus 34:6-7. I will quote it to you and ask you to please think about it, and your accountability to us, when you are gone.

"'The Lord, The Lord God, merciful and gracious, longsuffering and abundant in goodness and truth, keeping mercy for thousands, forgiving iniquity and transgression and sin, but who will by no means clear the unrepentant; *visiting the iniquity of the fathers upon the children, and upon the children's children, unto the third and fourth generation...:*'"

Yid stared in dumbstruck and mind-staggering silence as the images of Ralph and Carol began to fade. But then, as Mincy placed her work-hardened but loving hand in his, he suddenly found his voice.

"I'll... I mean, *we'll* do it," he shouted into the gathering darkness. "By Tophet, you youngsters can count on Mincy and me...!"

PART SEVEN

BACK HOME

30

For Yid and Mincy Francom the journey back was secondary to their journey home. At 7,000 feet on the rocky side of Dickey Mountain in the Big Lost River country in the year 2009 they stared in silence at each other. The night was hushed and cricket-chirpy all around them, the purple shadows were black in the valley meadows below, and a fourth-quarter moon, big and loomy as a ripe-cut cantaloupe, cast its last rays of light upon them.

They were alone, and they stood again on the elusive road of the Future-Compass. Or rather, they stood upon the trail, the narrow one that seemed so seldom used.

They realized that, digested the implications of it, squeezed each other's hands, stepped forward along that self-same trail, and found themselves, of a sudden, lying side by side in the old feather tick in their cabin, the sun streaming in upon them.

"Eeeeyagh," Yid yawned deliciously as he stretched his arms and arched his back against his pillow. "Morning, honey-darlin'."

And it was morning. In fact, according to the calendar on the wall it was the morning of September 2, 1899. Further, it was a morning to make a man glad that God had thought up Adam and Eve and the whole, wondrous idea of the world in the first place. This was surely the sort of day where a feller had to know that Somebody gentle, sensible, and kind was running things up there. A day like this just didn't happen, it was caused on purpose.

"Listen to those larks," Yid grinned. "Every last one of them has his tail in the air. You'd think it was spring, the way they're chewing the cud. You reckon they're wishing us happy anniversary?"

"More than likely," Mincy sighed. "If they aren't, I'll do it for them. Happy third anniversary, Yid Francom."

"Thankee, ma'am. And the same to you. It's been a mortal pleasure, being in your gorgeous company this past while. Fact is, it's felt like spring the three years long, entire."

"Well, I wish it *was* spring," Mincy sighed. "I've a mort of plowing to do before snow flies."

"You'll get it done," Yid declared, slipping his arm beneath his wife's neck and drawing her closer across the pillow. "Fact is, I'll wager you're finished plowing before I get through sewing Wiley Smith's new suit."

"You're daft," Mincy giggled. "Nobody can plow *that* fast."

"Nobody but you."

Mincy sighed contentedly and snuggled a little more. "Yid," she declared as she looked at the wall peg for the first time that morning, "for being a tailor, you don't do very well with your own clothing. You're missing a button on that shirt over there."

"Well, sew I am. Har har. Get it? So and sew?"

"Oh, no," Mincy groaned in mock dismay. "Yid, how many times do I have to tell you not to try so hard to be fun... Oh! Now that's passing strange. I just remembered something. Or maybe I dreamed it...I think...

"Yid, did you have a funny kind of button on that shirt? I mean, one that sort of took us to other places?"

Yid gazed at the rough-hewn log-beam rafters above him, considering long and carefully what Mincy had said and how he should reply. "That's a mighty strange question," he finally responded.

"Well, I recollect dreaming *something*, sweetheart, something that I think happened to the two of us. Seems like we got us a compass of some sort, too, and I remember people—children, *our* children, if only we had some, and..."

Yid sighed with relief at the diminishing of Mincy's memory. "You tell folks a yarn like that," he drawled then, interrupting his wife, "and I'll plead you was took temporarily insanitary. I'll tell the neighbors, happen they ask what ails you, that you was afflicted with a terrible fever. I'll say that you've been out of your head for forty-four hours and that the doc said to keep you dog-chained in a dark room for ten days before letting you out."

"You'll do no such thing," Mincy giggled. "You start spreading tales like that about me, and no one will stop at the station to buy our feed that I'm trying so desperately to get in the ground. Now I've got to get up and get Peaches and Cream harnessed to that new plow."

"It'll keep," Yid drawled easily.

"You're right," Mincy giggled as she took Yid's hand, "on our anniversary the plowing will keep. But don't blame me if your biscuits burn."

"I thought you were asleep," Yid declared, squeezing her closer. "Those doggone biscuits were my surprise for you."

"Wish I *had* been asleep," Mincy groused teasingly, "what with all I have to do today. You're noisy enough when you make biscuits to awaken Rip Van Winkle. But I'll still be surprised if you'd like me to be."

The two people laughed easily, and then Yid pulled the perfumey form of his wife closer yet and buried his unshaven chin still more excitingly deep into the night-dark fluff of her hair. Which hair rested, soft as raven down, against his small and bony shoulder.

Mincy sighed contentedly, kissed him beneath his chin, and Yid smiled. Or maybe he grinned slyly, which is not altogether the same thing.

"I think we're going to have us a son," he said quietly.

"But sweetheart, we've tried before."

Yid looked at the chest of drawers next to the bed. "I know, Mincy. But something's changed."

"Do you think so?"

"For a Big Lost Country fact, I do."

Mincy snuggled closer to her husband. "I hope so," she whispered tenderly. "There's nothing I'd rather give you than a son."

Yid's grin grew wider. "I love you," he declared emphatically as he held his wife, and he rejoiced with all his heart and soul that the only image that built in his mind was of his honey-darlin', the forgiving-sweet woman who lay comfortably beside him. By golly, he *was* changing, and he would keep after it until he was as pure as his great grandson Ralph had become, as pure as...

"Hallelujah for that," Mincy sighed joyfully as she turned toward him.

"For what?" Yid asked, surprised once again in his thoughts.

"For your love, silly," Mincy responded as she rejoiced in the light that was in her husband's eyes. "Hallelujah for your love!"

"Amen!" Yid concluded, and grinned even more as his eyes rested once again on the strange-looking button that lay innocently on top of the nearby chest of drawers.

"Amen, Amen and Amen!"

Author's Note

In the April 1950 General Conference of The Church of Jesus Christ of Latter-day Saints, President David O. McKay made the following statement.

"We are spinning our own fates, good or evil, and never to be undone. Every smallest stroke of virtue or of vice leaves its never so little scar. The drunken Rip Van Winkle, in Jefferson's play, excuses himself for every fresh dereliction by saying, 'I won't count this time.' Well, he may not count it, and a kind heaven may not count it; but it is being counted none the less. Down among his nerve-cells and fibers the molecules are counting it, registering and storing it up to be used against him when the next temptation comes. Nothing we ever do is, in strict scientific literalness, wiped out. Of course this has its good side as well as its bad one. As we become permanent drunkards by so many separate drinks, so we become saints in the moral [sphere], and authorities and experts in the practical and scientific spheres, by so many separate acts and hours of work."

When David O. McKay made that statement, little was known about the human genetic code. Now, thirty-seven years later, according to *U.S. News & World Report* (13 April 1987, pp.58-62), "scientists are turning up an impressive evidence that heredity has a greater influence on one's personality and behavior than either one's upbringing or the most crushing social pressure."

The article continues by reporting on genetic research done at the Minnesota Center for Twin and Adoption Research. It reports:

> "After exhaustively testing 348 sets of twins, including 44 pairs of twins raised separately, the institute's researchers concluded that how people think and act — their very personality — is determined more by the DNA in their cells than by society's influences. Such attributes as respect for authority, a vivid imagination and a propensity to talk to strangers were found to be largely preordained at conception. 'The evidence is so compelling that it is hard to understand how people could *not* believe in the strong influence of genetics on behavior,' says psychologist David Lykken of the Minnesota project."

Though much research remains to be done in this area, the implications are obvious and profoundly impacting. If, as President McKay states, our actions for good or evil affect the physical makeup of our bodies, then it takes no great stretch of the imagination to see how the tendency to those very actions can be passed along genetically to our children, our children's children, and their children after them, the third and fourth generation spoken of so very frequently by the Lord.

And after all, since the Lord organized or created our bodies in the first place, isn't it natural to conclude that He will use every physical aspect of them in furthering His work and His glory; the bringing to pass of the immortality and eternal life of man?

The author believes that it is.